Also by Neil Stanners -

'The Magic Room'

'Visions'

'Assigned Climes'

Somewhere
Night
Falls

NEIL STANNERS

Published by Garamonde (new edition) *2019*

GARAMONDE

Production by Media Services

Neil Stanners was born in Sydney.

He lived and worked in Europe.

He now resides once again in Sydney.

CONTENTS

Author's note: The dates in brackets represent the year in which the story is set.

SOMEWHERE NIGHT FALLS

It is 12 noon in Lacey Street on January 12. I am twelve years old today. I am the only person in the street. It was the same a minute before and an hour before. There is a war. Men have gone away to fight and our Mothers and Sisters have started running things or joined the Land Army. Grandparents look after some of the shops and businesses.
Mr Fletcher, the past school teacher, came out of retirement because Mr Harry Pollock, the current schoolteacher, couldn't wait to fight the 'damned Japs.' I think the first one he met shot him dead. Now he is decaying in the soil of Asia and his young wife has locked herself-away in their house. Mr Fletcher looks constantly distressed as his tranquil senior years slip from his grasp.

It's hot. Sticky hot. I can feel sweat running down my spine.
I'm wearing my army khaki school shorts. That's all. Shoes are too expensive. In summer, shirts and singlets stick and itch too much.
The shorts are a bit big. They took a lot of coupons, so they're the 'grow into' type.

Mum says they're in 'short supply.'
My Grandmother often runs her fingers over the faint
fuzz on my shoulders and says, "The boys gone native."
Personally I like it. Part of nature.

I guess this town is like any on the coast of northern
Australia. One main street with a couple of other little
streets running off it here and there. It sits on a ridge. One
side drops away to the Pacific Ocean while the other side
dips a little then goes pretty steep as it makes its way up
to the coastal escarpment. The main street is named after
Lacey Duncan who first settled the area. A lot of people
reckon he wasn't settling the area, he was making himself
scarce due to some interest in him by the police. I don't
know. People love finding fault and making up stories as
the situation demands. 'Drunk's dribble', is what Dad calls
it.
Either way, the town got started because he was here, so
having one street named after him is fair enough I think.

It's a street with lots of trees. Most of the shops have
awnings and piles of leaves hanging over the guttering.
And little bits of greenery growing out and hanging down,
till they get too long and somebody walks into them and
snaps them off in annoyance. The Fish and Chip shop is
the exception. Charlie the Chinese owner decided he was
sick of leaves blocking his gutter and constant shade. One
night a few years back he got an axe and chopped down
the big fig tree in front of his shop. There was a real carry-
on about it. One theory sprang up that he was using it as a

signal to Jap subs. Except that you can't see Charlie's shop
from the ocean and anyway he's Chinese.
"Drunk's Dribble", Dad said. "Everybody north of here till
you get to Europe is Chinese? Ignorant bastards."
The Council held a special meeting and Charlie had to
go along and explain why he did the deed. They passed
a resolution demanding that he not cut down any more
trees, which seems unlikely as he'd already achieved his
objective.
Now his shop gets really hot in the sun but he says he likes
it that way.
Charlie is given to crying every so often when he thinks
about his homeland and what the Japanese have done.
When this happens everybody leaves him alone till he gets
over it because he doesn't concentrate and overcooks the
fish.

Late in the day a few people come out and walk around
but right now, not a soul. If you want some fish or chips
for lunch you have to slam the screen door of the shop
and call out to Charlie. He comes out and then has to fire
everything up. It just isn't worth it.
Jap soldiers could march right in here at midday and take
over. Nobody would notice. That's probably why they
haven't bothered.

For my birthday I was given a pair of swim goggles and a
couple of books. Grandma wrapped a two shilling piece
in a bit of paper and put it in my card. The card said,
'to fuzzy, my little native grandson.' Grandma's sense of

humour at work.

Mum says she's extravagant. My sister, she's fourteen and a half, gave me a kiss and said that's all she could afford.

It's the goggles I really wanted, so I'm pretty happy at the moment. Mum must have really hunted around to get them. I first saw them nearly a year ago and I've been asking about them ever since. Each time I brought the subject into the conversation Mum would get that desperate look on her face and I knew it was not a good time. With everything either rationed or absolutely not available it's probably not a good idea to ask where she got them.

They're black rubber, with round glass eyepieces. There are little metal bands that hold the glass in place. I've seen pictures in the newspaper of navy men wearing the same type. I guess my head isn't too big. I've had to adjust them a fair bit to make them fit.

I'm truly busting to try them out. Not many people go down to the beach. The walk puts them off the idea. I can't go to the beach unless I have someone older with me but nobody said anything about the lake.

To get to the lake without being seen requires a detour round the back of some houses. Since everybody in this town makes a point of 'keeping a look out', it is worth the

trouble. Then you have to bush bash through to the cliff at
the bottom end of the lake and climb down. Easy really.
So here I am. From about twenty feet up I put on my
goggles and looked down into the water. Deep green/blue
water. So quiet. Sitting like a jelly.
I imagine some ugly pursuers, with guns and knives, intent
on my destruction. Intent because I had um......... killed
their captain. Yeah, that would do. They're right behind
me. "There he is," they scream. I dive.

The water hits me like rock. Shit it hurts. I seem to be miles
down. When I work my way to the surface I have lost my
goggles. My shorts and even my underpants are missing.
Sheer, blind terror. Everywhere I look I expect to see eyes
peering back. Perhaps even a person with a camera. There
is nothing. Not nearby, not on the far side of the lake. Just
the dark expanses of bush and rocks. It is midday. Too
damned hot. A quick prayer of thanks and then time to
think.

The lake is an inlet from the sea, held in by a big sandbar.
The bottom is white silvery sand with a few green plants
growing out of it here and there. The water is clear and
partly fresh from Johnson Creek but it's deep and that
makes getting to the bottom hard work. Also the top is
warm like a bath but the bottom is cold. My predicament
is not insoluble though.
I hang in below the cliff, treading water. It feels good in a
way, the water sloshing around my dick. Sometimes I go
with some of my mates and have a swim on the way home

from school. We all strip off so our parents won't know.
Everybody turns away and then dives in the water. Once
you're in, it's okay. You can wrestle and do anything. As if
the water covers you up. We dry off in the sun. Nobody is
supposed to look but everybody does. As far as I can tell
I'm pretty average.
This is different. They'd laugh till they burst if anybody
knew about this.

I'm sucking in air, breathing fast until my lips start to
tingle. Then duck dive. Pushing hard to get down.
Christ, the bottom never seems to arrive. The sand is not
so silvery. Every time you touch it clouds of silt stir up.
Poking around, I'm near bursting. Grabbing weeds and
little rocks, anything that looks like goggles. I have to get
out. Just as I'm heading up my thumb hooks the strap of
the goggles.
Halfway I lose them and grab them again.
On the surface the moment of truth. They're okay. No harm
done. And the air is so good.

The second trip down is a whole lot easier. I can see. It still
takes a while to find my shorts. They're lurking behind
some driftwood. And I'll never find my underpants. Nor
will I ever tell Mum when she works out that I seem to be
missing a pair.
I throw my shorts up onto the rocks then climb out and
put them back on real fast. Sitting on the edge of the rock
shelf I pull the tabs at the sides through the metal clips as
far as they'll go. Stand up, tug down on the legs. This time

they stay put.

Then I hear the giggles.
"What a nice bum you've got!"
The Anderson sisters are looking down from the top of the
cliff.
"We followed you."
"Bugger."
"We heard that."
"You're not going to tell are you?"
They begin climbing down the cliff.
"Naw, you're safe. Loose lips sink ships."
This has nothing to do with the subject but I am grateful
that they have taken the spirit of war-time cooperation into
personal relationships. They sit down beside me. Deborah,
eleven and Kerry, ten. Deborah nudges me and gives a little
laugh. "Pretty funny though." They're good sports I hope.
"We won't tell if you do it again."

Walking back, the sun seems to have gathered itself and
launched all its' forces into the surrounding bush. It is
rainforest, my Gran said. Tropical. It grows so fast and
covers ground so quick, you can bury a body out here
and in a week there will be no sign of your doings. Gran is
always one for the dramatic side of life. She says the Japs
tie prisoners over bamboo shoots and the bamboo grows
right through them.
The Anderson sisters trudge along with me. They have
bare feet. Kerry wears a dress but Deborah has on shorts
and one of her father's old shirts. I imagine she sees herself

in some role in the armed forces but I don't ask.

With the town up on a ridge, the ocean in front and a lake on the northern side, a road, the only road, comes in from the south west. Everything comes down that road and goes out the same way.

There are plans that if the Japs invade we will blow up the bridge at Merrick River and drop trees across the road. I don't think it would cause them much distress but every little bit helps I suppose.

The Japs of course are horrible little people. They're short and very ugly. Most of them need glasses to see. As a race they have very poor eyesight. They are incredibly cruel and quite often eat small children when their supplies are running low.

As they will kill me at a moments notice, I have plans to live in the hills. Mum could no doubt bring Gran along. If we were separated I could live in a cave with the Anderson Sisters. Deborah is quite pretty and if we stayed long enough, would make an excellent wife.

These are my plans at present but they require constant revision as the situation in newspapers changes.

I am whistling 'A Fine Romance' as we walk. It's one of my Dad's favourite songs and it helps me remember him.

Kerry says "Shoosh" and in an urgent voice adds, "Quiet, will you!"

We stand stock still. The earth about is creaking in the sun. The bush is bright where the sun hits and mysteriously dark in the shadow. You can 'hear it growing', as Gran says. Further up the track someone is crying.

We creep forward. In a little clearing overlooking the gully
Mrs Phelps is sitting on a log. She is screwed up into a
strange sort of pose. In her hand she is twisting a piece
of paper round and round. Her dress is real messy. She is
really sobbing and occasionally gives little moans.
It seems like something we should leave alone. Just as
we're about to back away, she looks up and sees us.
There's this funny silence. I can feel my ears getting hot.
The girls aren't going to speak. They're transfixed. (One of
Mr Pollock's 'words of the week.')

"Sorry, Mrs Phelps." I'm searching around for more words.
"We've just been swimming," I add brightly. "Well, I have
anyway. Um ...."
Mrs Phelps swallows hard. Her eyes are all red and
swollen. I don't think she can speak.
"Is there anything we can do?"
She looks at us for a moment, as if trying to work out
what I've said, then she holds out the bit of paper. We're
all focused on the outstretched hand. From across the
space of the clearing I can make out one big word. It says
'Telegram'.
None of us have seen one of these before but we all
immediately know its meaning. People in this town would
only get a telegram for one reason.
"It's my George," Mrs Phelps whispers.

Once we get Mrs Phelps to her home, the neighbours take
over and there's a great deal of tea making and patting of
hands. It's a strange ritual. The Anderson sisters fit right in

and stay. I can't wait to get away. I feel sorry for Mrs Phelps
but I hardly knew Mr Phelps and it scares me that people
die.

Up behind the town on the slope of the hills there are some
tin sheds. There is a bit of a road up to them and beyond.
The Moxleys and the Packmans live up there. The first
place you come to is the Moxleys. They don't seem to care
too much about anything. They're always happy and give
you a wave and say hullo. The sheds where they live and
the surrounding areas are a real mess. Not dirty, just a
mess. Everything stays where it was till they need it again
then they go and find it. This can often be a major problem
in the long summer grass, complete with snakes.
I've often been called in by Billy Moxley to help in a search.
When I walk past today, all the little Moxley children run
down to the fence and say, very slowly and deliberately,
"Hullo, what's your name?"
They know my name but it's a game that must be played.
I say, "Gee, I can't remember. Have you got any ideas?"
This produces lots of laughter and smiles. The game
continues, with the whole gang of Moxleys hanging off
fences and gates all along the way, guessing strange names
for me. I've never kept track of the Moxley kids but there
seems to be hundreds and they all seem about the same
age.
Billy Moxley came back from the war. He had been in the
thick of the fighting in the Pacific Islands. Though I have

not seen it, the story is that he had his knee shot off. Billy used to be real happy. Never wore any thing but shorts (like me). Now he is really moody and wears long pants. He walks with his leg straight as if he can't bend it. He gets drunk a lot and yells, "You white bastards did this to me." He was eighteen when he left, cheerful, fit, looking for some adventure.

Further along the road, at the end, there is a large flat area under the cliffs. This is the Packman place. I got to know Russell Packman at school. It is a real contrast.
Neat and tidy. Rows of vegetables. Fruit tress. Pumpkin vines. Bananas along the edge of the clearing. There's a cow called Rita and goat which is usually referred to as 'you miserable bastard.' The goat has a mind of its own. Neither the Packmans or the Moxleys are particularly dark skinned but 'native is native'. It's your label and you wear it.
Mr Packman sells his stuff in the town twice a week. He wheels it down the hill in a big cart. Charlie always gives him a cup of tea while he sits under a tree and recovers. Nobody goes near him till he's had a rest then he sets about selling the lot. It goes real fast because Mum says its good.
Some busy-body once mentioned to the police that Mr Packman should have a license. He was told that the job of the police was to keep the peace and if he stopped Mr Packman selling his vegetables and fruit there could be a hanging in the town. The busybody didn't comment after that.

Dad said they're the sort of abo's that can make a difference for their race. Know their place. Willing to adopt the white man's ways and knuckle down to a bit of honest work.

There are two times I hated my Dad. Once when he gave me a belting for something my sister did and when he talked about the Packmans that way. Russell Packman and I have been mates for six years. My Dad doesn't know. He probably never will.

There are calls and a lot of noise from a big tree near the house. Mrs Packman waves hullo from the verandah. Russell is in the tree on a wooden platform built in the fork, his legs swinging over the side. He directs me round.

"Big brown snake just there."

The Packman's are pretty casual about snakes. Vegetables equal rodents and that equals snakes. If they kill the snakes then nothing will kill the rodents, so the all get along together. They've never been bitten. Maybe the snakes are too fat and happy but it scares the hell out of me every time I go there.

Russell's two younger brothers, the twins, are hanging from a rope swing, arguing about whose turn it is to swing. Neither will give in so they both swing while the rope creaks.

Sitting up next to Russell I can see right down the slope. The tops of the houses in the town poke up through the trees and the ocean is glittering beyond.

"Any Jap subs?"' I ask.

"No mate, just a lot of water."

I drag out the goggles to show him. He fingers them as if they're gold.

"Oh mate, they're beautiful."

"You want to try them out?" I tell him about the Anderson girls catching me without my shorts. He is the one person I can trust not to repeat the story. While he is rolling about laughing I begin to question my judgement in the matter.

Sitting on the Packman's verandah, eating tomatoes with lots of salt, it is really peaceful. Hard to believe that over the horizon people are creeping through jungles, killing each other. My dad is out there somewhere. Russell is weird that way. He catches me looking off into the distance and says, "Thinking about your Dad, eh?"
I don't answer. Mrs Packman walks past and ruffles our hair in turn. It's quiet for a while. Summer is like that. Without warning, it all just stops, frozen. My Grandad knew. Little bits of summer were still locked in his mind when he died. Just hanging about, waiting, for anybody who cared to look. Lots of people don't even know they're there.

"Hey fella, we got to try them goggles. If you don't use 'em they gonna go off."

"What?"

"You know, rot away through neglect."

I'm never totally sure with Russell. Is he saying something really dumb, is he being very witty and intelligent or is it a strange sort of nothing talk just aimed at making conversation?

"They won't rot, they're brand new."

"Yeh, I know but hey, we gotta give 'em a go eh."

If Russell wants to try out my goggles why doesn't he just say so. I'm busting to go out with my friend and go swimming with them.

There are plans made for the next morning. Russell will come down before breakfast and we'll sneak off to try out the goggles. If we time it right we'll be back before Mum, Gran and my Sister get out of bed. Morning is a good time for swimming. Everything is still and quiet.

The twins are now wrestling in the dust, grunting and grinning, the game running like a Saturday matinée picture in their heads. Watching them it seems there is a cowboy theme involved in the scene.

Russell is settling down in the chair. He puts his feet up on the verandah rail. The movement catches the eye of his Dad working away out in the lettuces.

"C'mon son, time you did some work."

"But, Dad ....!"

"Now!" There is a telling rumble in the voice. It does not invite further negotiation.

Russell turns to put in a word to me.

"You want to give me a hand, mate?"

I'm already sliding away.

"I think I hear my Mum calling."

"Liar, nobody has hearing that good. You just one of them lazy white buggers."

"See you in the morning, mate. Bye Mr Packman."

Mr Packman waves easily without looking up. Russell is making gestures at me from the balcony.

"Russell !!"

Now he is running to his Dad. He leaps suddenly, no doubt over a snake and keeps running.

All at once I am focused very intently on where I am walking.

The house is quiet. Mum is sitting deep down in the lounge, listening to the radio. The news bulletin from the terribly terrific ABC announcer. She listens every day as if they'll mention how Dad is going. It's been ages without a letter. I used to listen but I never really heard anything about the war that I didn't know months ago from the blokes on leave.

"What you eating, Mum?"

"Shush. What? God, you've got a nose like a ferret. How did you know?"

"You had your mouth shut hard, it didn't look right."

Down beside Mum's lap there is a bowl of nuts and raisins left over from Christmas. I slide in beside her. Mum always smells of soap.

"Where have these been hidden?"

Mum looks down her nose. "Any other child would be out playing with his mates."

"I was, now I'm back."

"Don't get smart, child." She pinches me, as only mothers and sisters can."

The nuts are walnuts.

"Look Mum, they're like little brown brains. You can even see the veins."

She's looking at the ceiling. I look up.

"Well, I'll never eat walnuts again will I."

After an hour of rolling about in my bed, looking at the ceiling in the dark, waiting for sleep that doesn't come I head out to the verandah. The back of my neck is wet with sweat from the heat of the house. The verandah is great. Dad has enclosed one end in fly screen. There is always some air movement and no mosquitoes. On the old bed, in my underpants I can feel myself cooling down. Punch the pillow a few times, laying on my back. There are possums chasing each other about in the pandanas tree next to the house and across the roof.

Mum is never keen about me being out here. She talks in guarded terms about 'being carried off', 'snakes', 'spiders', and creepy crawlies, all geared to warning me off the idea. I found sis' out here one night last year. There's only the one bed so I lay down next to her. She got all funny and pushed me onto the floor.

I started yelling about how she 'must be kidding herself if she thought I was up to anything', then she yelled that I was 'kidding myself if I thought that she thought .....'. It was then that Mum and Gran appeared, going on about what the neighbours would think and we both finished up back in our bedrooms.

I sometimes wonder about women and girls, what exactly they all think they're up to. Is it some sort of plan to make life really even more complicated than it is already?

I'm dreaming, I think. It's wonderful. I feel just great. I'm not sure why.

"Jesus!"

Russell's face is right in front of me. I'm awake, now. Yep, awake. Russell is giggling quietly. There is some light. The sky is pink.

"You lover man," he says. "You rollin' around. What were you dreaming about, eh?"

I'm still trying to wake. Shaking my head. Deep breaths. Sitting up.

"Did you .... I felt something?"

"Yeah, I was using this feather. Should have seen your face. You were smiling away there." He pauses to break into another fit of stifled giggles.

"Shit," I say. My heart is thumping. "One word about this and I'll punch you till your knees fall off. No I won't, I'll tell everybody something about how you do strange things with your goat."

Russell just sits there on the floor, grinning in the half light.

"No you wouldn't," he says, still grinning.

He's right. I stomp off to grab my goggles, hitching my undies as high as possible, then remember the time and start to creep again.

Gran calls out, "Who's that? Who's there?"

"Only me Gran, goin' to the toilet."

"Lift the seat, boy."

Being early we don't have to do any detours. Straight up the main street. The town is all shadowy and gold and empty. Off through a paddock and down the track to the beach.

The tide is on the turn. Round the cliffs directly below Lacey Street there is a pool. It is a big scooped hole fed by an underground fault line. The sea bubbles up through this tunnel and spews out to the surface. Mum says its dangerous. There are always a few confused fish in there, sometimes something big. Russell told me at school one day that he saw a shark in the hole. When we raced down at half past three, there was nothing.

This morning it is all quiet. The surf seems far off. Behaving itself due to the early hour.

Russell walks round the pool, pausing every so often to stare into its' depths.

"I'm checkin' for sharks. You never know when there might be another one down there."

"I don't think there ever was a shark."

"Yeh, sure there was, honest. He was a big bugger too, cross my heart." Russell is only half hearted in his defence, preoccupied with the water.

"Every time you tell me it gets bigger."

Russell refuses to be drawn further.

"Hey, I think there's some fish down there, some good fish.

Maybe we can get a spear or something."

We look around. Nothing on the rocky shelf presents itself as a possible spear.

Russell's enthusiasm hardly shifts.

"Hey fella, we can catch 'em in our hands. They gonna be so stuffed from swimmin' round all night, they gonna just sit there and let us catch them."

Russell picks up the goggles. He hesitates and looks at me.

"Go ahead. You've got to wet them first."

He dips them in the water, shakes them then spends some minutes putting them on and taking them off to get the adjustment right.

"Hey, how do I look?"

"Fantastic,' I say, without much feeling. It's a lazy sort of morning. The sun is low and hazy, the water in the big pool is still with just a little fluffy ripple on the surface.

"I'm goin' in now." I wave okay, sitting down on the rock. Russell is in his school shorts like me. It's all we ever seem to wear. They fade with constant use and the metals clips rust. Eventually they fall to pieces.

There's a slight splash as Russell disappears into the water. He's a hell of a swimmer. Part fish. I keep checking under his arms for fins or gills. They're there somewhere.

Laying back I'm looking up, soaking in the warm air. Deep blue, a black cliff edge. The sky stretched across my eyes from corner to corner. A rock is digging in my back. Ignoring it makes it go away. A deep breath. Flicking eyelids. Vision, black, vision back. Through my eyelids it is red. Good blood. Sunlight filtered blood.

I'm thinking of my Dad. Where is he right now? Somewhere,

there in the Pacific. Doing something, fighting, hiding, shooting, crawling through mud, talking to a mate. Does he think of me, of Mum or sis'? I can't help it, a vision of him lying on a stretcher. They put a blanket over him, over his head, then walk away. I'm squeezing my eyes. They sting. Open, the sky is blurred.

I remember him on early mornings. He is always up before it gets light, shuffling and bumping about. The kitchen light usually wakes me. Sooner or later if I lay there long enough he'll come in and grab my toe. That's all he does, not a word. Eventually it drives me crazy.

"Dad, I'm awake. Dad!"

"Just makin' sure young fella." I can smell the cup of black tea he drinks

There's a faint noise. Where? Blinking, looking up. In the sky crossing from the black edge of the cliff. A tiny speck. A plane. Making it's way across the space. Squinting. What is it? Then there are four more, in pursuit of the first, sliding out from the cliff edge. I gasp. The intruder is about to die! Oh God. A part of the war is going to take place right above my head. Our magnificent air force. I watch as the gap narrows. Already there are flames, a smoke trail, a parachute. Will the Jap be dead? Or will he come ashore and try to kill us.

Today the war is calm. No gunfire. No flames and screaming metal. The pursuers gather around the first plane. They drop into a formation of two and three. Flying on, heading north out of my sight.

With my eyes closed again, I can shut out the world,

examine the insides of my eyelids once more.

Water is splashing on my chest.

Standing over me is Russell. The goggles are pushed back on his forehead. I have to shade my eyes. He is framed in light. In his hands is a large wriggling fish.

Russell caught three more in the next hour. With goggles and determination and increasing desperation I caught none. It's those damned gills he has.

Walking back round the cliffs on the rock platform, the surf crashing below us, carrying two large fish. Russell has given me a share. He couldn't carry four anyway. They are slippery, the rocks are slippery and we have to get round the headland before the tide comes in. There's piles of seaweed starting to stink in the sun.

None of this long trekking would be necessary if our parents could understand that we are now twelve years old and being almost adults we are able to take care of ourselves quite easily. We have to make our way right past the town and come up near the road that runs along from the south. A major waste of time and effort.

We're about in the middle of the work on our story about how we came to be in possession of four fish -

('This bloke on a truck gave 'em to us. Said he'd caught stacks of 'em down the coast a bit.') when there's a big crash behind me.

We both jump. There is a shattered piece of rock. The dust from its landing is spread out star-shaped on the wet surface. For a second I just stare. As I'm about to look up there's bash on the side of my head and on my shoulder and a lot of pain. Russell's yelling.

"I saw you Clancy, you bastard." He's yelling at the cliff above us. Dancing as another rock spatters near his feet. He looks across at me. His eyes widen. "Oh, shit. Oh Shit!" I can see my two fish on the rocks at my feet. They're blurred and seem far away.

Now Russell has my arm and drags me across the rocks, falling and sliding, under the cliff. More rocks are thumping about. I'm wet. Blood everywhere. It runs in a pool all over my shorts. A sort of buzzing starts in the back of my head, my lips feel strange. They tingle. That's it I'm gone.

"Oh shit, wake up buddy. C'mon, now. You not gonna die are you? Oh shit, oh shit."

I'm looking at Russell, who's not looking at me. He's patting the side of my head. It hurts. Blinding, stabbing pain each time his hand strikes.

"Jesus Russell, stop that."

Now he's looking.

"Oh thank Christ, I thought you was gone mate. Fuck, you been out to it for ages. You were makin' these strange noises and gurglin' and breathin' funny. I didn't know whether to run for help or what."

Russell holds up something red.

"I borrowed your hanky, mate. You're still bleeding everywhere. I can't stop it."

This must be serious. Russell only uses the 'f' word when extremely distressed.

We look at each other for a second, then the buzzing in my
head starts up to a roar again.

This time as I wake up there's more voices. I'm looking
into Charlie's face as he carries me up the cliff path. Mrs
Woolley from the grocery shop is holding something under
my head and Russell is leading the way.
I immediately thank Charlie by being sick all over him.
Not particularly put off by this occurrence I'm cleaned up
with fingers down my throat and the journey continues.
The town is empty except for the postal delivery man
who gives various opinions about my condition and what
should be done to the persons 'what done it'.

Mum and Gran and Sis' are all home when we arrive
and I'm quite amazed by the onslaught of efficiency that
ensues.
Mum takes me and lays me on the verandah bed which I'd
left only a few hours before. A towel goes under my head.
She coos and comforts and wipes me clean while I mumble
some detailed story about fish on the beach.
Charlie is totally taken over by Gran who has him out of his
clothes and into a dressing gown before he can summon
up suitable words of protest He sits sipping a mug of tea
with a plate of biscuits at hand, destined to stay until his
clothes are dry on the line.
Various neighbours put in token appearances.
Russell angrily and excitedly relates his story of the
incident with much vitriol directed at the Clancy brothers,
then unexpectedly bursts into tears and sobs away for

some time.

"I thought he was gonna die," he weazes. His nose is running. Probably sea water.

My sister wraps him in a blanket and sits with her arm around him saying what a good friend he is and how scared he must have been.

That picture stays with me forever.

The next time I'm awake there is more pain as the doctor from Leeward down the coast puts some stitches in my head and two in my shoulder. He gives an injection and that's it for me again for a fair while, I believe.

Through the blur of it all I can hear voices at one stage and a man's voice saying, "Crikey, the lad's certainly copped it." Russell is involved I think but I really don't care, it is so peaceful and warm and I'm happy to slip back to nothingness.

The next time I join the world Mum is giving me a sponge bath in bed.

"Mum, what are you doing? Mum, stop it!"

"Listen young fella, you came from inside me. There's nothing new or different about you." She has me in a vice like grip. "Now keep still or you'll bump your stitches."

Just as she says this I do and it hurts like hell.

"Serves you right."

I'm feeling the crusty lump on the side of my head. Squinting I can just see the black stitches sticking out of my shoulder. It looks well healed.

"How long have I been asleep?"

"Days my dear, days. You were concussed."

Sis is standing in the doorway looking at me.

"Get her out of here!"

"Oh well, sorry for breathing. I'll just throw the little rat's dinner on the floor."

Mum cuts across the conversation. "Just leave it on the hall table, love. You know he's a bit touchy about his manliness."

"I just wanted to know how he was," she calls down the hall.

Mum fixes me with a look that says it all. "She really was worried about you, you know."

"Oh bum, I'm sorry. Tell her I didn't mean it." Mum would have anyway.

The bath bit over and my dignity reinstated, she gets the dinner from the hall.

"Lot's of people have been asking after you. Look, Russell dropped in some lovely fish. Just what you need to get your strength back."

There's the plate on the tray. Butter and white sauce. Yep, it's one of them. Say nothing. It looks good.

"You were going on about fish the day it happened."

I shrug. "Must have been Because I was delicious um ....."

"Delirious dear, you mean delirious."

In the late part of afternoon Russell puts his head up to the verandah screen. I motion him in.

"Where did the fish come from?" I ask urgently.

He looks me up and down. "Don't you remember, we got 'em off a man on a truck."

"What, everybody believed that? So what were we doing

down on the cliffs."

"Oh that was easy. We were walkin' back to town from down the coast. After you got hit we dropped the fish. I went back for 'em later."

I lay back. It all seemed pretty plausible. Quite simple. Those were the best stories, the simple ones.

Russell suddenly has my arm. His eyes are lit up.

"Listen mate, here's the best bit. Your Mum, she got really cranky with them Clancys and bowled round there. She made Clancy's Grandad come back here and look at you. He got so pissed off he went stormin' back home and took to the Clancy kids with an electric cord. He was raving. The neighbours had to come in and pull him off them. Reckoned they were idiots. I've seen 'em workin' in his front yard, they've got black and blue stripes all over 'em."

Life was really good. The Clancy kids really were bastards and I was glad.

It took another week before I was allowed to even get up for the day. That was a week of my holidays wasted. I was pretty sorry for myself. Laying about planning how I could murder the Clancy kids was my only time occupation. Well not only, I read a lot of books. We had all these dusty things in the corner of the loungeroom. Some were pretty dull but there was some great stuff in there. Mysteries, ghost stories, sailing ships, a whole stack about the outback. Mum sort of looked sheepish when I queried their existence.

"It's your Dad, he's a bit of a bookish type. I don't know were he gets it from."

She made it sound like a disease.

Once you get tied up in a good story it's hard to come back. You lay to one side then turn the page and lay to the other side. Just for something different, you can lay on your back and hold the book up but it makes your arms ache.

The ghost stories were a bit of a challenge. The night after I read one I lay awake watching the shadow of the trees on the wall. There were things under my bed, behind the door and even at the bottom of the sheets. I kept saying it was just imagination. But how do you switch it off.

One of these nights I couldn't take sitting in bed any longer so I wandered down the hall toward the kitchen. Perhaps a biscuit would give my mind something else to concentrate on.

The tall lamp was on in the lounge. Mum was sitting quietly thumbing through the newspapers she had been collecting since the war began. With my bare feet on the carpet she didn't hear me. Standing beside her I was about to speak when she put out her hand and said, "Jack." She half turned her head and then jumped violently.

This made me jump and I fell back on the floor.

"Oh, it's you dear," she said, looking down at me.

"Did you think Dad was here?" I asked.

"Why luv?"

"You said his name."

"Did I?"

We sat for an hour or more reading the newspapers. Last year had not been a good one. Singapore fell, Darwin got bombed, Jap subs in Sydney Harbour, the 'Canberra, was lost and some guy called MacArthur turned up from America. Everybody was convinced the Japanese Army was about to land.

That was last year. This year it seems quieter. Could it nearly be over? Maybe the Japs have packed up and gone home.

The Anderson sisters came round to visit me one day. They brought a bar of chocolate and said they were very sorry to hear of my mishap. There were quite a few awkward silences but we sort of muddled through a conversation for about half an hour. They said how nice it was on the verandah and how pretty the jacaranda looked and I said some really dumbo thing like not as pretty as them. The moment it was out of my mouth I just wanted to be a hundred miles away. They took it very well I thought.

In the end Deborah said "Well, we really must be going. Don't want to be late for tea." She gave a meaningless little laugh.

Hopping up from sitting on the bed she then fussed around for a bit tucking in the sheets and mucking about with the pillow. All of a sudden she leans over me and says, "Mum said I have to," and kisses me on the forehead. Kerry dives in and does the same. Then the both wave goodbye and run off down the path calling goodbye to Mum over their shoulders.

Mum appears wiping her hands on a tea towel. "That was nice of them. Did you enjoy your visit from your little friends?"

She puts a cool hand on my forehead. "You're quite
flushed. Still a bit sick, eh?"
As she walks back inside I think I hear her say, "Not quite
the ladykiller yet, my baby."
I don't think she said it, I know she said it. Shit!

It's in all the papers. Not across the front page. That's
taken up with some more profundities from General
MaCarthur. If all he says is true the war will be over in no
time. He knows exactly what to do for the best.
The item that has me interested is on page 5. Several
hospital ships will be docking at Leeward in two days.
They are carrying sick and wounded from the Pacific
'Theatre of War'. There may be a surprise in store for
some families when they have their soldier boys home, it
says. I am not stupid, there are many thousands of soldiers
and my Dad is just one of them. He will be fine. So I don't
mention the newspapers and nobody else seems to notice.

Late in the night the heat drives me out onto the verandah
bed. The secret with this move is not to allow yourself to
fully wake up. It must be accomplished in a sleepy state
with eyes all but closed. With my pillow under my arm I
close the screen door and flop onto the bed. Roll up, punch
the pillow, toss around a few more times, lay and look at
the ceiling for a bit, wipe the moisture from my top lip,
then all of a sudden, I'm gone.
I have no idea how long I am asleep or what makes me

open my eyes. There is something at the screen door.
My heart is pounding. A dark shape. Just standing there.
Screwing up my eyes. It is hard to define.

"Dad?" I whisper.

"Give us a hand, son," the figure says.

Sitting on the front steps with my Dad I try to hold him
and hug him. He still has a haversack on his back and
ammunition pouches and he's holding his rifle. His sleeves
are rolled up. I can see that tiny little heart tattoo with
Mum's name. He is having a smoke and gazing out into the
night. It is quiet as always in our town. His hands are large
and strong. I always liked his hands. Seemed they could do
anything.

"I'm hurt, son. It's bad. So I thought I'd come and visit me
little mate."

It is now that I see the holes in his shirt and leggings.
His breathing is laboured.

"This smoke's good. I needed to take a rest. Got to lie down
now. Careful, you don't want any of this mess on you now,
do you. You, my boy ......"

He puts out his hand, reaching ahead, then tumbles
forward and falls down the steps. His rifle clatters over the
side.

"Dad," I scream in alarm. "Dad!"

Sitting up in bed, looking about the dark verandah. Eyes
flicking from side to side. Breathing fast. My heart is going
to leave my chest.

"Who's there?" Gran calls out from her room. "What?"
I can't answer and she does not call again.

So I sit for the rest of the night, hugging my pillow to my

face, rocking and crying. Nobody can see me. I don't care. And in the morning as birds begin to stir outside and the room lightens I know without any doubt that my father is on one of those hospital ships.

A trip to Leeward will not be easy. It is a fair way down the coast. A bus travels the winding road once a day. Down in the morning back in the afternoon.

Russell's initial reaction is pretty much on course.

"You bloody crazy, fella. How the hell you know he's gonna be there. Your Mum have a fit. How we gonna do it you reckon? When we gonna leave?"

"Tomorrow morning. We can grab the bus down the road, outside town. Only trouble is I haven't got much money. We can only get the bus one way."

To this news Russell is skeptical. Shadow from the banana tree above us hides his face in the glare. His father is calling for him to do some work.

"You got lots of money, mate. This is your friend Russell you talkin' to here."

"Mum makes me put it in the bank. She can't believe how much we get from bottle refunds. I've got one and six left."

I have never collected bottles. One of the ways I have of making a little money is by putting on a performance at the town club. Somehow my whole family has managed to miss the gossip on this one. It's a sort of Fisherman's Club and Office. It doesn't really exist. It has never had a license but it's been selling beer and whisky and sherry for the ladies, for years. The town policeman leaves things alone.

He told my Dad he has to live here and keep the peace and it seemed pretty peaceful to him. Now he's away in the war so I guess the question is no longer of any consequence. As for law and order, well the town just fends for itself.

My act at the Club is to sing. One of the curses of my life is to have been born with an affliction called perfect pitch. A former schoolteacher discovered it one day. She seemed quite excited at the time. It did not occur to me as a talent. I could just sing. Once I discovered its earning potential I immediately exploited the possibilities and the other kids stopped making remarks about it and became suitably jealous.

The method in its present form is to hang around the Club entrance pretending to play until one of the older members arrives. On almost every occasion (once my credentials were established) I will be invited in to give them a song. With Miss Renshaw at the piano I do a fair rendition of 'A Nightingale Sang In Berkeley Square', 'We'll Meet Again', 'Stardust' and that sort of thing.

One thing I learnt really quickly is to leave them wanting more. I stop when they're getting enthusiastic and complain I'm tired and it's past my bedtime. About then the ladies all start on about "their little crooner being tuckered out" and I let the men reluctantly talk me into one more. This is invariably, 'Silver Threads Among The Gold' (my mother's favourite), which brings forth great sentimentality. I sing this unaccompanied and embarrassing comments like, "beautiful voice" and "angel" start flying about.

Notwithstanding the unsolicited commentary I slip out with a good mix of pennies, threepences, sixpences and the odd larger amounts when my pure, honest conniving has affected some listener to paroxysms of melancholy and subsequent generosity.

'Paroxysms' was a word of the week last year when Mr Pollock was still teaching. He reckoned you could never have too much word power. I miss him. I've got a lot of great words to use when the moment is right. He was a real good bloke, Mr Pollock. I could tell him things I would never tell my parents. You didn't know you were learning when he taught. You sure know it with Mr Fletcher.

So it is duly arranged that Russell and I will meet at dawn under the big fig tree at the top of Lacey Street. We'll bring some sandwiches and walk down the road to wait for the bus at eight o'clock. Somebody on the bus will no doubt recognise us and Mum will find out eventually but I'm hoping by then to have Dad to sort out any problems. Russell's Dad is raising his voice with regard to finding Russell and getting some work out of him.
"I 'spose you'll be off, white boy. I got work to do."
"No, you're helping me so I'll help you."
"Shit," says Russell, "double shit," as we slide out from under the palms and into view.

The Leeward dock is a great long wooden wharf that stretches out over the shallows of the bay to the deeper water beyond. There are a lot of ships in the bay. Quite a number are tied up along the wharf. On the side nearest, two grey naval ships, with rusty strips and twin guns are alongside. Partly hidden on the other side is a much larger ship. It is painted a milky brown colour. A lot of greysmoke comes out of its funnel. On the side of the ship is a white square that runs from the water line to the deck. On the square is painted a red cross. Seeing it makes me greatly optimistic.

We watch as a convoy of trucks begins grinding their way through the gates and out onto the wharf. Others are arriving and lining up along a side street waiting their turn.

"We never goin' to get on that one." Russell is not being optimistic. "They got guards everywhere and take a look at all that barbed wire stuff."

He is right, though I am not going to admit it. Military Police are checking everybody and every vehicle that wants to enter.

I briefly consider a swim out under the wharf and then climbing the pylons but they provide their own security with oysters and barnacles all the way up.

"We can watch for a while," I say, "you never know what ideas we might get."

We lay under a tree in the shadow. Trucks continue to roll in. As each comes up to the gates a soldier climbs up alongside the driver. The truck then proceeds to the gate,

stops again and then moves off onto the wharf. It is too far
to make out any more detail. For a long time the sun beats
down and the procedure at the wharf does not alter.
"We've got to get closer." I look round at Russell for
approval. He is laying on his back with his eyes closed.
"Russell, this is important, mate. Can you help me please?"
So Russell opens his eyes. He looks at me without moving
his head.
"See that truck with the torn canvas." He points back over
his head. There is a truck near the gate with a rip down
one side of its canopy.
"It was here before, it came back. Wherever they goin' it
not very far. We just go to the one at the end of the queue
and jump in the back, then get a ride onto the wharf, we
get out and wait till they load up then we jump back in
and get a ride to where they goin'. I surprised you haven't
worked it out yet."
Of course he's right. All the detail, everything.
"When were you going to tell me this wonderful plan?"
Russell shrugs. "Better later than sooner, people get lazy
after a while. They don't watch so carefully, eh."
It seems sound. I run through it again.
"Wait a minute. When the trucks come out they're full of
soldiers"
"We got to take a chance fella. They all wounded blokes,
with holes in 'em and that. They all gonna be too sick or
they won't mind some kids on board. Might even know
your Dad. Hey, he might be on the one we get in, eh."
Russell's face screws up. "Oh shit mate I didn't mean your
Dad gonna have holes, he just got a sore foot or broken

arm or something."

Diplomacy is never going to be Russell's strongest characteristic but he has ample other redeeming features. I take his points in the nature they are intended.

From the hill I can make out the town's clock.

"Ten o'clock. I can't wait."

"They gonna get hot and lazy. You look now, they all efficient. Gotta wait mate."

We lay there this day, under a tree that offers little shade, on top of a hill and wait. From watching people walking, shopping, going out in small boats to fish we lay back at last aware that the town clock is not one to be hurried. Hands behind heads I watch Russell's chest rise as he takes a deep breath. It is a signal that he is about to say something difficult or profound. When he takes a breath his belly button (it's a navel, Mum says) lifts up. Mine never does. He has an outy, I have an inny. We have discussed this in the past. Deborah has a sort of an outy. I would love to touch it but I'm not sure whether she would think that was okay.

"Alright," Russell says, "tell me the ten best things about your Dad. We'll swap, eh."

He is good, this mate of mine. It's a topic I need to talk about.

"Alright, let's see."

You would think that such things would come easy but it takes some minutes to shuffle various aspects of my Dad around in my mind. Russell continues at rest with his eyes closed, like some indulgent doctor.

"He's strong."

"All Dad's are strong, mate." Russell intones. "They bigger than us due to their age so naturally they gonna be stronger. That the best you can do?"

"No, there's more. I'm just getting started. He makes my sister and me get along."

"You mean he threatens you with a belting if you don't stop fighting."

"He explains things to me and shows me how to do things." Russell continues his role as the interpreter. "What does he explain or show? You got to give me some evidence."

"When I was real little he showed me how to piss without getting it all over my hands. He told me how car engines work. He fixes my school shoes. Buys lollies and comics. Built me a billy cart, showed me how to kick a football straight."

"That all pretty average Dad stuff, mate. My Dad made the billy cart that beat yours, remember."

"It's his smell," I blurt out, shocked at such a personal admission. Now Russell has an open wound to dig and poke about, causing me great pain.

"Yeh," says Russell? "Now that somethin'."

No ridicule. My friend understands.

"It's a mixture I guess. Tobacco, soap, sweat, smoke, dust, tree sap .... musty but ...."

"My Dad smells of the earth and eucalyptus."

Looking across at Russell, he is still laying with his eyes closed.

"Does your Dad talk to the trees?"

Russell's eyes slowly open.

"No."

"Mine does. Calls them his mates. Big and strong. Always there. Hold you on their shoulders. Provide nice clean scent in the bush. Look after possums and bears."

Russell looks at me, his head on his hand.

"Maybe he does, I'll have to watch him a bit closer."

It comes easier after this revealing patch of creative honesty. My list includes Dad's squashed old toothbrush, his shaving mug with the cocker spaniel on the side, old football boots with the missing sprigs, his copy of the 'Great Tunes of the Century' songbook and the item I found in the shed, hidden under a great deal of carefully placed timber, Sun & Health's Special Edition of 'Maiden's of the South Seas.'

Russell counter attacks, after extracting a promise of a look at the hidden Sun & Health magazine, with his own impressive list. It includes his Dad's way of winking when he's pretending to be serious and his method of getting attention by bending Russell's finger when he is serious. What really catches my attention is the revelation that Russell's Dad has a kangaroo scrotum tobacco pouch. For the first and only time in my life I have to admit to Russell that he knows a word that I have never heard.

"A kangaroo's ball bag?!"

"Yep."

There is much rolling about while I wrestle the truth from this native mate. By various means I deduce that he has produced a fact. Scrotum, what a top word.

In the meantime the town clock has shifted considerably.

For over half an hour we do a big circle and find the side
street where the trucks begin to line up. On the edge
of the main street it is really a long laneway. There are
warehouses and a fish market but they are closed. Because
the streets are empty it is hard to stand around with no
reason for being there.

After several groups arrive together we see an older truck
making its way slowly along the street. This is the chance.
As the truck turns into the lane we wait to cross the road.
The driver waves us across but we give him a friendly
wave back and motion to keep going. He swings on into
the lane and we run behind and climb in. It's higher than
expected and takes several attempts. From under the
canvas we look back. Nobody has seen us.

Time seems to slow down. The back of the truck is like an
oven on Sunday roast day. We lay on the floor and sweat,
not daring to open the back. Periodically the truck starts
and our hopes rise. It moves forward then stops, starts
forward, stops, then the motor goes off again and we sigh
quietly.

Russell checks the damp patch under me.

"You were gonna wear a shirt to look proper."

The truck starts again. The gears grunt and the frame
shudders, then it changes again and again. We're rolling.
There are voices. Banging on the side of the truck. A loud
yell next to us.

"Okay, take it away."

Some other voice says, "Move it soldier!"

The truck shudders and bumps forward.

We hear the driver talking. "Jesus, don't hang onto the wing mirror, I knocked it off on the last run."
Another voice says, "Shit Lionel, if they ever give awards for the world's worst fucking driver you're gonna win it, no contest." There's laughter at this statement.
The truck's tyres are rumbling. "We're on the wharf," Russell says, "That's the planks. Those soldiers have got weird voices."
For once, I have the answer.
"They're yanks."

Now there's a lot of noise. Yelling, trucks moving and a more subtle, deep sound which is probably the ship's engines.
"We gotta get out." Russell's eyes are wide. He creeps forward and lifts the canvas, then urgently motions to me. "All clear, we facing the water. We can hide behind that junk there."
We're out, clambering down and running from behind the truck. The junk Russell spotted is a big pile of army packs. Each has a name tag tied to the top with a piece of string. They're stacked along the edge of the wharf as if a decision has to be made about what to do with them.
Australian Military Forces, Army No., Rank and a person's name. Moving in the tiny wafts of breeze.

From two big doorways in the side of the ship there are zig zag companionways leading down to the wharf. The hospital ship is still further down the wharf. To move closer we will be going past the two warships on our side of the wharf. This time I have a plan.

Walking past the warships we are both carrying an army haversack. It works. From one pile to the next. People on the wharf are engrossed in their work.

Now we are right opposite the big ship and in the shadow of the second warship.

"Sit down and look like we belong here," I suggest.

From our small hill of bags it is easy to see the lines of stretchers and the men working like ants to bring them down to the trucks. In one door and out the other with another. I can see the faces of a lot of the men. Some are bandaged, some sit up and smoke, some don't move.

Russell points out the obvious. "He could be anywhere, mate. How you gonna find him? Might be gone, might be still inside, might be wrong ship, maybe not here at all."

We edge a bit higher on the pile of bags.

"What are all these bags down the front, mate. Oh bugger, no, you don't look at them." Russell is vainly trying to put a hand over my eyes.

For the first time my gaze drops from the ship to our immediate vicinity. Lined along the wharf below us are longer canvas bags. These too have tags. Some are an awkward shape and there are dark stains on some.

"Russell, I've got to know."

My heart is hurting. I feel sick. Moving down to the nearest bag. There is a name. It is not my father.

"What the blue fuck are you doing?" The voice has come from in front of me. There is a soldier with his legs spread, his hands on his hips and his chin thrust forward, staring

at me. He is so close his shadow stops at my fingertips.
At this same moment Russell yells, "RUN!"
Back over the duffle bags. They slip and the pile falls but
we scramble to the other side. Now heading down the
wharf round the next pile. Crouching, looking back.
"We in trouble," Russell pants beside me.
The soldier is swearing and pointing. "Jesus Christ, what
is going on. Get them!"
We're off again, dodging in and out of trucks. Now we dive
behind a truck, just as the biggest man I have ever seen,
walks round the back. He doesn't catch us, he just scoops
us up.
"Well shit, I got some little Aussies here." He is black and
stinks of cigar smoke.

The lecture is long and tedious. Safety, stupidity, could
have been killed, there's a war on. The officer is Australian.
It's a tin shed and we're seated on two hard chairs, heads
bowed, sweating.
Finally he runs out of abuse. Winds up with, 'bloody little
idiots, you could have been shot.' Realises he is becoming
repetitive and stops.
"Orderly!"
"Yes, Sir."
"Get these kids some water before they melt."
All at once he changes. The anger seems to have drained
out of him.
"Why didn't you ask?" He takes note of our surprised
expressions.
"Not everything is a secret. We tell people about their

families for God's sake. Here drink your water. It's warm
but that's the only type there is."
"Orderly!"
"Yes, Sir."
"Any word on this boy's father."
"Not listed sir. Not on this ship or the last one." The man
called 'orderly' then whispers something to the officer.
"Righto, good. Dismissed."
The officer walks over to us and kneels down.
"Look blokes, you've been misinformed. We don't know
everything that's going on out there. But all the wounded
and otherwise are out of the area your Dad was in and
…….." he lowers his head, "I shouldn't be giving out this
information but your Dad's group is in a fallback position
at the moment and so they're not near any action. People
who get hurt out there are ……. it's not always possible
to help them. Those unfortunate people you saw on the
wharf were the ones who died on the voyage back. There's
been nothing happening up there for several weeks. Okay,
nothing to worry about. Go home. Don't come back."
He takes both our hands and squeezes them then rises and
becomes an officer again.
"Orderly!"

It is late. We lay in the park again, high above the harbour.
At dusk the ships begin to merge with the sky and fade
away. There are few lights. Soldiers are still working, using
torches. From the distance I imagine mice with small lights
scuttling about.
We don't talk. Sleep just comes without notice.

In the first light of morning I am cold despite the climate. One of the ships has gone. Stolen away by the night. Somewhere out there, over the curve of the horizon, my father is coming out of the night. Did he see Venus in the twilight. I watched it for a while knowing it was something we could share.

In Europe now they will be entering another of their nights. Cold and frightening. Their war too has days and nights, seasons and changes.

Now Russell sits up. He has been bitten by an ant. I see him flick it off from under his arm. He is marked by the rough ground. He says nothing, just hunches over and stares blearily out to sea. So we look, watch the light increase on the bay.

Eventually he puts out an arm, without looking. His fingers, absently pat my face.

"Better get back, eh mate." His voice is husky.

Our return journey takes on new dimensions. With no money for the bus we trust our luck to the road. The distance seems to have tripled. Perhaps we are tired or more in tune with each step and our surroundings. Russell at first suggests we sing and in a valiant attempt at light heartedness we begin a soft rendition of 'Chatanooga Choo Choo'. Apart from Russell's trouble with the word Chatanooga which he persists on pronouncing as Chamanuga the melody fades and silence creeps back on stage.

I can hear my breath as we walk up one of the many narrow tunnels the road makes through the foliage. It is a deeper green than I have noticed before. Layer and layer of varying shades. Beneath our feet the red clay of the road contrasts dramatically with the plants and trees it sustains. Once again our neighbourhood is in its slumber. There is no sound. No traffic, cars, trucks even horses. We're alone and the world is elsewhere. Two figures in a hot, creaking landscape. History is being made somewhere. I guess for there to be history somebody has to be there to notice it happening.

A farmer, a very old and sour man and his huge wife in gumboots had delivered us miles back on the road. They turned off into a track that led to wherever they were going.

"Yer'll get a move on an' you'll be 'ome before youse know it, childs. My day wern't no fancy transport for stray childs."

The woman's lips are squashed by her fat cheeks.

Her reference was to a stinking old Ford truck with no springs. In the back we felt every hole in the road and tried desperately to keep our feet and bums away from whatever creature's shit rolled about with us as we progressed.

The town, our town, did eventually come into view. It seemed reluctant to be found. From the last bluff where the road climbed past a steep part of the coastal cliff, it lay below, smaller than I recalled and still.

We had been travelling since before the first light of the

day. We had no story for our disappearance but with local communication being poor at best, people whose job it was to be concerned for our well being, would hopefully be only curious as yet.

Probably stayed at a friend's place. Other possibilities occurred in other places.

Notwithstanding, we approach Lacey Street with caution. It is midday. The street is hot and deserted. Above us in the intense blue sky, the sun spotlights our world casting huge deep shadows under everything that bars its way. Trees are blocks of bright green sitting on fat black bases, too deep for our eyes to penetrate. It is under the first tree that we stop to take stock. If we make it to halfway, to Charlie's Fish Shop, it will appear quite casual to be walking about.

Our current position implies that we have been 'down the road', 'out of town' and that is beyond our limits. All is quiet, however. It is good.

This changes almost immediately. Russell yells and falls sideways. He is rolling on the ground clutching his calf, his face contorted. His yell makes me jump. A small rock pings the ground in front of me.

My head travels around and then up. Fumbling to get the next rock into their catapults are the Clancy kids. They are half-hidden in the leafy branches, their pockets bulging with ammunition.

"Youse two are gonna be dead, you fucking little creeps." The older boy spits out his message and brings his weapon up to fire. He is a huge lumpy kid, given to bouts of incredible rage. It appears to be his current mood and he does not intend to miss.

Though no words are exchanged Russell and I find ourselves pelting down Lacey Street dancing in an erratic zig zag pattern. Russell takes another blow to the foot of the same leg and hobbles on. Another rock, intended to brain me, whistles past my ear so close I can hear its trajectory. Their threats and their rocks pursue us for some time. The catapults must be good and I find I have some grudging respect for their expertise. Despite their best efforts no more rocks find their mark and we finally make it out of range.

On the steps outside Charlie's shop, we're both panting. Russell is rubbing the two great lumps on his leg.
"Shit they hurt. Oh mate, I think me foot's broken."
I can offer little but sympathy. Pain is not a pleasant thing. It could be me with a rock buried in my skull. It occurs to us that the Clancys must be down out of their tree by now. The street is empty. Nothing much is moving. A solitary black dog walks aimlessly round one of the trees. Three times he circles it then flops down. The heat he is trying to avoid is still there.
"What we gonna do?" asks Russell. "They gonna hunt us down for sure."
I have my mouth open, the words about to escape my lips. I've never known why I closed it again. What does it matter? Silence serves a greater good.

The Clancy's do not bother us that summer or ever again.

They move away shortly after the telegram arrives. Their untidy white weatherboard cottage stays empty. There is little concern that they have gone or where, only their going sparks interest.

On the wharf that day as I lay nose down with the nearest of those long, canvas bags, mere seconds away from being discovered, I read a name. 'Herbert Alfred Clancy'.

He had died on his way home to his house, his mousy wife and his horrible children. No kids deserve to lose their Dad. Some do.

On the last day of January it rains a lot. Puddles form and disappear into the thirsty ground. The rain keeps on falling. Soil becomes mud. Mum is sitting with my sister and Gran on the verandah. All three are too hot to move.

"I'm going to talk to that husband of mine," says Mum, as if he's in the house somewhere, "dragging me up here to the tropics." Mum is Melbourne born and likes to restate her birthright whenever things aren't quite right.

I've been sitting with them for a while but a man can only take so much of this idle chatter.

"Where do you think you're going?" Mum asks.

"For a walk."

"But it's raining, son."

"I know."

Now off the verandah steps and onto the path, it is to be a test of wills. A point where I'm called back to my senses or I break free of her influence.

My sister is incensed. "Are you just gonna let him go?"
"Oh, so he'll get wet. I'm past caring. God this weather."
Mum is rambling, unsticking her dress from her chest and
I'm away.
I hear Gran with her standard line.
"Look at his back. The rain's makin' little lines through all
that fluff on 'im. Someday you're going to have to get him
into a shirt and some clothes."

By the time I have reached Lacey Street the rain has all but
stopped. Black clouds are rolling out over the Pacific. Sun
is breaking through, turning the landscape gold. With the
dark backdrop it has an odd painted effect. Something you
can never quite explain, just admire. Turning the corner I
have the whole street to myself once more. Every colour
has been washed and brightened. It is a new view and
like other randomly chosen images in life it stays in my
memory forever.

Well Dad, here I am and there you are. I may be looking
straight towards you. Who can tell? I love this hopeless
town. When you want to be alone, it is no problem at all.
Right now I am on the headland beyond Lacey Street. It is
a fair guess that the Clancy kids stood right here trying to
kill Russell and me with their rock throwing. And there is
the track that Charlie used to carry me and the remains of
my blood supply back to the top.
Turning my head hard down, there's the scar on my
shoulder. It's sort of pink.
Sitting on the edge, clutching my knees I can rock back and

forth. My own form of a trance. Imagining my way around
the islands.
If the war is still going when I'm old enough I can take
over from Dad, give him a rest, drive the enemy back and
restore peace.
Jesus, if only we knew. No word at all. Please come home,
mate. I don't want to grow up alone. Two things a kid needs
is a dog and a Dad and I don't have a dog.
Now that's done it, I can feel my cheeks getting wet.
Rocking, rocking, blinking my eyes. Well I really wanted to
cry. A sort of therapy. Dogs eat grass, boys rock.
Am I a lonely, pathetic, little figure in the landscape?
That's a line from one of Dad's books.

I will sit here for many hours. A couple of people will
notice me and leave me. In the end I will get hungry, the
sky will brighten and with little else to do except dream
fleetingly of impossible, simplistic outcomes in my narrow
world I will head home. Sometimes it's all you can do.

THE WHITE BOAT

I don't normally read the weekday newspapers. There's just not the time. Today is different. Catching a train. Something I haven't done for years. It's the only way to this particular town, for this particular meeting and in a child-like way, I'm looking forward to it.

After the initial feeling of the movement and the viewing of the passing countryside I realise there is little to see from a train. Shake the newspaper into shape and see what range of offerings are served up for today's reader. On page 6 one column is given over to the death of a very old lady. The rest of my journey is lost as I sit with the paper limp on my lap.

It arrived overnight. When we woke in the morning, there it was sitting out in the middle of the inlet.. She was a big job. White with a single funnel.
Robbie saw it first. He saw everything first on account of

him waking at 5am every morning. Banned from making a
noise until 6:30am at least, he occupied himself by sitting
at the bay windows with Dad's binoculars.

"Hey, Screwball, look at this will ya." He is shaking my
shoulder. (My name is Stewart, after Jimmie Stewart but
when Robbie feels important he gets cheeky.) I took the
binoculars to the windows.
"Geez, she's a beauty." I had to admit it was worth being
woken for.
"Do you think it's sinister?" Robbie asked, his eyes wide.
He gazed again at the fat white hull contrasted against the
blue/green waters of the Pacific.

Being fifteen my opinion was considered valuable.
"No. I doubt it. Just some rich people who don't know
there's a war on."
We both used American accents. Sydney was full of Yanks.
Everybody was trying to sound like one. Except perhaps
for Aussie soldiers who thought they were a giant pain in
the arse.

That's why dad brought us up here, to the cottage. Getting
away from Sydney was like moving to another planet.
When Dad's leave ended he had to return to service. He
said he'd be happy because he could think of us up here,
nice and safe. If we were safe we were also bored. There
was not a lot to do in this part of the world.

We said nothing about the boat at breakfast. There was the porridge to get through. Mum had obtained a sack of the stuff and even though it was early summer in the tropics, she force fed it to us on the grounds that it built stamina and set us up digestively for the rest of the day.
I remember all that because I heard it so often that year.
So, with porridge sitting in our stomachs like cannon balls we staggered outside to greet the day.
We always closed the screen door quietly. It acted as an alarm and switched Mum's mind to thinking about times out and times back. Once the silence of the day set in she got going on housework and we were, for a while, forgotten.

Erroll had not seen the boat. His house was behind a big clump of coral trees at the bottom of the hill.
Although it was on stilts and had quite a high verandah going right round, the coral trees, banana trees and other palms had beaten it years before.
We sat on the steps and gave him all the details.
"A big white job, with a white funnel and a gold star. Lots of decks. She's magnificent. Can't see anybody. Looks deserted or they're all laying low. Pretty sinister if you ask me."
"Wow" said Erroll slowly, his eyes wide.

"Hey Screwball. I reckon ...." I punched Robbie hard on the

arm. He slipped off the step.

"Don't call me that you little speck."

Erroll was my mate, being fourteen, so it was considered okay to pick on little brothers. Especially those who talked incessantly.

Rubbing his arm and glaring at me Robbie tried again.

"Stewart," he whined, over emphasising the word, "I reckon we should set up a watch to make sure nobody tries to get off the boat with something."

He had a point.

Erroll warmed to the idea.

"Or tries to get on, with vital secrets," he suggested.

Our next stop was to the fourth member of our gang. Bill was thirteen, so he was sort of Robbie's friend and a little bit mine. He completed a set of ages from twelve to fifteen. While this was not an ideal situation and would not have been tolerated back in the city, there were so few kids around on this part of the coast that we allowed this breakdown in protocol for the sake of something to do. Bill had not seen the boat either. This made us pretty important. There was much prestige in our exclusive knowledge. It gave you power. The power to be first is part of life. I don't think it ever leaves us, it just changes in complexity. At this time it was simple and obvious.

"Lucky somebody's thinking of the country and how we'll all survive," I pointed out. "Lucky we keep a watch out."

Robbie took a deep breath. I knew what was coming.

He was about to claim sole credit. I hit him again.

"Hey," he yelped, "I didn't call you Screwball."

I hit him again for calling me Screwball. I was enjoying this. The last punch must have carried too much malice or landed in the same spot or both. Robbie started crying. He curled himself on the lawn in a little ball of self pity.

"Why are you always picking on me. Someday I'm gonna get bigger and I'm gonna fix you," he moaned from where his knees nearly touched his chin.

Now I was a bad guy. Nobody said anything. Robbie lay sobbing softly. Erroll and Bill gave that look. Suddenly I'm blabbing about how I was asleep and Robbie had really seen the boat and raised the alarm.

Robbie is really good at that. Winning when he loses.

Okay, I'm using my Yank accent. The binoculars are sitting on a stump pointed out to the water. The mystery boat sits there, hardly moving. Nothing is happening.

"Reckon we need a closer look," says Erroll.

"I'm having a closer look. That's what these things are for …."

Erroll, eyes half-closed, talking to an idiot. "I mean physically on board, not squinting through some old binoculars."

"Hey shithead, they're good binoculars. How do we get 'physically' on board? Fly?"

"I guess he means a boat," Robbie adds brightly looking around at all of us. He's like a little terrier. I expect his tongue to hang out. We both give him that superior older kid look.

"Where are we going to get a boat, Robbie?"

Robbie is indignant. "How would I know Erroll. You're the one who suggested getting out there." He has a point. Erroll shuts up.

Time for me to take charge. God, they're so hopeless.

"Alright, who's got a boat we can use?"

The long and the short of it all is that nobody has a boat they would even consider letting four kids have for one minute. This may appear odd seeing it is a coastal town and there are lots of small boats about but we just keep running into problems.

"What you want my boat for fellas? You just gonna mess about and break things then I got to fix it all up again ...... No, I don't think so."

"The skiff, no she's under the house. Got a .... big hole in her she has."

"My boat has an engine kids. You ever used a boat with an engine before? Course you haven't. Don't talk daft."

Finally Bill's canoe.

"It's here somewhere." We searched for quite some time to find Bill's canoe. Bill's family were not much into gardening and the yard was very big, sloping down to a little creek.

"Here she is," cries Robbie in triumph, his bum sticking out from under a mass of the endless banana palms.

"I'll pull it out. Gonna need a hand. Really jammed in here. Whoops .... Oh" There is silence. Robbie is still.

"Something bitten you, Robbie?" My little bother has no

fear or no sense and I'm always picturing myself carrying his lifeless corpse home after he's been bitten by a taipan or something similar with fangs.

Robbie slowly stands, lifting his head through the palm leaves. He holds up a section of wood. It is pointed and formed with some specks of blue paint still apparent.

"You pulled the front off the canoe. Robbie, you pulled the front off the damned canoe!"

Bill is more philosophical. "Forget it Stewart, it was rotten. It's been under there for years."

On the beach, staring once again at the big white boat. Still no movement through the binoculars.

"Maybe if we tell people why we want their boat. You know, national safety, secret business." Erroll, raised his eyebrows. "Well what do you think?"

"They'd tell our parents, Erroll. Within an hour we'd all be confined to our bedrooms."

None of our foursome returned home for lunch. There was the possibility that we may be held back or asked to work about our house. We 'borrowed' some bananas from Mrs Hendersons front yard then sat on the beach once more and talked about building a raft, stealing a boat, making canoes out of bent sheets of tin and melted tar, even knocking a quick rowboat together.

Robbie said, "I don't know why we don't swim out. We're all in the swim club. It can't be that far."

We resumed our discussions treating Robbie's suggestion with the disdain it deserved.

"I've heard that the local natives used to cut down trees and hollow them out. The wood is soft and buoyant so it's quite easy to do." Erroll is quite pleased with this bit of hitherto unknown local history.

"Where do we find these trees?"

"I don't know. They can't be too hard to find. Big, soft trees."

Behind us the coastal range, that runs all the way down the eastern seaboard, is covered in a mass of rich green foliage and tall timber. We all know it is there. No need to look round. Stay here, wait, and hope for some other form of salvation.

For quite a time we sat, heads bowed between our knees, the water lapping on the shore of the inlet. It always seemed to arrive and then fall onto the beach, like a drunk tripping over the front steps. Out there above the slap of the waves, across the fat lump of inlet water, sat the white boat. One by one our heads lifted, looked out to our goal, slowly turned and rested on Robbie. His eyes widened.

I said, "I guess you're right again, you little shit." We jumped him, held him down and tickled him until he pissed himself, then all jumped back. "Oh, you disgusting little person. Get out of here."

He worked his way up, covered in sand, strode down to the water, hitching his shorts with the dark stain and then flopped down. Smiling, eyes closed, he said, "Ah'" as he finished his piss.

"He's not really my brother, you know. He's adopted. His parents were mad people."

A great deal more work went into that afternoon. When the beach glistened and the heat became too intense we retreated to a grassed section under trees, then again into the creek that slid mountain water down to the sea. Floating in a circle four heads went round and round endlessly discussing the big swim we were to undertake that night.

Several times during our swim we have to stop. The boat seems no closer. Treading water, laying back and floating like frogs, our lungs full to add to the lift. Nobody talks of quitting, all pretending we're okay. We have wisely decided to leave behind, shoes (they'll make a noise on the deck), clothes (except for our swimmers, they create drag in the water), weapons (difficult to carry and they'll provoke the enemy into firing).
Before leaving we coat each other in baby oil, to aid flotation and make us harder to catch should escape be necessary. There is probably an easily traceable slick running all the way behind us back to the beach.
Robbie and I are late at the start, waiting for our mother to go to bed. She has discovered a story in some old copies of the Women's Weekly and started reading each episode. In desperation I wander past to the kitchen for a glass of water.
"Oh is that the one where the girl turns out to be a twin?" My mother's eyes lift from the page. She is glowering. It is a horrible thing to do but national security is at stake.

Soon after she is in bed talking of her idiot son.

Our final obstacle in the water is the unexpected surge of the incoming tide as we cross the mouth of the inlet. Swimming across saps our dwindling supply of energy. With a suddenness that stops us as we reach still water the boat has arrived. It sits there above us. We are within its faint silver shadow on the water. We are breathlessly silent. Looking up I am immediately aware of a hole in our carefully laid plans. No thought was given to the method of boarding this giant, once alongside.

With immaculate timing Robbie slides under water and emerges next to a large wood stepped, rope ladder hanging into the water, hidden near the boat's stern. The little terrier has done it again and is already climbing. I am too relieved to consider my ego.

Within seconds we are all over the side and on deck.

A task carried out with laudable silence. It is a moment to cherish. We have achieved our objective. A remarkable feat. Here we are, masters of our fate, able to carry out the task we have set for the good of the nation. Now, for a determination of layout.

"Don't bloody move! Stand completely still!"

I am frozen to the deck. I am crouching down. My heart has picked up speed. Racing. Making a noise in my ears. A quick glance at the others reveals that they too are crouching, as if it somehow makes you less noticeable. The voice seemed to come out of the air. Moving just my eyes I realise I still have one foot in the air.

At what seems great personal risk I lower it to the deck.

The alternative is to fall over.

There is a noise, ahead and above us. Now I realise where the owner of the voice must be. I chance a look up. Staring back down at me are the double barrels of a shotgun.

A sort of whimper escapes my lips. It is taken up by the others. If I am not brave then they apparently wont be. Silhouetted against the sky is large bearded man. He is at the railing of the upper deck that overlooks this back section.

Robbie starts up with a noise that has the potential to grow. I shush him out the side of my mouth, as quietly and distinctly as I can.

A very big light comes on. There we were, locked in various awkward postures across the deck, like a bad chorus line.

The man with gun was hidden behind the glare.

A thumping noise followed. I realised later that it was the bearded man stamping to attract attention from the cabin below.

A second or two passed then another man came out a side door onto our deck. He looked, not particularly surprised.

"Bloody hell," he said.

"What do you think Lloyd?" the man with the gun said, "Some local riff raff or German spies?"

This was too much. "We're not spies," I pointed out.

"You, shut-up!" The man with the gun seemed closer. His voice made me jump again.

The man called Lloyd looked back up to the one with the gun.

"So, what do we do with them. Throw 'em all overboard?"

"Nah." There was a sudden softness in the reply. I hoped this meant the gun was no longer pointed at my head.
"I don't know, you can't go anywhere without people poking around." He now sounded exasperated.
"How did you get out here kids? Where's your boat?"
I realised he was asking me a question.
"We swam." A pause. I pictured him measuring the distance.
"God - I'm impressed."
"We're all members of a swimming club," I ventured.
"No doubt," the voice said, "pretty good ones too. Wonder a shark didn't have you, you stupid kid."
"I've never seen a shark in here, sir."
"Well there's a first time for everything in this world isn't there."
The light was swung away. To my great relief I saw him put the gun down. Heard the clunk of it's stock on the deck.
"Well, I don't know what to do with you. Put you back on shore and give you all a kick in the bum. Damn bloody damn. I was just going to bed. You know you're trespassing don't you?"
Time for more explanation I thought. "We were just curious. No harm intended."
Bill suddenly came to life. "You see there's a war on. We thought we'd better check you out. They say you've got to be suspicious of everybody. Absolutely everybody."
"A war eh. Well we're genuine just like you fella."
The man with the gun looked at us. A long glowering look that commanded silence. He scratched his beard, then his nose, rubbed his forehead and finally took off his cap,

scratched his head and looked to the sky. He had a bald
patch in the centre of his black hair. When he looked back
to us there was a degree of disappointment in his eyes.
He really did not want us to be there.

"It's no good Lloyd we'll have to get the boat out and take
'em back."

Lloyd moved toward us. He too was unimpressed by the
night's events. "You lot, sit here and don't move a muscle."
He pointed with a stabbing finger. Did I smell booze?

We dropped were he pointed, backs against the railing,
knees under our chins.

He began untying ropes from a large canvas lump on the
deck. It was an upturned rowboat. It was at this point that
we all became aware of a third man on the deck.

The new man was tall with white shorts and shirt and long
white socks. He had quite thin legs and stood with his
hands on his hips looking about.

"What is going on?" he asked. The emphasis was on the
word 'is'.

Lloyd jumped and turned. The other man came down from
the upper deck.

"Sorry sir, I didn't see you there."

"I repeat, what *is* going on?"

"Some local kids, sir. Caught 'em on the deck." said Lloyd.

The other man joined in. "They made a lot of noise,
chattering away, so I was waiting for them. Lloyd and I are
just going to drop them back to the little beach over ...."

"A lot of noise? Of course! This can't be. This cannot be.
Why would guests sneak aboard? How could you treat our
guests so .... so carelessly."

"Guests, sir?"

"Yeeees, 'guests'. Been expecting them all day. And why, you've nearly thrown them overboard."

The big man looked neutral. I guessed he knew his place. What was this other character talking about?

We watched as the strange conversation floated between the three men in front of us. Four sets of eyes followed the action from our seated position.

Mr White Shorts obviously had authority and so had to be tolerated. Robbie looked at me. I raised my eyebrows. What else could I do?

The discussion was reaching a conclusion. "So, they're our guests."

"Certainly, sir."

"She needs a nice little diversion. You know how difficult things can be if we become bored. So don't be so tedious lads."

Suddenly we exist again. Our man in the fancy duds swings round with this big, broad smile on his face. His head is to one side, as if examining puppies in a store window.

"I'm thinking you should escort our guests to the reception area, eh.. We'll be dying to meet them."

This was all getting a little strange. The bearded guy turns to us and says, "Well now, if you gentlemen would all like to follow." His hand is outstretched, like a hotel doorman, to indicate the way. Do I detect a slight bow. We stay seated. First because we're a bit suspicious, secondly because we're confused and thirdly because we'd never been called gentlemen before.

Seeing our dilemma the man Anderson crouches down beside me.

"No mystery, there's this lady I'd like you to meet. She's beautiful and charming and she loves children. I'll drop you back afterwards, I promise." He gives one of those glinting, salesman's smiles. He seems okay.

"You're our honoured guests," the man in white is chirping. That's the clincher. We rise as one and follow Anderson, along the deck. This really is a great ship. The decks are polished and shine in the lights. We pass Lloyd who maintains a poker face and half closed eyes. Stepping through a door we are in a corridor. There are vases of flowers set into the wood paneling. I touch a few. They seem fresh.

Bill puts his hand on my shoulder. "Where are we going?" His voice has a slight note of urgency.

"Don't know, they seem okay though. I mean I haven't heard any foreign accents."

We turned into a larger corridor. It led to some large, glass panelled doors. The floor was now carpeted and soft under our feet.

Anderson ushered us through. The man in white squeezed past and assumed a position in front.

The room was round. It had dark panelling, big lounge chairs even a fireplace. The radio was playing dance tunes, very softly.

"Its' got a bloody fireplace." Robbie is wide-eyed as he whispers this information to me from behind his hand. Anderson I note has backed out quietly and closed the doors.

It is at this time that we realise that there is someone else in the room.

"Who's there," a voice inquires.

"I've brought you some guests, my dear." The white pants man is wringing his hands I note.

"Guests? At this hour?"

A hand appears over the top of a long lounge facing the fire. "Who might they be Dorian?"

The man we now know as Dorian is making rather urgent signals for us to move forward. His eyes too are flashing messages. He looked a little ridiculous but thankfully nobody deems laughter appropriate.

So, the moment of truth. We migrate in one lump around the corner of the lounge. There on the lounge is a woman. Everything about her is soft as is she is blurred by some smoky glass.

Stretched out, propped on one elbow, she surveyed us as we looked back. Her skin is soft, her hair is gold. She wears a satin gown and at the end of her long slender legs she has on dainty gold slippers. In the low light of the room she radiates and glows. She is the most beautiful person I have ever seen.

Her tongue did a slow circle of her mouth as we all watched its progress. Nothing on her face indicates emotion or much at all for that matter. She takes a long drag on a cigarette in a long gold cigarette holder. Possibly as a joint mental connection we all become aware of our lack of clothing, looking first at each other and then

down at our feet. Our hands creep across to our crotches.
"Oh, aren't they gorgeous!" She has spoken. Those lips
have moved. We're frozen once more.
"Where *did* you find them?"
"It appears they came out to check our boat, Diana.
Swam out mind you. Concerned that we may be spies or
saboteurs perhaps." Dorian is warming to the situation. His
boss is obviously pleased so he is quickly becoming a jerk.
"Oh how simply gorgeous," says Diana, taking another
puff on her cigarette, while her eyes stay fixed on us. "And
look they come in a matched set, look at that. Beautifully
balanced and arranged."
Her voice is husky and rather grand, as if she was talking
to somebody in the next room.
Somehow we were standing on a row relative to our height,
pressed together with our hands in front.

The lady Diana props herself up on some pillows.
"Now don't be shy boys. It's not every day a lady has four
handsome and obviously virile men attending her in her
sitting room. Stand up straight now, don't slouch."
We all snap to attention.
"That's better. So you think we're all spies. Sounds like one
of my gorgeous scripts."
The hand sweeps about in a idle gesture. There is hint
there that we may have expected to pick up on.

I chance a look around. Whoever owns this boat has a high
income. It even smells rich.
"You must have some refreshments, dears. Dorian darling,

some of those sugary drink things please and some cake, they must have cake."

There goes that hand again. This time it waves in a circular motion.

"Oh sit down boys. You look like the home guard."

Once again the hand waves about, this time indicating to some chairs. There are three. Robbie is left standing. Unperturbed, he asks the question we all want know.

"Are you famous?"

Only a slight pause. "Oh isn't he adorable." She is addressing no one. "You, the little one, come here."

This time the arm makes an all encompassing, sweeping motion. Robbie naturally hesitates.

"No, come, come, you can sit with Diana."

He moves forward slightly. Once within reach her arm encircles him and he is pulled in tight beside her. He does not look all that comfortable but her arm remains in place.

"I think I can trust you," she whispers into his ear, "you're too young to take advantage of a lady."

There is certain breathless quality to her voice, as if she is fighting for air. It is sort of a loud whisper.

She nuzzles her nose against his arm. "Oh you smell delicious sweetie, like a young puppy." She pulls Robbies head down and gives him a solid kiss on the cheek. It leaves the imprint of her lips in stamp-pad perfection. Robbie looks horrified.

"Don't squirm dear, there's a darling."

There is a brief silence. The lady is examining Robbie's arm.

"You have a bruise my dear. I hope that isn't the work

of some brutish person taking advantage of your undeveloped stature."

"No, its my brother." The little toad lifts a finger and wavily points in my direction. I am fixed with a quite malevolent stare from the lady.

"I won't enquire into the details young man, possibly your young brother was displaying some unsuitable behaviour. But he is younger than you and smaller and less mature. You should take such things into account when dealing with him. I could have Anderson box your ears. He is after all bigger than you. Would that be fair?"

"No, I guess not." I'm mumbling a bit, planning to kill the little shit when we get home. Robbie has a slight smirk on his face and is settling down comfortably in the clutches of this Diana person.

"Good then," she says, and flashes the most amazing big smile at all of us.

Dorian returned at this juncture. He had regained some token dignity by having Anderson carry the drinks.

"No, no, no."

Anderson poised to distribute cake and drink, looked up at Diana.

"Bring it here." Her hand moved in an imitation of a periscope. "They must sing for their supper, as it were. Each of my guests must step up and tell me his name, his age and a little about himself. Sufficient to be rewarded with supper, eh?"

Anderson nodded and left the tray beside Diana.

"You, the largest boy. You may go first." The tentacle finger pointed at me. Despite a degree of awe I felt the first twinges of annoyance at this persecution.

"My name is Stewart, after Jimmy Stewart. I'm fifteen.
I like drawing. Dad is a boat mechanic. He's down in
Sydney at the Naval Docks." This seemed sufficient for the
circumstances.

Diana looked at me.

"That's lovely dear. And he's a lovely man." As I pondered
the possibility that this lady knew my Dad she added,
"Jimmy dear, Jimmy."

With the hand that was not clasping Robbie she lifted a
glass of lemonade and held it out.

With cake and drink I resumed my seat. It all seemed so
formal. It all seemed ridiculous but it was not for me to say.
Bill was up, summoned to perform. He stood awkwardly,
looking at his toes.

"I'm Bill. I'm thirteen. I'm named after my Dad."

"Very nice too Bill." The drink and cake was handed over
with due ceremony.

"Now, there's this one here isn't there."

Skewered with the finger Erroll rises and is positioned by
various silent movements in the centre of the carpet.

"My name's Erroll. I'm fourteen. I'm a champion swimmer."
He paused and grinned. "Or a bit of a liar."

Diana raised her eyebrows. I don't think she totally
approved of people showing unsanctioned initiative.

"You're named after my dear friend Mr Flynn."

"No, after my grandfather Erroll from Larne."

Drink in hand Erroll backed away to a seat. Diana suddenly
jumped and began gesticulating in his direction. "Oh my
god, oh my god." She had her hand to her face. "Dorian,

will you look at that. He's sitting in the same seat. Erroll's seat. He sat there only months ago."

"Quite, quite remarkable," ventured Dorian.

"And you have the hide to cast doubts on my astrology. He was drawn to that chair. There is an astral connection." Erroll looked quite alarmed. Examining the chair for wires or trapdoors.

"I am sure Diana will remind me of this occurrence regularly over the next few months." Dorian says with an air of resignation.

"You're darn tootin," dear." says Diana, not looking at the unbeliever in her midst. "My guests no doubt all believe fervently in the influences of the cosmos."

We nod vigorously as her beautiful, narrowed eyes, move from one to the other in an inspection of our loyalty. I dread the possibility that she will question me about 'cosmos' but she seems content with blind allegiance. There follows some moments of silence. We fill the awkwardness by delicately biting into the sponge cake and taking very small, well spaced sips of lemonade.

Her smile rests upon one or the other of us at times as she smokes her cigarette. Robbie has adapted to his environment with the same cocky assuredness he has for life in general. He has deemed this person, who still holds him beside her, as somebody special and of no physical threat, so he is settled contentedly against her like a cat in control of its master. At other moments the lady Diana seems to drift, her eyes are far away. Dorian stands casually in the background. A decoration that can spring to life as required. Suddenly, there is a question.

"Do any of you dance, sing, act, tell humorous stories,
play a musical instrument etcetera, etcetera?" Her head is
now animated and jumping around as if she has produced
an exciting new direction for the evening to take. I almost
expect Dorian to respond with some polite applause.
Instead we are all doing the thing that most loyal mates
do in a tight situation. In this case we're all looking at Bill.
Diana picks up on the message quite quickly. "Your friends
are indicating that you have a talent Bill dear. What, pray
tell, is it?"
"I play the piano a little." He glares at us.
Robbie leaps right in. "He's terrific, best I've ever heard,"
he says, squirming round to look at the lady. Now Bill
wants to kill him as well.
Diana waves her hand majestically once. "Then we shall
have a demonstration. A private soirée. A recital by Bill for
his closest admirers."
Bill is a little perplexed. We are all thinking the same thing.
There is no piano. Bill is safe. But fate awaits the unwary.
Dorian pulls a velvet curtain back in part of the panelled
wall and there indeed is a piano, securely fastened in an
alcove. By undoing some restraining devices Dorian drags
it out into the room. He quickly produces a matching
swivel chair with velvet and tassels. Bill is before the beast,
his shoulders slumped.
"I hope you know some dance tunes?" Diana is struggling
to her feet. Robbie is up and moving away but not fast
enough. She has him again.
"Oh no my darling, you're my date for this evening. Can't
desert a lady. You stand with me." She positions herself,

leaning on the piano, pulling Robbie to her. "I want to feel your heart swell when I sing. You're delicious, I could eat you my dear." She bends down and kisses Robbie on the shoulder. Now he has two sets of lips on his person. "When I grow older and less beautiful I will produce children. My first child will be you dear."

Robbie once again is wide-eyed and horrified. My turn to smirk at him.

Bill, now seated, is staring at the keys. His parents had him at the piano from three years old. Technique is not his problem.

"Dorian, the boy needs loosening up." Diana has called for something. I wonder if Dorian will give Bill a shoulder massage. Instead he appears with a tumbler of pale brown liquid. It is bubbling with soda water.

"Drink it down dear. It will do wonders for your performance." Diana is pointing as Bill eyes the glass suspiciously. "What is it?"

"A tonic, dear. A tonic."

He takes a sip, as we all watch for a throat clutching reaction. He licks his lips and proceeds to down the lot. "That was nice."

"Good God," says Diana, "another alcoholic musician. Honestly, it must come with the music."

Bill tentatively taps a few notes with his right hand.

"Gershwin," says Diana, "you clever boy. I did his stuff."

We all got some of Diana's magic loosener as the evening progressed. She had us singing, harmonising beautifully without a touch of the squirming embarrassment that

should accompany such a revealing act. In turn we all danced with her, our faces pressed into the white sheen softness of her chest. Her voice was as beautiful as her face. Bill excelled himself. We had never dreamed how well he could play. He became quite unbearable and unstoppable and then, when the evening had reached its zenith, a point where you truly wonder what other delights can further enhance its perfection, he fell off the chair. "Dear me," said Dorian, holding his wrist. He looked up at Diana, his face awkward. "He's a little too loose."
"Oh, well that's torn it. Can't have a party without the piano player." Diana plugged another cigarette into her holder. She lit the thing and perched on the vacated piano stool, crossing those long legs. Puff, puff. She was deflated. Mumbled something. Put her hand to my face as a prop. "But see! The rising moon of Heaven again. Look for us, Sweetheart, through the quivering Plane: How oft hereafter rising will she look Among those leaves - for one of us in vain."
A brief silence followed.
I found the verse next winter. Quietly recited it to the lady in the library who recognised it.

Then it was over.
"It's 2am. Rouse the crew and we'll send the guests on their way. Parting will break my heart. 'Tis better to have loved and lost them all than never crossed their paths at all etcetara."
Diana seemed ragged. Less in control. The room swam about me.

In the boat still in only our swimmers, we are suddenly
cold. A surprisingly affable Anderson, stops rowing briefly
and puts a blanket round us. We each bear the Diana stamp
of approval, a large imprint of red lips on our cheeks.
"Goodbye my princes," she calls from the deck. Turning to
Dorian she says, "It's no good I'll have them all as babies.
Perhaps two at a time. It's in the stars."
"Of course," says Dorian.
Anderson is strong. The little skiff skims across the water
that took so long to swim. I look back once. Already the
lights are going out. Under the blanket we're warm and
drunk and fading as we bump onto the beach. Robbie is
fast asleep. Usually I would kick him. This time I lift him
out.
As Anderson is about to push off he calls us back, shakes
each of our hands and pats the unconscious Robbie. "Nice
to have had you on board kids. Hey, listen, do us a small
favour." His voice is conspiratorial. "Don't mention this to
anyone will you. Diana needs a bit of peace at the moment.
Okay."
We each solemnly agree to his proposal and then say
goodbye.
It's past caring time for all of us. Bill can barely crawl and
I have my little brother to carry home like a baby. We all
part agreeing to meet the next day.
Robbie doesn't wake until after midday. By then the boat
has gone.

TIDES

When the water rose, fields of summer green moved
oddly then turned brown.
It, the water, quickly reached the house, oiling its way
across the threshold, slipping into the carpet. Dismay and
resolve happened at once.
They moved upstairs, carrying all they could, as fast as
they could, to live above the lapping menace. Beneath
a grey-black brittle sky the water ran, like a mob
seeking satisfaction in a fruitless rampage. Not fast, just
purposeful. A cow, bloated and obscene, bumped past.
The house groaned under unrecognised stresses.
Their world had changed.
The sun set and the light went away. No power and only
saved water. When they slept they tossed about fitfully,
with half an ear to the possibility of the house crumbling
away from beneath their supine forms.

In the morning an unblemished bright blue sky sat on the
brown tide in a sliced line of separation. The urgency in the
water had eased. It was odd to walk down the stairs from
the landing and find solid water at the fifth step.

A fish darted away.

"So much ruined," said Mother.

Father climbed a ladder into the attic and from there through the skylight onto the roof. 'Parrot', the dog, stood at the base of the ladder with one paw on the first rung, in a show of concern for his daily companion. Father was above for some time, his footfalls tracing his position over their heads.

"We're an island in a light brown sea," he said, sitting on Susan's bed. "Nobody will be along to rescue us just yet"

Mother climbed out of her comfortable corner and became practical.

"You must take care on that roof, Louis."

"I am that dear, you know how I operate. Though if I fell at present I'd just be getting wet."

"We must make the most of our predicament until there is a change in the outlook," Mother continued.

She set up the two burner gas stove on the landing. Dragged a smallish table out to act as a workbench and prepared shredded potato, cheese and eggs.

"Umm nice. What do you call this?" Jeremy held a section on his fork.

"Anything you like, my boy. You give it a name.."

"Goat's bladder." And so it remained. None of the family ever considered asking why.

Jeremy needed to go to the toilet after breakfast. No suitable container presented itself and the need became pressing. Father shut the door to the main bedroom then

sat him on a window ledge with a rope under his arms
and let the water carry away the result. The search for a
suitable container consumed the girls interest after this
and a bucket was eventually located in the attic. Emptied
of its contents of string and pieces of soap it was placed in
the bedroom corner with as much dignity as a bucket can
bring to such a situation.

The day was an adventure of sorts, however by its middle,
very little of the excitement was left. Logs had begun to
collect about the house and in their bumping way they
found windows and broke them. Father cursed anew each
time another pane was shattered.

Mother read a book as father paced.

"Your crops were all in, Louis. The money is in the bank."

"The bank," he reminded her, "is next to the park by the
river."

"Wet money is still money, dear."

Susan began on the piano. It cut father short. The reply on
his lips turned to a smile.

"I've not heard you play for a while girl. All the effort
getting it up here years back. This water would have been
the end of it downstairs. Don't play anything melancholy,
please."

Jeremy sat with her as they performed a party trick with
'chopsticks.' Never one to be entirely at ease with the
situation, father then relented and agreed to a catholic
selection.

There followed 'The Girl with the Flaxen Hair', 'Scenes from
Childhood' and 'Londonderry Air', till Susan grew tired and
father was much relieved, feeling himself beginning to slide

into an unproductive reverie.

"Will we be rescued by sea or by air?" Beth looked at her parents. Mother continued in her book but her father could not let any query go uncovered by his ample knowledge.

"It is a matter of conjecture, dear. I would suggest that a rescue by boat may be what finally takes us away."

"There are no boats about, father. Not a one anywheres in Pallister or Manning. Why would there be boats way out here?"

"For the same reason that fish appear when a dry stream is flooded. It is the nature of things that such objects present themselves at appropriate times. Boats will come, I feel sure of it."

Father returned to the roof at dusk and reported back that nothing had changed, not the vanished land nor any dot of hope upon it. With this news in hand they all settled down for an early night, having secured their stomachs against hunger with the last of the bread and raspberry jam. Before he slept the father stared at the ceiling and made a quiet pact of deliverance with himself then turned on his side and patted the ample rump of his sleeping wife.

Another day came in the morning. In a continuing mockery of their weeks of rain the sky once again refused to produce a single cloud. Each family member in turn ran their gaze of the whole circumference of their horizon and said nothing. Mother set about sorting through the larder. She produced porridge made of a watery powdered milk and sweetened with treacle.

Spooning mouthfuls with annoying enthusiasm Jeremy

noted that the chickens must all have drowned by now.

"Is there a heaven for chickens?" he asked.

"Be awful damned crowded," his Dad noted, smirking at his daughters, who had just adjusted to the fact that 'Henny', 'Pecker', 'Clarice', and even 'Albert' that miserable rooster were no longer with them.

With the breakfast over these five people stood about unsure of the procedures. Beth and Jeremy ventured down the stairs and reported the water level unchanged except that now there was real smell.

"Give us a choon girlie." Father put his arm round the shoulder of his oldest girl but she shrugged away. This disappointed him. He felt he had a good relationship with this one. She often presented an alternative sounding board for his aspirations when Mother was unreceptive. He could chat with her for hours, hanging as they did on the rails of the roundyard. It was a sign he decided that their situation was parlous and in need of remedy.

Like the deck of the Ancient Mariner's ship the crew of this creaking wooden vessel lay about wrapped in their despondency. Below, unseen, the swelling lengths of timber cladding lifted their holding nails and edged away from the frame.

An oppressive heat worked up through the day until it reduced its captives to laying about on the floor, pooling their sweat. Jeremy stripped to his underpants.

"Can I go for a swim, Dad?"

"That would not be wise son."

Beth became annoyed. "Look at him, always running about
without clothes. What if somebody were to call?" In the
silence she flushed red at the stupidity of the statement,
then rolled over so as not to have the others see her smile.
Jeremy compromised and put on one of his father's shirts..
"I can still see his undies," noted Beth.
"We all have bottoms my girl," Mother noted, "even you."

At lunch they ate some apples that were brown inside.
Nobody noticed mother go without.
"It came with such a rush," she said. "I had little time to
find the children, let alone gather up food."
In the mid afternoon, with father on the roof, the heat went
away or was lost behind another advancing weather front.
On the south western edge of the horizon a black wall
approached their island.
Just then from deep in the bowels of the house a snarling
crack rose up to their ears. The house moved slightly
beneath their feet, transmitting its vibration into their
spines, up their necks and into their hearts. Beth and
Jeremy began to cry.
Father scurried down the ladder. He found his family,
his dog included, huddled round mother, on the landing
carpet.
"That was not a good sign, something is seriously amiss
below." He went to the landing window and stared for
some seconds at the clouds and lightning cracking across
the sky towards them.
"I'm going for help. It's the only thing to do."
Mother rose, shedding children and dog. "You'll do no such

thing. Leave us here while you drown."

Father had dignity added to his decision. "I can make it easily. There has to be dry land over towards Murchies. That will be where the rescue effort will be centred."

Mother was angry. "It's ten miles. Why would any 'effort' be set up on some barren hill in the middle of nowhere. God man, if you made it you'd just sit there."

As if accenting their dilemma, another pop sound came from below and to their terror they felt a tiny shift in the level of the floor.

Father stood with his chin thrust forward. He faced his steel set wife and the wide eyes of three children and a concerned dog.

"Are we going to all perish, Dad?" Jeremy' voice was croaky and soft.

Beth immediately set to wailing and Susan prepared to join her. A massive blast of thunder racketed across the sky, shaking tin on the roof.

Father was about to speak although he was unsure of what to say.

"What's that?" Mother's head scouted about, her eyes looking around the room, darting from one object to the next.

"Lightning, thunder, what?" said father.

Mother waved her arms about and then grabbed Beth and shook her into silence. In awe or perhaps fear of this odd behaviour, they all stood and waited while Mother tilted her head one way then the other.

"There," she said. Now they all heard it.

A low steady noise. Not a rumble, roar or threatening shake but a faint, rhythmic squeaking.

Susan looked at her feet and at the ceiling, concentrating, stretching her hearing. "It's from out there." She held her hand out, finger extended toward the window.

Father galvanised by the gesture, rushed forward. His large shoulders filled the space. They rose in exultation then fell in realisation. "Oh God. Oh Christ. Oh no. No, no, no."

He turned to his family. "It's Svenson."

The sky spat great globs of occasional rain at them but seemed unable to get going. Father pulled hard on one of the oars while Svenson handled the other. Father glowered at his family seated in the back while Svenson regaled him with every detail of the last week. The rain, the town, the people, the mud, the fish, the river, the goats, the cows, the sheep, the old boat he had in his barn. In the roof in case it rained.

Jeremy watched to see if it were true. Father had said once that Svenson never even paused for a breath and by crikey it appeared to be true.

Mother kept protective arms around her children for no obvious reason. Parrot had made his way to the prow of this stout vessel to gaze ahead and give advise on direction and speed. His barks went unheeded.

"I varned dem many a time," Svenson said, pulling hard on his oar. He had very little body hair and a thin annoying, wispy beard on his chin.

"Yairs," I said, "you all listen now, dat river has silted. She's running out of der room in her bottom. Little bit of rain and den she gonna burst her banks."

Father rolled his eyes back in his head. He could easily imagine Svenson in centre stage at the stock agents store. All the men of the town trying to slide out the door as Svenson gave them some more of his endless advise.

"Nobody listens. Now zay say, ho dat Svenson, he knows a ting or two."

They were heading for Svenson's farm. He had built his house and outbuildings on a rocky hillock. Tight together with very little yard and a steep road up, it was considered another example his eccentric state of mind. Now, apparently it sat above the water line and provided further fuel to the Svenson way of doing things. He had built a small levee around his homestead.

"I was sure you'd be flooded," said Father, almost hopefully.

"Noo not me. I rowed five miles to your place. I vill take care of you. I have lots of nice food." He smiled benignly at Beth. "All stored for such a day. I bet dis buildup caught you out, eh."

Father's dignity continued to be ground down. Like grain in a mill he could feel it turning to dust as he fought the oar that brought them closer to Svenson's prison. He would hold them captive and bombard them with 'dis' and 'dat' and 'de udder'.

"I told dem," Svenson continued, with no sign of a breath, "when Manning built dat giant earth bank. Where you tink

de vater going to go, eh? She gonna bank up all de way
back ..."
"What?!!" snarled father.
"Vat, Vat?"
"Manning built a dam?"
"Yairs and I said, she's gonna be like dis big lake ...."
"When? How? I didn't know about this .... dam? So all this
bloody mess is the fault of the good people of Manning?"
"Vell day didn't going around telling everybody but it was
known ...."
"Bloody Manning's fault!"
Svenson seemed perturbed by this repetition of the
obvious. Father slammed down his oar. "Those bastards.
They must have known the consequences."
He sat with his large hands cradling his head. Mother
noted the remarkable silence.
"Now Louis, it's something to be sorted out once this
predicament is over. Swearing will not help. Perhaps they
never expected this much rain. For now, let's get the
children under cover." Parrot barked.

Svenson took a breath. Jeremy definitely saw him do it.
"Ho, it vill fix itself real soon, you'll see. Do even I did
not expect such rain as ve hav had. I told dem down in
Manning, dey don't build her with a big enough base. De
vater vill undermine de whole ting ewentually. Den she'll
all joost flow avay. It's only dirt after all. Vont take much
to .... ummm". Svenson paused and looked up from his
rowing.
"Ummm," he said, again gazing outward.

"Dad, that tree is growing." Jeremy pointed to a nearby
gum, full of snakes and other wet beasties all keeping a
watch on each other.

"Look. Something's happening."

Indeed the tree grew bigger. It was emerging and they were
descending. Very slowly but obviously.

As if some giant over their horizon had pulled the plug in
his bath they continued to drop. No huge rush or surge,
just easing down. They sat, mouths open. watching pieces
of landscape appear as minutes ticked by.

"Ho, ho, ho." Svenson slapped his knee. "It has happened.
Manning vill not be a pretty site. I tell you sumpzing ..."

And he did, for many many minutes.

Then the boat bumped and started to list. The girls cried
out and father reached over to hold his family as they
skewed round and stopped.

They were resting in a small gully. Just on the edge of their
farm.

By the time they had all scrambled, slipped and clawed
their way out they were covered in mud.

Svenson looked down at his boat. "How de hell am I gonna
get dat out of der?"

"Later Svenson. We'll get it much later." Father shook
his neighbour's hand. "Very good of you. Decent and
neighbourly. We'll be off then."

"You can com to my house. It's dry and varm."

"No thanks. Can't wait to get back to our little place."

They left Svenson peering into the gully and squelched
away across the fields.

Their house was a brown, putrid mess. One side beam had
snapped and an upper room hung at a slight angle. Boards
were missing and the skeletal frame was revealed. No
downstairs window remained intact.
"Not too bad," said Father making the best of it.
"All repairable. Prop that section up straight. Brace it with
some extra framing. Replace the cladding. Bit of glazing
work. That will take a while. Coat of paint."
He paused, putting his hand to his mouth. "Wonder how
the insurance company will get out of paying." He seemed
to almost relish the battle ahead.
They found a selection of flapping fish on the lounge and
mother set off upstairs to prepare them for dinner. Susan
played abstractly on the piano. Jeremy rolled in the yard
with Parrot and then inquired about taking a bath.

At 8pm they were seated on the landing eating fish and
potatoes with butter and parsley they'd washed from the
garden. The clouds had gone away. A late evening light
on the drying mud outside made the landscape into an
interplanetary experience.
"Like Mars," said Beth. "As viewed from the landing craft."
This interesting line of thought was interrupted.

A strangled noise came from below. Muffled yet urgent.
All looked about, seeking an explanation.
"It's the phone!" Louis jumped to his feet. He pounded

down the stairs. "The phone," he cried, "who'd have thought the thing was working."
The girls, the boy, the dog and mother listened to some conversation floating up in the dim light.
"Well he hasn't been electrocuted," Mother whispered.

Father reappeared. His face bland, his eyes unfocused.
"Concerned about us were they?" Mother ventured.
"Manning's pretty well wiped out." Father pursed his lips.
"They want to know how many people we can put up for a while."

DANCER

It picked up as soon as they crossed the gully. Dancing through the trees and rushing up behind, whipping their legs with the tall paddock grasses.

"Bitch", cried Hal, "we've got to run."

As they pounded forward up the slope its intensity grew. Now the trees shrieked desperately and the grass made determined tangles that gripped their clothes. Bits of old broken timber stirred up and hit them hard.

This time there was a noise they had not heard before. Indeterminate, a rumble as if a huge beast had been disturbed.

Lyle was falling behind. They ran on until well away from the steep gully floor.

Standing with his feet planted apart Hal screamed into the rushing air.

"You won't stop us. You own nothing. This is the time for it."

Alison, 'Ally', looked at him with some admiration.

She pulled strands of hair from her face. His eyes were wet. Curious, she touched his cheek.

"It's the wind, I'm not crying," he said, clutching his dignity.

He reached out to pull Lyle up with them on the slope.

All three turned their backs on the angry sky. Winding away and up the hill they could now make out the faint line of the old track. It was much higher and steeper than they had imagined. Or had their perception become distorted. They had not made it this far before. And fear was a factor. Below them a tree branch gave up and snapped, cartwheeling in a shower of leaves as it ran down into the brush at the base of the gully.

Lyle yelled grasping his face. It took both their hands to hold him down and pull the fingers away. A finger-thick piece of white gum wood from the shattered branch was sticking from his cheek. It still glistened with sap. Hal pulled it out before there came time for discussion. Blood rushed from the hole. Ally, as was her nature, continued to hold Lyle's hands away while Hal produced a rag of a handkerchief and pressed it on Lyle's face.

"Now Lyle, small cuts on your face always bleed more than on your knee or elbow so you'll have to hold this on till it stops. Don't take it off. I'll tell you when."

Anticipating the way of the conversation Hal added.

"Just a scratch. A splinter really." He did not look at Ally.

As they stood, Lyle appearing quite dramatic with blood down his neck and staining his shirt, the wind gusted again, spraying them with dirt.

Hunched, they made their way up the track. A slight bank on one side. The late afternoon light threw shadows around the frantically active landscape. It seemed that each step closer to their goal brought some increase in the frustrated roar of the wind.

Perhaps this was the child, with powers beyond its
maturity.

Hal trembled, making an effort to walk. Like the drunken
purposeful steps of his father after a night in the town.
It was hard to see. He squinted with his hand to his face
staring at the ground. Dirt flew about trying to reach his
eyes. He had never known such fear.
All they'd heard, all they'd been told, appeared true.
This was not like any previous attempts but they had been
younger and had not ventured so far or so close to it.
His was the sudden act of bravado that had brought about
their pact. They would cross the gully and keep going.
They would reach it no matter what the consequences of
their actions. An easy thing to say sitting quietly under the
water tank by the safety and the still of the house.

High overhead towards the ranges there is a cry. The
two older children keep their heads tucked down. Lyle
automatically turns his face to the sky seeking out the
wedge-tail eagle. He knows their ways. It is unusual for
them to make a sound but he has heard it before echoing
off the ranges. As his neck tilts back an unseen hand
reaches across his shoulder. Briefly he is aware of a small
piece of blue sky surrounded by boiling black clouds.
Through this coloured patch the unmistakable silhouette
of the bird slides across his view. It appears to be circling.
Smash. His face and eyes are covered in dirt. Reeling
away he steps off the track. His arms go out and Hal's
handkerchief is snatched away.

Without sight and spun round he falls heavily, rolling till his jacket hooks onto a tree stump.

The air knocked from his lungs he lays gasping as more dirt is thrown into his face.

Both Hal and Ally have turned at the yell from behind. They have time to note that Lyle is no longer with them before their faces are stung with vicious grains of soil attacking their skin.

In an effort of protection they drop to the ground and crawl together, head to head.

"I saw him," Ally whispers into Hal's ear, next to her mouth, "he's down the hill a bit. I think he fell."

With Hal's jacket over both their faces they slide over the edge of the track, across dry autumn grass. Even under the shield of the jacket the air is active. Dust and grass seed flutter about the space. Hal is spitting and blowing.

Reaching Lyle they can unhook his jacket and drag his head under their coats. Afforded slight protection by the stump, it is time to take stock.

"What happened?" Hal demands to know.

Lyle is blinded, screwing his eyes tight trying to clear them.

"Don't." Ally advises. She spits on the finger of her spare hand and awkwardly wipes at the small boy's eyes. He gets one half open then flinches and closes it again as more dirt slips into the eye socket.

Lyle tries to explain, their heads jammed together under the jackets.

"There was a wedge-tail. I heard it cry. When I looked up."

Hal is angry.

"They don't cry, they're silent. That wasn't a bird.
It wanted you to look, to uncover your face."
Too close for eye contact Lyle squeaks in that voice of his,
"Are you sure about this? I've heard them ……. "
"Yes, I'm sure." Hal's own voice is at a much higher pitch.
"I'm very sure."

Ally is waving her hand frantically in the small space.
They all stop. There is nothing. No sound, no movement.
Hal's eyes skip about the tiny area. He can see past Ally's
shoulder. The grass is not moving. There is no rush of air.
No dust.
"Wait. Let's wait for a while. I want to be sure."
Six legged and coat covered they lay for a time, ears tuned,
waiting. A daring growth of optimism is creeping into
Hal's belly. It may be that they have come through. Ally
is prepared for a longer stay but Hal has to know. With a
witless boy's impatience he backs up and turns his head.
Looking cautiously from under his coat wall. Nothing.
Okay. He straightens up on his knees. All about him is
calm. No movement. Calm as daybreak on the lake. Far off
he can make out cattle in the big front paddock. Allowing
himself a small laugh he nudges the others.
"We've won. It's given up. C'mon, have a look. It's okay."
Ally straightens up next to him, gazing across the
landscape. Lyle is still cowering beneath his jacket, peering
out from under like somebody trying to see the circus for
free. He has just got the last dirt from his eyes. His cheek is
caked with dark globs of drying blood.

Now all three are together, kneeling side by side, looking down on the part of their journey that is completed.

"We can get up there easily now. " Hal is feeling his confidence returning. He is quite calm. In the late afternoon light their world looks remarkably peaceful.

There is a massive bang from behind. Before they can react and turn a sheet of roofing tin smashes past them and gains altitude before seesawing its way into the gully trees. All three figures spin round. It is as if the whole earth is rupturing. A great screaming roar descends the hill. A fist of knotted power slams down upon them.

This time they cannot see. Dust, leaves, twigs, rip and tear about, dancing around them attacking viper-like, hitting and scratching.

The girl makes to cry out but the devil's fingers are thrust down her throat the moment her mouth is opened. She falls forward unseeing, choking on the mix of alien matter lodged within.

For an observer, these three figures appear to be drowning. Silently they fight, arms groping. The actions are slow without purpose save the necessity for movement, the need to reply to their tormentor.

They could be frogs boiling on a stove.

Now they are all down, heads together. The larger boy has his jacket pulled over their faces.

Lyle is crying. He has lost the handkerchief and his blood is getting everywhere.

The others do not know this yet, eyes clenched against the

turbulent air. Waiting for some relief.

"I'm going back," Lyle cries out in his despair. For his brief statement he swallows more dirt. He prepares to move away, feeling for the path. At this point Hal rears up, stung, blindly angry.

"No," he screams, "you little bastard. We agreed. This time we do it."

He is raining hard, vicious punches on the younger boy. Without sight, he hits at anything. He is crying out in his own way.

"We're not stopping, we're not, we're not, not . . . . ."

Lyle whines in genuine pain, rolling from side to side in an effort to escape. He is hit in the eye and in the stomach. Ally joins in. It is not a time for words. With her fingers gouging Hal's face from behind she causes him to stop. Her grip is locked and in fear she will not let go. In this slow motion ballet they fall on top of the smaller boy.

All are hurt. It is not the pain of a fall or a schoolyard taunt. They are assaulted. Their senses stolen and now their minds turned brother to brother, sister to brother. This power has an edge. Way back down, across the gully the first lights of the house are on. Too far and unseen by their dirt blinded eyes.

"I hate you, you bloody shit," Lyle hisses from the bottom of the pile. His face is red, bruised, bloody, tear stained, dirty. They lay together, panting and waiting.

Hal, and perhaps the girl are aware, that this is not within the experience or learning of their lives. For this Hal has all

the cockiness drained from his body. He begins to shake
and cannot do anything about it. He rolls away from the
others and sits clenching his hands together, his head
bowed between his legs. The terror will not leave him. He
realises that he is urinating. The warm liquid is pooling
under his pants. Still the trembling does not subside. He
curls his body tighter against the foul wind, wanting to be
taken away. So sick and so afraid. They will not be allowed
back.

It is their father's fault. In a melancholy mood over a year
before he related the tale by the fire. His evening stories
were many and varied and provided special entertainment
in the family. The children gauged their father's capacity
for truth, accuracy and comedy content by looking to their
mother.
On this night, the story of the truck, her face was white.
Expressionless and disapproving she left the room.
Later they overheard their father in the kitchen, defending
his actions. She would have none of his explanations.
It was not something to be discussed let alone passed
onto children. Those poor men should be left in peace.
Everybody about must know that now. It is dangerous
and well he knew when he opened his mouth. God, hasn't
enough happened to silence him.

There is a change. Lifting a hand to his face Hal is able to
shake clear his right eye. This wind thing is plucking at
his shirt. He is a victim in an alley, waiting for the gang
members to hit again. Looking, wincing. No, it is not there.

Grabbing his companions he drags them sideways then stands pulling them to their knees.

"It's stopped."

The girl's head turns, listening. She still cannot open her eyes. Lyle, on his knees, turns his blinded head.

"It's regathering," Ally says quietly, "in the gully. It won't go away."

Hal cannot lose the moment. Pulling the others clothes, pleading, he gets them to their feet.

"We've got to go now." He is screaming in their faces.

A roaring noise commences in the gully. Guttural and threatening.

"C'mon. Lyle hold Ally's hand. Yes, c'mon!" Fearfully he looks over his shoulder. The trees at the edge of the gully are thrashing about wildly, shedding leaves in a stream.

The group, still with just one functioning eye, moves off. Cajoled by the leader, kicked physically and mentally, unable to hurry, unable to resist their mad brother.

A shambling beast-mix of crouching bodies.

Ally can feel the shaking in the boy's hand. The fearless warrior of this afternoon's planning has vanished. And as he is frightened so she has the fear transmitted, causing her legs to waver in their strength. Her feet are not in contact with the earth. She steps stupidly, placing each foot and unable feel the tread.

Once again there's a raging noise coming up behind them.

They have moved no more than fifty metres. It hits them very hard. Now there is pure hate in the onslaught. Deranged at the impudence of this intrusion the whole hillside is raked by the power of the attack.

There is a small indentation in the land. In this they lay, able to breath, their faces covered in the huddle.

"Are we going to die?" Hal turns his head. His sister's face is close to his. Alison, tough, practical 'Ally' had asked the question. The teacher had called her his little pragmatist. They had proudly looked it up in the dictionary. He did not know the answer but he wished she had not asked. He could not lie to Ally.

For a moment they are all lost in their own thoughts.

"Can you still see?" asks Ally.

Hal blinks the one eye.

"Yes."

"Then I have an idea."

It is quite a feat. Ally struggles out of her light cotton singlet and then replaces her shirt and jacket and woolen hat. She does this while they cower under Hal's coat. She wraps the garment tightly round Hal's face, feeling her way, using his nose and ears as a guide to adjustment. Finally she is satisfied.

"Well?"

Hal pokes at the singlet searching for openings close to his skin where further assaults may be made on his eyes.

"Yes .... yes."

It is time for their final assault.

"Lyle, do you want to stay here?"

Hal is asking with a mix of guilt, kindness and a lessening of his burden. To Lyle the possibility of being alone on this dreaded hill outstrips the trepidations he has about reaching its summit.

"No," he cries!

They stand together. Their goal is in sight. Hal has a faded, gauzed view through the singlet cloth. With his available sight he can see the tormented landscape thrashing itself about. Far off, too far to see, on the flat, by the homestead, the trees are calm. Ally and Lyle are attached white-knuckled to his coat. The hill summit is just there. They can do it. Turn to face up to it. About them the wind now rants and pounds the hillside in a tantrum of defiance.

"Here we go!"

They are running, stumbling to their goal. The world in which they move is in chaos but Hal is focused only on the top.

Their universe has paused. Calm descends. The monster holds its breath.

It is there. As described in their dreams and imaginings. They are stopped at a deep crevice on the uppermost rise of the this giant paddock. A crazy, high, isolated corner that has no purpose to it. The area is like the top of a well cooked cake, split on its highest point.

Overgrown in parts the hole is home to a spindly blackberry bush. They have come upon it suddenly, as the others must have found it. Without warning. No time to react.

The cab is below in the darkness. Just visible is the tray, an old, wood spoked, wheel with its solid rubber tyre and part of a light, buried in the earthen side.

In the story that night by the fire, the men and the boy were removed nearly two weeks later. Trapped they had

been imprisoned by the earth. Growing pale and exhausted
from their calling out, till eventually, as the searchers
looked elsewhere, they fell silent one by one till none but
the boy moved at all.

This useless portion was fenced off between the two
properties. Left alone in respect and peace.

Rather traditionally, as things do in the country, parts of
the story floated in and out of people's minds, mouths and
homes and slipped into generations.

The boy, whose name was Stuart Dancher or was it Dancer
had wanted the emblem from the front of the truck it
seems. From the day the family acquired the beast with
its impossible gear box, the boy eyed with envy the silver
metal object on the truck's bull nose. His father often
remarked in company that he'd leave it in his will.

"You'll have it a good many years," he'd said.

He hovered, this pale, light framed child, feebly holding
death at bay with bony fingers. Such was his silence,
staring blankly, running the pads of each index back and
forth on the sheets. Laying hot on the bed with eyes that
searched the ceiling.

Mrs Larrop, the midwife, took on the challenge and
nursed him. She eased life and strength back into him. She
gazed long hours into his translucent skin, watching and
willing the veins beneath. At night she held him when he
whimpered at the memory of it all.

Town advice was that the event had sent him quite mad.
It became common to add a sorrowful, finite note to the
conversation with regard to his health.

Mrs Larrop won out. A month later he returned to his
mother and large family.

Now the town talked of the silent boy Stuart and his wish
to fulfill the need to collect the emblem from the front of
the doomed truck.
Whether he ever wanted the thing and felt obliged to leave
it be or was scared of the place or the townies simply
created the story, the truck stayed intact and undisturbed.
Too difficult to retrieve. Besides, there was the saying that
the hill was cursed and that it should be left alone.
He grew and when of age found work on various properties
of the district. Though reclusive and a man of little word
power, he worked well and was in demand.
From the town he bought and moved to a ten acre portion
at the corner of Dutch Creek.
Over the years he a built a substantial stone cottage and
lived alone in it until he died last week, still alone, in his
sleep, less than a mile from the paddock and the truck.

The oldest boy looks with his one functioning eye into the
black opening. The wind plucking at him, sliding its fingers
round his cheeks. He has come with all that bravado for
the piece on the front of the truck. Down below buried
in dirty darkness and time. With his blinded companions
hanging from the sleeves of his coat, awaiting his decision,
he hates all at once, his father, his stupidity, his ego and
his brother and sister. The sum of these things, he knows,
are a greater force than all that around him.

Hal does climb down into that terrifying darkness. In his mind is yet another of the stories of the body that is still there. He loses his grip at one point and his ear is ripped on the rusty door. It hangs in two pieces. Much of the work in the dark is carried out with the surety that there is a person who breaths and moves behind him. There is a hand that is about to be placed on his shoulder when he twists and dislodges the metal truck insignia. An involuntary shudder runs the length of his body as he waits to be struck down. He pictures himself tossed by malevolent force and cast down to be lost forever. Above, his two blind companions hang over the edge, listening. The silence is more threatening than all that they have been through.

Ally is first to clear her eyes. She tests them, surprised at the light. When she turns back to the hole there is her brother's face below her. He is holding the emblem from the truck. Struggling up the short distance to the top. One side of his face is covered in blood from his ear. He is not grinning in triumph.

At the edge, lying on the grass Ally now binds her brother's head with the same singlet.

"Let me see." Lyle is reaching for the emblem. He has eyes again.

In the twilight their world is still. The gully is dark. Far away the lights of their house are on. All three slip into silence as night moves in around them. Alone on the hill. Silhouetted, victorious, they are empty. A great sadness moves unseen into each of the warriors and lodges in their chest.

Now, with the last his strength washed away, the younger sister and brother hear Hal begin to cry. His head is buried in his arms. Wordlessly they move in and with heads touching hold him tightly.

"It's done," whispers Ally.

It is Lyle who stands at last. Holding onto the chromed metal piece in his hand he walks to the edge of the crevice. It vanishes into the dark hole. There is a tiny metallic noise as it descends.

"There you are Stuart. It's there when you need it," he whispers.

As they make their way back, the moon begins to break through the clouds and brighten the landscape.

LIAISONS

Three times I stood on the wharf wrapped in a heavy coat
and long socks. (They always seemed to leave in winter.)
My pockets were full of streamers. (I kept them rather than
threw them.)
Three times I watched huge ships with portholes and
rivets and rust and people waving insanely, pull away.
I stared at the water. It looked green and oily and
dangerously deep.
I tried hard but I could never make out who we had come
to bid farewell. Their faces were lost in the mass of action
and streamers on deck.
Then the ship (it's not a boat it's a ship) was gone.
We always waved as it made its way down the harbour.
(Long after anybody on board could see us.)
We were generally silent on the way home. Conversation
was monosyllabic.
"Judith's dress was nice."
"I thought Archy was a bit cocky."

Afterwards would come the postcards. Silly messages on
the back of pictures of little old Chinese men in Singapore
or Snake Charmers in Colombo, as the ship bounced

from one outpost of the Empire to another on its way to
headquarters.

The fourth time, I was on deck and the others were below
looking up from the wharf.
I still kept the streamers. It still seemed a waste to throw
them to people. The man next to me had written a message
all the way along his streamer and then rolled it up again.
It must have taken him ages. I was very impressed.
"For my lady love," he confided with a wink.
He waved frantically to somebody on the wharf. "Catch."
he called.
With great ceremony he threw. The streamer hurtled
out from the ship for about six feet then snapped and
plummeted into the water way down below.
"Bugger," the man said, gazing after it. He looked down
at me. "Didn't work. Bugger it." He wandered off in a huff.
The lady was still below, still waiting, her hands out in
anticipation.

My parents, the irrepressible Steve and dizzy Doreen had
parked me near a life boat davit while they rushed about
making much ceremony of the occasion. It was their first
trip 'overseas' and already Steve was on about getting
beyond the three mile limit so he could go to the bar.
Life of the party they were. Anybody's party.

The ship finally 'departed', as they say. I hung through
the rails, fascinated by the widening gap between the
wharf and the ship's side. Tugs belching black smoke

hauled us out into mid-harbour, shoving and snorting as
if determined to be rid of us. Progress was slow down the
harbour.
The wharf faded quickly though. I imagined all the people
waving at nothing in particular.
"There you are kid, we've been searching the boat for you."
Dad was in an expansive, loud mood.
"I'm where you told me to be. I haven't moved."
"C'mon kid let's get to the cabin. You can see the harbour
some other day."
He reached down for me. Mother was leading the way
trying her best to look like a seasoned veteran of the seven
seas. Steve grabbed my hand.
"It's a ship Dad, not a boat."
"Okay, it's a bloody ship. God you can be a pain at times,
son."

The cabin was pretty small but mother was impressed to
death. It opened straight out onto the deck. "Just like a
stateroom," she suggested. There were two bunks.
A set next to the porthole that were narrow and
immediately given over to me and a larger set on the
inner wall. Steve and Doreen decided the bottom one was
wide enough for both of them. It wasn't. Dad then got the
top bunk. I could see a problem with this arrangement
but not how to tactfully explain. Let events take care of
themselves, I decided.
A sink and a locker and that was about it. My top bunk
became the only place to put the suitcases.
The ship started to move about dramatically as they were

hauled up.

"Whoo, we're outside the heads. Europe, I hope you're ready for us?"

I looked at Dad with his thin moustache and black shining eyes. No, Europe wasn't ready but I was sure they'd manage.

Kneeling on my bunk and leaning to look out the porthole I watched the clifflines of Australia, my home for the past ten years sliding away. They were deserted, much as the first sailing ships had no doubt seen them centuries before.

"Why are you looking out the porthole, son? The bloody deck's just outside the door."

"He likes his little porthole, don't you baby?" Mother followed this outburst with a big wet kiss that left a huge red set of lips on my cheek. She then spat on a hanky and proceeded to wipe it off.

"Your Mum and I are going to take a quick trot round the deck, son. Boring stuff, eh. You'll be right here, eh? Stay in the cabin now. Don't want you going overboard and holding up the boat um ship. They might back up right over the top of you, eh."

With a pretend punch to the upper arm from Dad (his ultimate in fatherly gestures) they swept out the door and were gone. I wondered if they would remember to leave the bar to take me to dinner. Laying on my bunk looking up I closed my eyes and let the motion of the ship take over. When I opened them again it was dark and I was hungry.

'B Deck Dining Room' it said, then added in smaller print, 'Second Class Passengers'. I had arrived late. The sound of cutlery working on soup bowls greeted me at the double doored entrance. The Head Steward, all in white with gold trim finally noticed my pathetic figure at the entrance.

He assumed quite a lot.

With hands on knees to lower his height he stated, "You're travelling alone, eh?"

"Why would a ten year old be alone?" I pondered.

He blew out his cheeks. "Nobody told you the meal times. The Cabin Steward should have known. Supposed to take care of 'lones'. Dear me. And we're packed."

I said nothing. I was his problem. He blew out his cheeks again.

"Wait," he said, raising a finger. He backed away looking me in the eye. Much conferring followed with another person in white. They waved their hands about and finally the other person shrugged his shoulders and ended the conversation.

"Right," said my man, back and staring me in the eye, "You see this dining room is very full. We could squeeze you in at the end of a table but it would be 'awkward'. " He screwed up his face to illustrate the point. "I have a much better idea."

He led me away. I caught a glimpse of Steve and Doreen as their soup bowls were being cleared. Up two big staircases, the second being roped off. Along to a splendid room with large glass lights and paintings. More conferring, this time with the diners. The tables here were much smaller. It was quiet and there were a lot less people. The four diners at the table being talked to, were all looking at me.

The Steward turned and beckoned me over.

So, fortuitous timing and a certain innate cuteness had
won me a place in first class. My dining companions turned
out to be Sir Robert and Lady Mayberry, their daughter
Patricia who was really ugly and a lady called Dorothy
Prentice. I introduced myself as William Baxter and
explained that I accepted 'will' but would not abide 'willy'
or 'bill'.

"That's settled then, Will," said Sir Robert with a pat on
my back. "I'm just glad to have another male at our table.
"Remember to back me up on everything. It's them and us,
you know." He was a kind man. I liked him immediately.
"Another consommé please Reggie". He half-turned and
raised his hand slightly. A steward went scuttling away.
What command he had.

I spent the rest of the evening talking to Sir Robert. Turned
out he only had daughters and they kept producing grand
daughters so he craved male company, even mine. He
taught me the basics of cheating at bridge, which I frankly
found boring, then he fell asleep. It was my chance to move
on.

Our cabin was empty. I washed my face, brushed my teeth,
put on my pyjamas and climbed into bed. Then I got out
again, sneaked outside and lay on the deck with my head
through the railing. After looking for some time at the dark
ocean washing past the ship I spat into its inky depths and
went back to bed, content that I had done something this
day.

The next sound, no doubt many hours later, was my
prediction coming true. The sound of father falling and
banging his head as he attempted to scale the heights
to the top bunk. Much slurred muttering and cursing
followed. Mother bent over me and shushed him loudly at
the same time.
"You'll wake the boy." I felt her tuck me in. "Asleep or not
he can't miss another meal, poor thing."
Father grunted a response. He had messed up. There was
no place for me. Too late parents, I had moved on. It had
been a complete day.

I feigned sleep in the morning.
"Poor lad, not used to the bracing sea air," said Father,
feigning knowledge of such things, "we'll bring him some
brekky, from the table, in a paper bag. I've seen people
doing it already, for seasick companions."
Steve and Doreen made their exit, in that 'trying to be quiet
and making a lot of noise doing it' style.
Once I was sure they had gone and that Doreen wasn't
rushing back for her handbag or sunglasses, I slid out
of bed and hurried with my preparation. It was a rather
superficial cleaning. Under the armpits and slick back the
hair. I chose a subdued polka dot bowtie.
"Good gracious young Will, you can't come to the table for
breakfast whilst looking so splendid, you'll show us all up
as being common and lacking sophistication."
Sir Robert was taking umbrage at my use of a bow tie?
He winked. "Save it for dinner."
I slid the offending item from my throat and awkwardly

into my pocket. Was I blushing? A cursed family trait. Everybody was dressed casually. The sort of casual that costs a packet and takes hours to choose.

The Sir Robert hand went up and the fingers snapped but Reggie was already in mind of his end of voyage tip and appeared at the table's edge with my sliced melon before the hand was down.

"Good Reggie, good," said Sir Robert with the tone of master to pet spaniel.

We passed the rest of breakfast in relaxed, idle conversation on all manner of interesting topics. The Mayberrys were going to stroll the deck after breakfast and then play deck quoits while Dorothy said she was about adjusting her 'pale pallor.'

"Me? Oh I'm going to curl up in a deck chair for a bit more of Mister Conrad."

"A splendid choice," said Sir Robert. "Couldn't get enough of it when I was your age. Or was I younger or older? Top man anyway. Writes stories with guts and very few women."

By this time Lady Mayberry and the ugly daughter (who had an outgoing personality as a compromise) were dragging Sir Robert away.

I had mentioned earlier that I was a great fan of Joseph Conrad then moved the topic onward to avoid further examination and probing for details. The truth of the matter was that Uncle Roy had given me a book of Joseph Conrad stories on the wharf as we left.

"Something to help you through those long tropic nights,

Old Bean," he confided, slipping the parcel under my arm.
I had never actually heard of the man before and had no
idea what a 'Nigger' or a 'Narcissus' could be.
Dorothy walked with me part of the way back.
"As a writer I commend your reading," she said suddenly,
"especially 'Mr Conrad', who appropriately set much of his
writings in the waters we'll be passing through, however,
don't be a book-worm Will. We're travelling round the
world through amazing and exotic places. Drink it in as
much as you can. It can't be seen from inside a book. You
may only get one chance. Nothing in life is that certain.

I decided the Purser looked a learned man so I put the
question to him.
"I wondered if you'd ever heard of Dorothy Prentice? She's
a writer," I added, "I'm curious."
He looked at me as if I had asked him whether we were
travelling on the top of the ocean or along the bottom.
Perhaps he was simply trying to look into my eyes to see if
the question had some jocular intent.
Finally he decided that it was the question of some odious,
ill bred and uninformed child. To some extent it was.
"Miss Prentice is a brilliant and famous writer. She is
a passenger on this ship, as you may well know from
your sudden interest. I suggest that as one of our more
illustrious guests she would be acutely annoyed, in fact
angry, if she were 'bothered' in any way. Any way at all."
He was looking down his nose at me, which given our
comparative statures was not the least bit difficult for him.
"Fine," I said. "Thank you for your assistance."

Of course I could have added that we dined together in 'First Class' and that she would be more likely to be 'bothered' by his manner than my presence but I did not. I was acquiring a certain tolerance in my senior years.

On my bunk was a vomit bag. It contained two rather squashed ham rolls. I fed them to the seagulls hanging in the air at the back of the boat. They could catch just about any throw I tried.

"Don't feed 'em kid, it just encourages 'em." The man stood with his wife on his arm. He had a cigar.

"Your wife feeds you doesn't she?"

The man's wife opened her mouth, then laughed.

I stomped off. After the Purser I was in no mood for any more of this oafish behaviour. Away from the scene I suddenly saw the cleverness of my retort.

It takes another two full days and a night before my parents summon up sufficient concern to be translated into motivation and action. This is in the form of an inquisition in the Games Room where a very exciting Bridge Tournament is drawing to a close. Having been eliminated early by some ladies who cast doubts on my playing methods I am watching Sir Robert 'defend the male honour' in a tight final tussle with these same ladies. He is much better at cheating so they haven't noticed anything awry as yet.

"William, there you are. What the hell are you doing in here."

Dad's noise and his comment draws a collective scowl and

he retreats with me by the arm. Mother is waiting outside in the corridor. She launches into an immediate series of statements and questions.

"What have we done? We thought you'd be happy. Not many young boys get a sea voyage in their lives. You can't keep doing this. I've been so worried. Why do you do these things? You should see a doctor. Get vitamins. That's it. Is there a doctor?"

She is pacing about, wringing her hands. Father keeps adding the word 'yeh' to the speech and at the end says 'strange kid', shaking his head.

For my part I remain silent. Then comes a real question of sorts. Dad puts his hands on his hips and says, "Well?"

"Well, what?"

"Why have you bloody well decided to stop eating?"

"I haven't, I'm eating very well."

A complete silence descends. I can hear the ship's motors rumbling away beneath us as we stand in a little group. At last Dad says, "How?" Then in a deeper tone. "You're not stealing are you?"

Well, it was an interesting exercise in human relations and in a way I am relieved that my parents do have some latent concern for my well-being. Plus I don't wish to become a completely obnoxious little brat. So I confess. First Class. No room in the B-Deck Dining Room. Only solution. Quite okay. Nothing to worry about. I'm fine. Discretion decides that I leave out the part about travelling alone.

Now begins a new dilemma for both me and my parents. Some maternal/paternal ethical code suggests that they demand their child be returned to their side in B Deck.

But they are having such a great time and have become such a hit with the others at their table, they are reluctant to introduce a child into the equation. Some funny little fellow who could cramp their expansive style and look askance at some of his father's more bizarre inventiveness. Time to take matters in hand.

Providence provides a brilliantly executed entry onto our little stage of Sir Robert Mayberry. He peeks out, looking at our group.

"Everything okay, Will?" I'm touched. A concern for my well being in the clutches of these strangers.

"Mum, Dad," I say, "I'd like you to meet Sir Robert Mayberry."

Had I ever managed to script part of my life, what followed would have been about the perfect exchange.

Sir Robert was gracious and asked Steve and Doreen to simply call him Robert. He assured my parents that I was no trouble at their table and they very much enjoyed my company. It would be a great shame if they lost my input to their convivial gathering.

So it was that a flustering, blustering pair of parents departed for the lounge bar, much relieved and also unburdened.

I returned to the Games Room where Sir Robert related the tale of his Bridge victory over the ladies. I shook his hand.

"Travelling alone, indeed," said Sir Robert, still holding my hand.

Before I could begin a lame answer, he added. "God, if I'd had a son, Will, I think you'd be the one."

To cement my newly created freedom, I told my parents
later, that in First Class the service was very slow and you
had to be terribly quiet. This amused them.

The predictions of Dorothy Prentice emerge much
sooner than I had expected. The eastern and northern
coasts of Australia are freckled like a redhead's cheek
with pieces of land. Natives come out with a pilot boat
to help unload mail and provisions. Snaking through the
channels is wondrous to me. While Steve and Doreen
glance occasionally from the bar I must hang over the rail
and drink in the air, sound, smell, feel, always with a little
flavouring from the ship's engines. Dolphins, reef fish,
flying fish all join us at different times. As if the ship is a
giant toy cast into their playroom. The water is so pure
and has a bright pale blue/green hue that makes you want
to jump right in. The reef hems us in waiting for a moments
lapse in concentration.
From the bow deck I can look up to the wheelhouse.
They appear to be concentrating.
A map near the Dining Room entrance shows our
course in blue pencil and the progress we are making
running alongside in red. It is of little interest to most
of the passengers (or they wish to appear part of the
international veteran class and so refuse to look.) Sir
Robert catches me with my finger on the top of the red
line and gives a rundown on what lays ahead. We are now
round the top of Australia and pushing into the exotic
outskirts of Asia. The temperature has risen considerably
and the air is steamy with portents of mystery and

throbbing drums.

Dark shapes make their way past the ship at night.
Headlands, islands, perhaps boats? They are vague, filled
with the menace of unknown.

The names were secret sounds to be mouthed softly as
I strode about. Coral Sea, Torres Strait, Moresby, Saibai
Island, Badu, Moa, Arafura.

Occasionally there are lights in the darkness. Dots
scattered through thick green foliage. Whisps of smoke and
mist. Too far to ascertain their origin or purpose. Strange
and forbidden rituals fill my head. Beautiful women, clad
in seductively torn dresses, their hands tied, awaiting their
fate at the hands of callous savages. Suitably attired in pale
khaki with lots of pockets and a huge machete in hand,
I am able to effect a suitably clever rescue for which the
lady is mightily impressed and indebted to me.

Days are beginning to slip by. No other child of anywhere
near my age is on board so I must be content with idling
about, working my way into the creaking, salty world of
Joseph Conrad together with occasional forays into the
adult world of entertainment.

It is a time when a person should pursue a rich and
rewarding, mind stimulating hobby. Unfortunately I have
none.

I had noticed that the deck on our level was scrubbed
timber. Years of washing down with salty water had
reduced it to a bleached white with grooves where the
hard grain held out. On the First Class level the decks were

stained and had a certain sheen to their finish. How keenly
the eye becomes focussed on minutia as the lack of variety
begins to take hold.

My pyjamas were not helping with the heat. Mother
insisted on nothing but large (to allow for both shrinkage
and my growth) flannelette and was proud of paying for
the thickest and best. On a bunk, in a small cabin in the
tropics they were as impractical as it was possible to get.
Father had taken to sleeping in his underpants but I was
not allowed for some obscure maternal reason. I had to
stay fully clad for the night.
Tossing about, rolling my eyes at my father's snoring,
feeling that soon I would lapse into unconsciousness if I
could not immediately find relief from the heat I took it
upon myself to get out and explore the ghostly decks by
night.

The pyjamas presented another problem. This time to my
mobility. I had to keep hitching them up as I walked. The
decks were totally empty. Briefly, I imagined the bridge
in darkness with a thin beam of light highlighting the
abandoned wheel as it rotated one way then the other.
Ahead, set in regimental rows, were the deck chairs. In the
day they were a hive of activity and territorial claims. The
ship simply did not have enough and they were guarded
jealously. Now, all was quiet. They sat alone. All mine.
I took the nearest. It was my first experience with a deck
chair. While quite familiar with their existence and able to
confidently point one out, I had yet to actually sit in one.

The depth proved deceptive. My knees were up high. Once used to the odd angle I found I could relax.

With my hands behind my head I waited for the cooling effect of the night air. Sweat ran down my face.

I unbuttoned my pyjama top and flapped it about to create some air movement. My stomach was wet with sweat.

I checked my navel (it's not a belly button) to see if it contained a pool.

By moving my feet open and closed I was able to switch the ocean scene off and on as the ship pushed ahead. The water seemed slow in the moonlight. Thick, like lime jelly. I could see the propellers cutting their way through chewing it to chunks, the bow slicing into the rubbery surface.

A puff of air stirred along the dark deck. It was brief but its effect was tremendous. I closed my eyes. The ship was gently surging into the swell. Lick off the salt from my lips. Run the tongue round to give them a good clean. There was that puff of air again. This time a little longer.

"Will, hullo there." I jumped violently. I think I also let out a little cry. Looking up trying to focus. Dorothy Prentice stared down. I could just see a mass of hair.

"Oh, didn't see you coming."

"You had your eyes closed, that's understandable." She wore a strange outfit. It was sort of silky and very short I thought.

"I wasn't expecting company," she said, " bit pointless going out to cool off and then putting on one's gown."

"Yes," I agreed because I thought that I should. She sat down in the deck chair next to mine. With comparative ease I noted. It became silent. I wondered if I should speak.

We were both looking out at the sea.

"Oh this is lovely." I nearly jumped again. "A whole boat to ourselves, Will. Silly people stay in their cabins when there's a nice cool deck outside. We could be the only people on board. A clandestine meeting, it's rather sordid don't you think?"

"It's a ship. When they're this size they're not a boat."

"Of course dear." Dorothy put her hand on my arm. "What does clandestine mean?"

"Oooh secretive, slightly naughty."

Steve and Doreen were asleep when I got back. Steve had his head back and was snoring loudly. As I was trying to quietly close the cabin door Mum said, "That's a good idea, babe. Open the door, let some cool air in. God, it's bloody hot. I cannot sleep."

A minute or so after I climbed back onto my bunk she was asleep.

At breakfast Dorothy looked across the table. "Sleep well?"

Did I blush?

"Yes, thank you."

Lady Mayberry buttered her roll and looked across to Dorothy. "Your work on the pallor seems to be coming along nicely."

"I'm quite pleased," said Dorothy, moving her arm about.

I had to know, even if it could prove embarrassing.

"What's pallor?" I asked.

"Something you could do with less of yourself, Will."

Dorothy is looking me over.

Carrying a towel, clad in swimmers and a white shirt, I finally locate a set of stairs that appear to ascend to the highest deck on the ship. Halfway up a steward is coming down with a tray. Briefly we make eye contact and that sets off a familiar sequence whereby I am questioned as to my rights to be here amongst the first-class folk. I am now familiar with the procedure. As he takes a breath in order to begin the probe I say in my haughtiest voice, "Excuse me I'm in rather a hurry."

The effect is amazing. He slams his buttocks back against the rail in order to give me maximum room to pass. "Right you are, sir," he says, holding his tray high.

Oh the joy of the class system. Coming from a rather Bolshe, left-wing family I have always held great and grand views on the equality of all. But I had never viewed it from the other side. There is merit in everybody knowing their place. All depends on where your place is at the time.

The stairs lead up through the top deck. The effect is startling. In three paces you are upon this large, open stage next to the ship's three massive funnels.

"Over here, Will." Dorothy Prentice is on a towel, across the deck, waving to me. She has a triangular shaped cane back support that allows her to sit up. Dark, sunglasses with white frames, a book, small bag. She looks at ease.

"Thought you may not be coming," she says, smiling. "Here spread your towel out next to mine. Then all the other men will stop bothering me."

I am picking up on a little irony in that remark. This deck is dotted with other people 'taking the sun'. Some are on

towels, others more formally arranged with lounges and
a little table for their drinks. The funnels tower above us.
Two are issuing a grey smoke and have a certain amount of
black around the upper edges. The third rear funnel seems
clean.

"Well isn't this nice," says Dorothy, now on one elbow. I'm
sitting on my towel, unmoving.

"C'mon Will. Get that shirt off. Show everybody your
muscles. You won't arrive at Southampton all brown and
healthy and making people envious, unless you get to work
early."

There's no putting it off any longer. Slowly, deliberately I
unbutton my shirt, slip it off, revealing strange, dark blue,
wool, swimmers. Using my shirt as a pillow I lay back and
close my eyes against the sun. After some seconds I am
aware that Dorothy has not lain back. Opening my eyes
again I find her leaning over me. Our eyes meet.

"I'm sorry, Will," she says, "it's just that you're the palest
person I have ever seen. You're positively translucent. In
a healthy way I suggest but I can see blue veins running
beneath your skin. I'm sure if I look closely I could make
out your heart and lungs. It's very odd."

"It's the way I am. It's an inheritance."

"Now don't become all indignant, Will. You've simply spent
a lot of time away from the sun. You're a thinker and God
the world can use some more of those. You're not fat, nor
thin, you're in fact well proportioned and quite handsome.
Just somewhat lightly coloured."

"Maybe I'm not meant to be, what did you call it,
'bronzed.'"

"No," says Dorothy, leaning closer as if examining a
laboratory specimen, "you'll definitely come good.
Dark hair, totally unblemished, not even a scarred knee.
Perhaps not native in quality but we'll have you several
shades darker before this voyage is through, you mark my
words Will. Now lay back darling and let's get started."
And I do lay back, feeling the sun roll over me in bursts
of heat. Sleepy as the ship in turn, rolls beneath my
shoulder blades. She called me 'darling' I think. Famous
international author Dorothy Prentice called me 'darling'.
Oooh.

There is a nudge on my shoulder.
"Time to turn over, Will. You won't be impressed if you
burn. It can be agony."
I can feel a certain warmth emanating from my chest and
legs. They have taken on a faint pinkish hue. Dutifully I
shuffle and bump around until I am on my stomach. In
front of my nose is a glass of ginger beer, with ice and a
striped straw.
"I took the liberty of ordering you a drink while you were
asleep. Hope you don't mind."
"No," I say, reaching out, "Splendid."
Mental note: Must find some more 'up to date' terminology.
I know right now Dorothy is smiling quietly to herself, the
way she does.

Once again the sun slides over me like a thick blanket.
Odd view of life from deck level. An enormous woman in
one of the chairs is sitting next to her skinny husband.

She is trying to appear delicate, using her short fat fingers to eat a big cream sponge. He is half turned away as if distressed by the sight. He has black tea with a slice of lemon sitting on the rim of the cup.

Feet pass by, moving in different directions. Feet are probably the least attractive part of the human body. Certainly the First Class passengers are not shod with particularly fine specimens. Flat, veined, quite often with terrible growths of thick nails. Close the eyes against such abominations. Dorothy has nice feet, for an older person. She is tanned and appears healthy, smoking short, dark cigarettes and pausing to pick small bits of tobacco delicately from her tongue.

I'm woken this time by voices.

"Most terribly grateful. Didn't want to disturb you but I have been a devoted fan for so long. I'll get along now. Perhaps if we meet again I can ask a few questions about 'Face In The Moon.' There's a chapter that has puzzled me for years ....."

My looking up interrupts the conversation. A woman is leaning over Dorothy who is writing in the front pages of the last of three of her novels. She hands them back to the lady who smiles unconvincingly down at me.

"Your child?" she asks. Knowing no doubt that Dorothy is unattached.

"No." Dorothy places a protective or possessive hand on my head. "Will is a friend and confidant."

"Oh." The woman is not about to leave this alone but dear Dorothy has the situation in hand.

"I hope you'll excuse us now, we're both very tired."
Fixed with a kindly stare and my own squinting look from
beneath the eyebrows, the lady falls into a full retreat.
"Well, yes of course." She clutches the books to her bosom.
"I shall treasure these. Something to show my friends.
Good day. Thank you so much." She is backing away as if in
the presence of royalty.
"You handled that well, I thought."
"Why thank you, Will." Dorothy runs a fingernail across my
back. "Hmm, you're becoming a trifle coloured there m'
lad. We had better finish for the day."

Doreen is viewing me with alarm. She has me backed
against the cabin door. "You're all flushed, honey." She has
her nose close to mine, her eyes working their way over
my face.
"Jeez woman, he's just caught a bit of sun. Bloody calm
down." Dad gives me one of his matey punches on the arm.
It hurts but I don't wish to be examined any further so I
stoically remain unaffected.
"How's all your posh friends up in First?"
"Oh we hardly speak." Not going to give him an opening
there.
"Hope you've got a big tip for your waiter. They expect a
whopping great payout in First. That's what all the bowing
and carry on is for."
"I have the situation in hand, Dad."
"Oh well thet's awl rite then." As an actor my father would
have spent a great deal of time unemployed. His awful
British accent even draws a negative look from Mum.

At breakfast Sir Robert's daughter says, "My, look at you, you have the beginnings of a tan." I thank her for noticing. "We're one of those family's that stay pink all their lives," adds Lady Mayberry. Whether this is a statement of resignation or planning I'm not sure. It is odd to hear Lady Mayberry talk of a family. I had not pictured them as one. "I have taken Will in hand," says Dorothy, placing a claimant's hand on my shoulder. "He will arrive in Britain looking very much the part of the Australian cousin. Your relatives will no doubt be consumed with jealousy, Will." So, this whole sunbathing thing is merely a ploy by Dorothy Prentice to 'stick another one up the Empire' as my father often says. I'm tempted to use this term to amuse my breakfast companions but after a quick glance around the table I decide against such crudity.

Reggie arrives with a silver tray (on B deck they stack plates along their arms) and places compote of fruit, cereals, steaming racks of toast on the table. (on B Deck it is on a plate).
Placing the tray aside he reaches into his jacket and with white gloved hands and a little stoop, hands each of us a small white envelope.
"Oh, the Captain's Cocktail Party." Sir Robert is holding the gilt edged card under his half moon glasses. "And join him for Dinner afterwards. How nice."
There on my card is my name. 'William' spelt out, middle name and surname. Respectfully requests the pleasure of the company of ....

"Out with the old dinner suit and starched collars again."
Sir Robert is making conversation as he spoons Green
Ginger Marmalade onto his toast.

My cheeks are getting hot. "What's a dinner suit?" I ask.
The table stops momentarily. Sir Robert is quick to assume
control.

"Those ghastly black and white things, Will. You know,
black jacket and trousers, bit of a stripe down the
leg. White shirt, studs, stiff collar, bow tie. Not at all
comfortable. If you don't have one with you I can happily
lend you one of mine."

I can feel Dorothy looking to Sir Robert and to me, no
doubt doing a quick visual comparison of our sizes.

After breakfast, in the Mayberry's State Room, my
reservations concerning the chance of a fit are confirmed.
The jacket hangs round my knees. No amount of padding
on the shoulders will lift the sleeves sufficiently for my
fingers to put in an appearance.

"Hmm," Sir Robert is amused at my expense. "It's no good
Will, you'd slide right down one of the trouser legs and out
onto the floor."

He consults the ship's services register. "No good, they've
got a seamstress but it would take a proper tailor to lop
this down to size."

I'm touched. Sir Robert would allow one of his dinner
suits to be destroyed so as to fit me for one evening. Does
he expect payment? It is my 'confidant' Dorothy Prentice
who picks up the invitation and then consults her diary
calendar.

"It's not for another week and a half. We can pick
something up in Singapore."
Sir Robert is horrified. "Let those butchers in the back
alleys put together some dreadful, ill-fitting garment.
Heavens no. Let me see the diary." He peers at the diary
and the invitation.
"We can do it. It will be tight. If the ship loses time we're
sunk. No, it's for the best." He turns to me, still sadly
standing on their expensive rug in the baggy suit.
"Will, my man, I will consider it a great honour if you
could accompany me to the premises of the S'hing Bros in
Colombo to be fitted out for a superb dinner suit, befitting
your role as my temporary adopted son."
"Can Dorothy come?"
"Of course. I greatly value her opinion."
Lady Mayberry and her daughter have their arms folded.
"We'll just take tea and wait, shall we?"
"Best thing," says Sir Robert, "they're gentlemen's tailors.
No point." He eyes his daughter over his glasses. "Should
have been a male of the species, m'dear. You'd better find
a chap that I can abide when the time comes. Can't go
huntin' and fishin' with some namby pamby." He supplies
me with a wink that says these exchanges are all light-
hearted.

On the way up to our sunbathing spot I whisper to
Dorothy. "How much will all this be? I'll have to tell Mum
and Dad."
Her smile down is warm. "Oh Will, don't mention money.
Sir Robert would be upset. You've given him something to

do on this voyage."

For most of the day our ship works its way forward in the
Singapore Straits past rows of cargo ships, tankers, fishing
boats and many other bits of floating marine oddity.
By evening we are berthed at a big wooden wharf near the
city.
'Home of Raffles' Sir Robert had said. He also said 'Conrad
slept here.' I had no understanding of either phrase. Who
was Raffles? Where did Conrad sleep?
Steve and Doreen were revved up. Their first port of call!
Despite their concerns about all the 'foreigners', they were
about to see the sights. Dragged across the road from the
gangplank we all piled into a rickshaw with me sort of half
standing. The owner of the rickshaw looked unamused.
"Three too many," he said, waving his arms.
"Three, two, what," said Dad. When we showed no sign of
leaving the man's eyes narrowed. "Where you go?"
Dad had no idea. "Eat, eat, drink, someplace good. Clean,"
he added. "In town."
"Fifty dollar."
Now this bit was right up Steve's particular alley. He had
dreamt of the great white Australian taking charge in some
Asian clime, ordering the shameful natives about.
"I'll give you one good Australian Pound note. Look."
He held it up for effect. The native was so in awe of the
offer that he spat a large green glob of something onto the
ground.
In the end, sometime later, after all the other rickshaws
had departed, we wound our way into the city, dragged by

the muttering figure of our driver who had the comforting
knowledge that he had extracted a considerable number
of Australian Pounds from Dad as part of the transport
arrangements.

"Could have taken a flying boat for less," I thought,
though Dad was quite pleased with his deal. I admired the
rickshaw man's technique. He was doing us a favour even
talking to us.

We had a good meal in a crowded cafe, served by a surly
waiter. Steve just upset foreigners. It was his nature.

Later, shopping, Doreen bought some blouses and bangles,
Dad purchased an overly ornate ivory cigarette holder
and I was given a bamboo back scratcher. This latter
item, initially disdained, proved invaluable and virtually
indestructible.

By 11pm we were back on the boat, having walked the
return leg. Steve and Doreen headed for the bar and I went
to rest in a deckchair and delve into Joseph Conrad.

"Ah," said Dorothy, ten minutes later. She dropped down
next to me. "Been ashore?"

"Yes, we ate well. Have you?"

"Oh I went for a walk. Looked up some old friends for a
while."

"You have friends here?"

"I tend to bump into people all over the world, Will."

She sat for a minute staring out over the rooftops behind
the wharf. Rusted tin mostly. Not at all quaint. "I've just
thought, there's some others I could see. Would you like to
meet them?"

Several nights later as we chugged through the southern outskirts of the Bay of Bengal I crawled once again along the steamy decks through the rich tropical odours to find a deck chair and catch some breeze. Pleased with my now substantial tanning I left my pyjama top behind. Quite daring I thought.

Dorothy was already in her familiar chair, legs curled up, gazing out to sea. I was pleased to see her hair moving about. There was some breeze to be found.

This now familiar routine had dispensed with the niceties of greeting. We spoke when there was something to say. Eventually I cracked the reverie.

"The sea is 'running' I'm told. Nobody has explained whether it's running with us or against us."

Dorothy has her head back. I can just detect her half closed eyes in the moonlight.

"I have no idea Will. I'm not strong on nautical topics." The light breeze is flicking tiny strands of her hair.

"I thought authors knew everything."

A slight smile from Dorothy. "Heavens no, it's all in the research."

"What about confidant?"

"What about it?"

"You called me one, the other day when the lady wanted her books signed."

"It means, Will," she says placing her hand briefly on my arm," a person in whom you can have confidence, confide in, share your innermost secrets and thoughts without fear that they will be misused."

"Oh, really, well." I am lost in the grandeur of such a

revelation. Dorothy has her eyes closed, enjoying the night air.

"Are you a virgin, Dorothy?" Her eyes open quite wide then close again.

"No, Will, I'm not. Why do you ask?"

"I heard the man in the brothel discussing me the other night. They thought I was asleep."

"Little cloth ears Will, eh."

"What's a cloth ears?"

"Somebody who listens a lot."

"Am I a virgin, Dorothy?"

This question causes Dorothy to look round. She gives a small shake of her head then leans back again in the deck chair. Her friends in Singapore ran a thing called a brothel. It had lots of noise and fun and lots of customers coming and going. It seemed to be very successful. She had introduced me and explained that she met these people while working on the book 'Lost Soul Found.' They were all very friendly and the ladies gave me a large bag of sweets. While Dorothy talked I had lain down on a lounge and closed my eyes.

"It's not for me to say, Will, but my guess is that you're a virgin."

"Would you like to be a virgin?"

"Well, you can't become a virgin, Will. You stop being one."

This is becoming rather confusing. "You mean you were a virgin and now you're not?"

"That's the way it is Will."

"Is it good to be a virgin or good not to be one?" There is a pause this time.

"I would say, neither. It is something that happens to most people as they get older. When it happens to you I'm sure you'll approve."

I can feel a trend in this conversation. It is one of limited information.

"You're not going to tell me what a virgin is, are you, Dorothy?"

Now Dorothy sits up. "Well, knowing you as I do, Will, you're not about to let this topic alone. So here is my answer."

She moves round to face me. Takes both my hands. I can see down the front of her nightie. She lifts my chin with her finger, so that we are eye to eye.

"The word applies to many things, Will. Generally it means anything that is fresh, new, unbroken, like the unbroken soil of a new field on a farm, entering a new, unexplored area, thus you hear the expression, 'virgin territory' ...."

"Are you going to summarise soon Dorothy?" This brings forth a small snort of laughter.

"Oh God, why me?" she says, squeezing my hands.

"In the human context Will, it has to do with sex."

Now this becoming quite engrossing. I have heard a lot about sex at school from uninformed bigger boys who are transparent in their ignorance but it is a very hard subject to pin down.

"In what way, Dorothy?"

"Once you have sex with another person then you're no longer a virgin because the spell has been broken. Just the same as virgin soil on a farm is no longer virgin soil once it has been ploughed. So, you're born a virgin and at some

stage in most people's lives they have sex and then are no
longer virgins."
She lets go of my hands and sinks back, as if some burden
has been lifted from her shoulders.
"What exactly is sex, Dorothy?"

At Dorothy's suggestion I have discovered the ship's
library. Her other suggestion of asking my parents has
been taken into account and rejected due to my doubts on
their ability to answer a straight question.
Thumbing through the large two-volume Oxford Dictionary
I keep happening upon new and interesting entries.
Wandering away down sidetracks of information I
take some time to find 'sex'. When I do, the answer is
unsatisfactory. It assumes some prior knowledge for the
reader. I am beginning to suspect the basic machinations of
the 'act'. Why do they call it an act? Are they playing a part
in some stupid play? And what is intercourse?
The dictionary goes on about communication. There
seems to be a conspiracy of misinformation.

We approach Colombo late at night. There is a lot of
messing about. Several boats are alongside and dark
skinned people seem everywhere. All of them have an
opinion about something. They point in various directions,
wave their arms about and the ship's officers seem to
understand what is going on.
"When are we going to enter the port?" I ask one as he
strides past.
"Not until morning," he replies over his shoulder.

Fascinating though all these strange foreign happenings
may be I am too tired to watch any longer and wander off
to bed. Mum wakes as usual as I come in.
"Keep the door closed, hon'. I don't trust these natives.
We must be getting near Ceylon eh. That should be
interesting. I wonder what you can buy there?"
With that she is asleep once more, dreaming no doubt of
the untold riches and shopping opportunities that await
her in our next stop.

As it turns out the ship's officer had not told the truth.
When I wake and look out the porthole we are sitting in the
middle of Colombo Harbour. There are passengers moving
about and looking over the sides. Strange little hooks and
pieces of rope are attached to the rails.
Dressed in my one pair of shorts and a long sleeved shirt,
I daringly put on sandals to go to breakfast. Close the cabin
door quietly. Steve and Doreen always go to the second
sitting for breakfast, if they make it at all.

"Oh you look sweet." Patricia Mayberry is no doubt being
friendly but I have never been called 'sweet' before. "Look
at your brown toes," she adds, "you look terribly healthy."
Quickly sitting down to avoid any more of her looking, Sir
Robert puts it in perspective.
"Wise choice, Will. Hot, dusty, steamy here."
Even Sir Robert has a slightly casual tone to his wardrobe.
He has a cravat inside his shirt and the shades of his outfit
go from beige to white.
"Well we made good time, Will. Neptune was on our side.

Quick bit of toast, then we're off. Do you want me to speak to your parents?"

Oh hell, I'd forgotten about mentioning the whole dinner suit / captain's party to my parents! Perhaps this is not entirely true. Subconsciously I had probably avoided the subject because of their feelings. Little son slips into 1st Class, gets invited to something that they won't see and then has an act of charity performed on him in the shape of a tailored dinner suit. Yes, I was definitely avoiding the issue.

"I mentioned it the other day. I'll remind them again. I'm pretty sure they want to see the sights and have some lunch."

Steve and Doreen have skipped breakfast. Woken by the noise of the busy port they have made their way out of our cabin, to be immediately waylaid by the people at the other end of the ropes and hooks hanging from the rails. Down below in the water are numerous boats and water craft. Displayed on their decks are large assortments of rugs, brassware and carved tigers, elephants, even set scenes involving the mongoose and the tiger. This I know from my days in Cub Scouts listening to tales of The Jungle Book.

Doreen has just hauled up a rearing elephant. It is being assessed for positioning in our parlour back in Sydney.

"I think the tiger would look better," Dad is saying, "more colour."

"Oh, you males with your virile tigers."

They commence a bargaining session involving hand

signals, shouting and the waving of money. Despite being in possession of the goods and on an upper level the small grey haired man in the boat below is calling the tune to which his customers dance. He has several contractual arrangements going at once.

"Just take the bloody thing and go." A man behind Dad is holding a large carved elephant umbrella stand. "Dumb buggers want to hand over the stuff, what do they expect. That's how I got this."

Occasionally even the oddest parents will do something noble in their lives and unseen and unrecorded, restore a great deal of credibility in the eyes of their offspring. Dad spun round, grabbed the elephant holder by the neck and the pants and marched him along the rail to a very upset, gesticulating, young vendor.

"Pay him five quid, you low life," said Dad. As I watched through distended eyes, the man put a five pound note in the little sack and lowered it down to the now very happy trader. "Now take ya bloody elephant and get out of my sight."

The man hurried away, clutching his expensive prize. Dad returned to Doreen. "Some people," she said.

Leaning over the side of the boat Dad called out. "I'll give ya ten bob for the elephant or ya can have fifteen for the elephant and the tiger."

Next thing I knew we were all back in our cabin, deciding where to display our elephant and tiger. Dad had accomplished the entire proceedings without touching the cigarette that still hung from his lip.

S'hing Bros. tailors really were two brothers. They met us at the door. One was stout, the other, tall and slim. I thought it odd that they produced suits and trousers yet wore Indian leggings, with a sort of long grey coat.

"Sir Robert, what an honour," they chorused.

"No good chatting me up this time lads. Here's your customer." Sir Robert pointed at me, as Dorothy pushed me forward. The S'hing Bros smiles widened still more.

"Oh, young man, what is your pleasure?" Their sing-song voices and nodding heads made them slightly comical.

"A first class dinner suit,"said Sir Robert.

"Perhaps with a little room for growth," added Dorothy, indicating with her hands, the future width of my shoulders.

The tall S'hing brother brought out different bolts of cloth while the other extolled the virtues of each sample.

We were all obliged to feel the quality and pass comment. It appeared that Sir Robert was aiming for the best. Measurements were then taken. Much licking of a pencil stub and notating on a small pad. Neck, shoulders, arms, chest, waist, they measured my legs outside and inside. A slightly disconcerting experience.

"On which side does Sir dress?" The S'hing brother with the tape measure, his face close to mine, has his eyebrows raised in anticipation of my answer. I can only look round at my benefactors. "At his age I don't think it really matters," Dorothy points out.

"Oh but I'm allowing for growth," says the S'hing brother with a smile. There is condescending chuckling all round. Sir Robert stands in front of me with his hands on his hips, head to one side, one eye closed. "Hmm, let's say left. With most fellas it's left."

Upon completion of the measuring, ordering, choosing of the cloth, a question is asked. "When would you wish to return for the first fitting, sir?"
"Return?" Sir Robert is in charge. "Heavens lads we're going to wait. Damn ship leaves tonight. We must be on board, with the suit."
The S'hing Brothers jointly give a weak smile, then rush about ordering staff here and there. Chalk lines appear on the cloth. Large scissors flash into action.
"I'll sit outside," I say. It is becoming oppressive in the tailors with their one slow ceiling fan, failing to move the air.
On the steps, sniffing strange pungent odours. Along the street, rows of jacaranda's are dropping their pulpy purple flowers onto the roadway. A small shop opposite my position is taking delivery of sacks from a cart. They look heavy. The bony delivery man seems to buckle slightly each time he lifts one from his cart.
Time to reflect on my guilt. Confronting my parents in their cabin as they admired their carved animals I had plunged into my story.
" .... some stupid party I have to go to. Would be rude if I said no. Apparently you have to have a suit. Sir Robert knows where to get these cheap ones from a factory.
Says it's his shout. Have to go with them to get the right size off the rack."
It is quiet in our cabin. Dad looks at the wall. Mum brushes

her finger through my hair. I have softened the story as
much as I can.

"Sure babe, if that's what you want. You can't let your
friends down. Hey, they've been very nice to you, haven't
they. We're just going to look around, go for a walk, you
know, that sort of thing." Her voice is quiet. I can tell
they're hurt.

A small girl in a faded yellow dress. She has dusty bare
feet and is standing before me with her hand outstretched.
My eyes travel up to her face. There is a small gold ring
through the side of her nose. As our eyes meet she gives
a tiny lop-sided smile and moves her hand closer to my
face. I have no local currency. She looks at the Australian
sixpence then clutches it and runs off, round a corner, out
of sight.

Back to my reverie. The cart opposite is now empty and
the store keeper is examining the bags perhaps with a
view of adjusting the price to the delivery man. On the
corner, two local policemen are talking. They seem to be
interested in some overhead wires that are hanging down
very low. Their uniform is khaki with a turned up hat and
baggy shorts. It looks a lot like the Australian Army.

They have appeared as if blown by the wind. At each side
and now in front. Children, my age and younger. All have
their hands out. Their expressions are neutral. Crowding
closer. To escape I decide to walk across to the shop where
a lively discussion is now in progress over the contents
of the delivery. The shop owner is pouring whatever

the substance is, back into a bag, while applying critical comment as to the quality.

Now I am surrounded on all sides by these begging children. They are jostling for the best position close to me. Like a white knight there is suddenly a S'hing brother beside me. He is yelling and the children all scatter. "Time for a fitting young sir. You should not encourage these children or they will never leave you alone." As we walk back to the tailors I note that the parents of these beggars are all sitting round the corner in a shady spot. The children run back to them with the money they collect and are sent out again.

That night as we make our way round the tip of India and out into the Arabian Sea, it is time for the Captain's Cocktail party. My mother is suspicious.

"You've done awfully well honey. You reckon he paid ten shillings. This is not a ten bob suit. Well it's not a suit, it's a dinner suit."

"It's an odd size. The only one they had. They were glad to be rid of it. Lucky timing."

"Should have gone myself," Dad puts in. "Crikey at ten bob I'd have bought a couple."

"No, the normal size ones were hellishly expensive. Even Sir Robert was shocked." This bit of news seems to placate the parents still wounded by the absence of their son while they went for an elephant ride and saw a snake charmer. We have some brass objects to add to our souvenirs and Mother has some clothes she will never wear. Perhaps a ride on an elephant would have been more fun than a day at the S'hing Bros.

Dad supplies braces for the trousers, adjusting them up to the maximum amount. The shirt, studs and bow tie are a gift from Dorothy. My black school shoes have been buffed up to a mirror finish.

After three goes Dad finally works out where he is going wrong with the bow tie.

"I'm looking at it arse about," he says. He kneels behind me and puts his arms round to the front then positions us both in front of the wardrobe mirror. "That's better, now it's like I'm putting it on, ya see."

So, at last I am trussed up in this black suit of fine cloth, with its satin lapels and subtle lines on the legs. Dad sternly hands me one of his white monogrammed handkerchiefs. "Gentleman always has one of these on board. To dab the ladies crying eyes when he's leaving them."

"Oh my," says mother.

In the mirror I look at the suntanned, wind swept, fine figure in the black suit. It's me. The shoulders have special pockets to add or subtract padding, depending no doubt on the growth or ego of the wearer. The S'hing Bros have padded mine up quite severely to bring my hands out of the sleeves. I look like a miniature boxer.

Captain Braithwaite, in a dazzling white uniform is greeting people at the door. To my relief all the males in the line are dressed in dinner suits. It was not, as I suspected, an exaggeration of the case by Sir Robert. Now I'm in front of him. He beams down. For a horrifying moment I think he is going to get down on his haunches and treat me like a two year old but to his credit he keeps everything on a professional footing and simply shakes my hand. "So good of you to come," he says.

"I'm delighted to be here," I reply. Boy did that sound pompous.

Dorothy is standing talking to Patricia Mayberry. Patricia looks me over as I approach. "God, he's the best looking, unattached male in the room. If only you were a bit older William."

"Don't worry," Dorothy says, indicating out and beyond, "your man is waiting out there somewhere."

"Well, I wish he'd fire off a flare or something."

Dorothy grabs my hand. "I've been invited to sit with the Captain. Seems he's a fan. Now if I have to spend the evening answering questions about my writing, you must join me and give me someone else to converse with."

At this moment the band starts playing a dance tune.

"I'd be honoured, Will."

"But I can't dance Dorothy."

"Well neither can I Will but I've been faking my way round dance floors for years."

She's right as usual. On a crowded little dance floor we simply walk around. Dorothy spins on my arm a few times which is quite flash. Sir Robert appears dancing with Lady Mayberry and looks me over with some proprietorial pride. Even Patricia slides into view in the arms of a 'man'. Forgetting the style of gathering I wink at her as she leans over her partner's shoulder.

Many hours later upon my return to our cabin the lights
are on. Perched on the edge of the bunk are my parents.
"Okay," Steve says, "we're going out to the bar." Situation
normal I think. "Care to join us for a night cap?" What? My
father wishes to ply me with alcohol?
"Not quite," he explains, "I'm not the world's greatest
parent but I'm not about to get my 10 year old son pissed.
I'll buy you something that looks like it might be booze."
Mum is like a schoolgirl. She grabs my hands. "You can tell
us all about the party, eh babe."
"Aren't I too young to be in a bar?"
Dad guides me out the cabin door. "Me and the barman are
like that." He indicates with entwined fingers.
Now that part I can believe.

It was a splendid party. The Captain has Dorothy sign a
book 'for his wife' and bathes in the reflected glory of
somebody famous at his table. My novelty value ensures
that I dance a lot with various matronly ladies. None
appear to be great dancers and with the slight roll of the
ship and their curiosity about the relationship between
myself and Dorothy there is little time for footwork.
"People are talking about us," I whisper to Dorothy at the
table, "and I'm very hot in this suit," I add. She dabs my
forehead with a napkin. "That will give them a little more to
be getting on with," she says. Dorothy has had a little too
much champagne.

As we are leaving, Captain Braithwaite shakes my hand
and finally crumbles to curiosity. "Your Aunt Dorothy is

a wonderful person and so talented," he says. Nice try captain.

"Oh, she's not my aunt. We're just mates."

From this pinnacle of time and place, the line on the map outside the Dining Room moves inexorably toward its goal. Aden is another dusty, dangerous stop. Port Suez is my mother's best shopping chance and she collects an assortment of dubious items to assess with a clearer head at some date in the future. Steve buys me a particularly splendid knife. Possibly he would have liked this dagger himself but could not justify an adult with such an item. My nights on the deck with Dorothy continue right through the heat of the Red Sea. We solve what problems of the world that are of interest to us and leave the rest for others of a more dreary nature. Dorothy fails time and again to answer some of my questions about life matters. There is a point beyond which information will not go. My tan progresses on the upper deck to a point where I appear to be in danger of outbrowning my host. I rub sun oil on her back and she does the same for me.

"Should give our fellow passengers a bit to be getting on with at their dinner tables," she whispers to me as she massages my shoulders.

It is on one of the nights as we head north, away from the African continent that a sudden cold finger of air slides along the deck and plays about our necks.

"Europe is just over there. I'm afraid this may be our last need to cool off, my petal."

"You look sad Dorothy."
"I am, my little deck-chair buddy but only briefly. Life is just a series of chapters. We're not at the end of the book."

With a haste that is both unseemly and unforgiving we are back in scarves and coats, chugging rapidly like a horse returning to the stables. There is activity about as passengers retrieve cabin trunks to repack with the items they have acquired on the voyage. Boxes line the corridors and deck. Steve and Doreen begin worrying that their letters to all the relatives we intend visiting and hopefully staying with (thus negating a great deal of the accommodation costs) have been received.

Southampton does not appear so much as ooze out of the morning light. A soft grey dawn, lacking brightness but with an antique quality I like. It is time for our 'last supper.' Dad has given me a white envelope from our cabin stationery set. He will not say what is in the plain white envelope with a ship's funnel in the corner.
"It's adequate," he replies, to my enquiry. "Besides, by the time your mate opens it you'll be gone and never see him again."
At the end of our breakfast we all thank Reggie for his sterling work. Dorothy shakes his hand and presses a handsome wad of notes into his palm. The Mayberry's to my relief, say their farewell's and hand him a white envelope. Reggie is not sure what to do with me. I shake his hand and I say thanks for being so nice. He wasn't especially but it seems appropriate. He is shocked when

I try to slip the envelope into his hand. It flutters to the floor. We both bend down to retrieve it and nearly clash our heads. There is much laughter and we part with what I imagine is the usual run of tired jokes about ships, waiters and passengers.

Outside on the wall the line that has made its way across the world map day by day has been taken right onto the coast of England.

Sir Robert squints at it. "That's a bit presumptuous, we may founder yet."

Lady Mayberry looks about. "Well my dears, we may not have time for such things later. Let me say what an enjoyable voyage this has been, thanks in no small part to our delightful table companions."

"Here, here," adds Sir Robert.

Lady Mayberry shakes Dorothy's hand warmly and then, in an unexpected move reaches down and gives me a big hug. "Bye bye, Will."

Patricia, gives me a peck on the cheek. "If only you were a big person little Will."

"I will be someday. Say what about that man I saw the other night?"

Patricia looks coy. "I have his name. I shall begin pestering him the moment we're settled in."

Sir Robert shakes my hand and to my surprise gives me a friendly punch on the arm. "I sincerely hope we bump into each other again, Will. Who knows, eh?"

Then they are gone.

"I've got some last minute packing to do Will. I'll see you on the wharf. Don't you dare zoom off until I catch up with you."

Now Dorothy has gone and I'm alone in a totally empty
foyer.

By mid morning, with a pale orange glow penetrating the
hazy sky I am standing looking up at the ship, all rivets and
steel and dark green, oily water.
There are people and boxes and crates and officials and
customs and mild chaos on all sides. Steve and Doreen
are relieved. Outside they have glimpsed a whole swag of
relatives anxiously scanning the crowd. It appears we will
have somewhere to sleep tonight.
We can only wait as the throng of passengers is slowly
dealt with. First Class are receiving priority treatment.
Distantly I see the Mayberry's following some porters
piled high with luggage. There is a sudden commotion
near the exit. A fight? Men pushing forward. A flashing
light. Climbing on a large crate I can make out the centre
of the storm. It is Dorothy Prentice. Surrounding her are
two policemen and a lot of people asking her questions
and taking pictures. As I watch another flash bulb goes
off, then another. She seems to be ignoring them. She is
looking about, holding her hands up. Her eyes search the
crowd. Then they're looking at me. She smiles. I wave from
my high vantage point. Using great command Dorothy
strides through the people and makes her way across. As
she gets closer I can see she has a tall man holding her
arm. Looking up at me on my crates, she says, "Will, I told
you I'd find you on the wharf. Here, climb down a bit." She
holds out her hand and once I am on the wharf, she turns

to the man at her side. "Ted, this is the other man in my
life. Remember I said I'd met somebody on the ship. Will,
this is my fiance, Ted."
We shake hands earnestly. Damn, she's already taken.
"I guess I'll have to grow up and marry somebody
else," I say.
"Thank you for looking after Dorothy so well." Ted has a
very correct accent, to go with his tweed jacket.
Dorothy takes a large package from her shoulder bag.
"Here Will, this is to help answer all those unanswered
questions. I had Ted pick it up for me."
Inside the brown paper is a two volume set of the Oxford
Dictionary.
"I've signed it for you. Read it later."
We stand looking at each other while everybody else looks
at us. The silence becomes awkward. Then Dorothy holds
out her arms.
"Come here lover boy. Give me a big hug." It is a big hug
and I hug her back through her thick coat. This lady
who has the world on a string and holds it so easily. The
cameras pop. Steve and Doreen are open-mouthed.
Dorothy squats down and takes my hand. She has piece of
paper. "I insist that you write to me. This is my address. I
want to know all about the rest of your life Will. It's going
to be a good one."
"Are you going to put me in a book?"
"Perhaps, with your permission?"
"Sure, as many as you like."
She hugs me again and the bulbs flash.

In the parlour of a starchy old aunt in Bridport.

We have risen and are taking tea. It is the morning after our arrival. Steve and Doreen have lost any concept of their surroundings as they continue to question me on my relationship with the world famous Dorothy Prentice. They have fingered her inscription in the Dictionaries as if they were touching the work of the creator.

"For God's sake Will, stop calling her Dorothy. She must be in her mid thirties at least. Miss Prentice, please." Mum has always been a sucker for fame.

At that moment Uncle George pokes his head round the door. I have just met the man but have taken an instant shine to his likeable manner.

"How about this then, look here ...." His accent is thick west country. "We've made the front page of the London papers."

Yes there I am, being hugged and handled by Dorothy. The caption reads. 'A young admirer gets the thrill of his life, in a brief, impromptu meeting with famous author Dorothy Prentice on her arrival at Southampton, yesterday.'

Since that day I have not believed a single thing that appears in newspapers.

A VILLAGE IN THE SOUTH

There was a neat fishing fleet in the harbour. No rust
or algae. No barnacles. A well maintained collection of
successful trawlers. From the park that sloped gently
to the sea-wall a whole section of the town is laid out.
Seabirds, whose types or names I could never remember,
dot the sky.
She is waiting, under a tree.
I could see her legs and bare feet, slim, pretty, pale against
the rich grass. As I walked round the tree she turned.
The sun had broken in pieces through the clouds after
an attempt at rain. She looked up from beneath a creamy,
wide sun-hat and slipped her thumb into her book to mark
the place.
"Hullo." An enigmatic half smile.

I had not seen her over those years. Her beauty was quite
chilling. Perhaps there was an expectation that she would
look a lot older. She held me in her gaze, pretty mouth,
poised. What did she think of me?
"I don't try to go brown," she said brightly, "for me it
doesn't work. I feel I should just be iridescent. What do you
think?"

She extended an arm.

"So far, so good. There's a hint of sunlight I think. Slightly warm toast brown." It felt odd, to be so casual.

She continued to hold out her hand, now squinting slightly in the sunlight.

Momentarily I considered taking it and kissing her fingers.

I realised in time that she wanted to be helped to her feet.

Walking barefoot (I like the feel of grass) back across the park to the house, she was quite at ease.

"How was the trip down? The railway is odd, isn't it."

"I feel lost without a car. You were right though. Wooden carriages. They still have those water jugs in the racks. Train windows equal reflection time I guess."

All this stilted talk.

There followed a tiny silence. On the nape of her neck soft hairs caught in the light.

"Imagine all the stories in that wood. Tucked away in the corners of the compartments."

"I think you just took my line."

She skipped round in front of me.

"Well I know the way you think." Her eyes are the most intense green, confronting. "Don't I."

My face is flushing. She lays the back of her hand on my cheek.

"Mr Perrin."

There is that slight smile. And the eyes never leave mine.

"I wonder how much longer a nostalgic train trip will pay enough for it to continue?" I say. "The train was nearly empty."

"I suppose the train's a bit like this town. You won't notice a great deal of change in the place. The town or the house. Sluggish area this is, too caught up in itself. There's a new market with a bit better selection of food. That's about it."

Apart from the newspaper headlines outside one shop, the main street was still smug and quiet and time locked, as we passed through.

We turned into Cliff Road, one of the aptly named streets and landmarks of my youth. Those utilitarian members of the first town council had reduced everything within my early existence to very practical terms.

She danced beside me now. Now with her slip on shoes back on her feet. She never could walk with a normal stride.

"Your schooldays are over. What does life hold for you now, Susan Hughes?"

"Stop sounding a lot like my grandfather, you're only two years older than me, Mr Perrin. Remember?"

Her eyes met mine again in this game. No expression gave a hint to her intent. She had always been an actress of sorts.

"I'll sell up and head off to make my fortune. If you consider that prospect it gives me great scope to do pretty well anything."

Gulls called overhead, swooping on the currents of air that pushed up the cliff face as we moved up the hill. It seemed to add dramatic effect. Susie smiled up at them. In a note of thanks I suspected, for their timing. No more difficult questions.

"Here we are." She held out her arm like a tour guide, encompassing the four cottages This oasis above the town. I disguised the stab of memory. Here it was, as I had left it.
"The walk didn't seem so far."
"Your perspective has changed. You're older now and wiser."

We had lunch in her home. The cottage I knew so well. It belonged to her alone now. The meal was as expected. Salad and an exotic high grain bread. My own appetite was limited. Sitting next door to my old home, in this room that I had not seen since that night. The last sight of the houses had been through the frosted rear window of our car. Late at night, skulking away, criminals in our own minds. My brothers pushed in beside me, already half asleep, for the journey north.
"I was very sorry to hear about your Mother's death. So soon after your father. Did the authorities try to interfere?"
"No. They no doubt had a look at the situation with a view to getting involved. But I was old enough to look after myself. Perhaps with the past they put me in the list of lost causes."
This time I did not meet her eyes.
"What were your new neighbours like here?"
"A dull fishing family whose children have all refused to follow the tradition and moved on. Quiet and bitter I guess you'd call them. Just get an occasional nod. The other two cottages have been empty for a while. Nobody wants to live up here."

After the meal we sat on the clifftop opposite the houses and viewed them as a group. It seemed even the rocks and indentations were familiar.

"Are you worried that we might be seen?"

She looked surprised. "Not particularly, not at all. I stayed, I've paid my penance. It was a lot worse for my mother. Didn't help her health in the end. And don't seek out some bitterness in that statement. There's none."

"I wrote to you."

"I didn't know that. My mother was a 24 hour guard dog. Nothing got through. Suppose that explains your surprise when I wrote to you."

Tugging small pieces of grass by her feet, her confidence was ebbing away. This meeting had been planned for some time. I doubt she had thought of our conversation much past the initial greeting in the park.

"So, have you got yourself a girl up in the big city?"

"No," I said.

It was windy, always damned windy up here. When we left, I missed the wind most of all.

Like brother and sister, people would say. Her with no father. He's so protective of her. And no wonder, she's so pretty. Lovely children.

Our own world lay about us. Secret places, rituals that meant nothing and everything. I was the one that had to keep her and protect her, up here on the clifftops. There would be trouble if I was not aware of where she was at any time.

We grew older. The world did not expect that. On summer

days, alone.

"Do you ever think about it?"
"Don't call him 'it'." She sat straight backed, indignant in her pose.
"It was a boy? I heard nothing until your letter last week. How did you know it was a boy?"
"I have eyes Mr Perrin. Through the tears of self-pity I could see. While they cut the cord. The nurse let me hold him briefly before they took him away. He'd be into his school years now."
I put my hand on hers. She pulled it back.
"I'm in charge now," she said, not looking up. She waved her hands about. "No, no, that's wrong. There's no guilt, I'm not bitter. Please, just ..." The hands again, moving. After a moment she added. "Perhaps you're reading more into this than I intended. I thought it would do us both good. Do you know you're the only person I know outside this town. I need help with disposal of the house."
Suddenly she spun round and lay on her back. She hitched her shorts down and pulled her shirt up. I was staring at her torso.
"I worked very hard after it was over. No sign that it happened. Look. No marks. Slim and flat. I rubbed cream into my nipples to make them soft. I wanted to be a little schoolgirl again."
The houses across the road sat in mute judgement of the scene. I had always imagined the two upstairs windows in each to be sets of eyes. Now I was sure.
She rearranged her clothes.

"Now, that Susan girl from Cliff Road is leaving. The final
act in cleaning the slate. You're here. I was sure for years
that I loved you. It was just something for me to mull over
on long evenings. Perhaps I see you as a brother. Is that
okay? With some guidance from you the house will soon be
gone. The leash will be taken away."
She gave the sweetest smile. Her green eyes drilled into
mine. They glittered. She was back in charge. But then she
always was. The purpose of the meeting.

She came up north two months later. Moved into my flat
near the University. Took charge. Our childhood came
back. Playing at living. She was an accomplished cook
tending to odd and healthy.
I couldn't study. She was still my pal. The person I had
played with and with whom I had sought and found the
wondrous joys of another's body. We had pursued the
game for months, every chance we had, unaware that there
were such things as consequences. I was a late and totally
naive pubescent. Now there could be none of that. Her new
rules did not allow intimacy.
As I lay at night I hoped that at least she was going through
the same restless, fitful notions in the next room. Was it
pride? Was it an evening of a score?

"I am employed." she announced after about three weeks
of searching and actually turning down two offers. "I am
Marketing Research Officer."
Trying not to sound incredulous I inquired, "Do you have
some background in that area?"

"No, but I learn fast."

"You lied?"

"Marketing is rather like that, don't you think Mr Perrin."

She did survive. Each day I returned expecting her being discovered and unemployed. She simply triumphed.

Her confidence grew. She became a child again, so happy with herself that she dropped into areas previously cut off. We had wine with our meal on one night. Into the evening we giggled like naughty children waiting to be sent to bed. Remembering, out performing each other with feats of recollection.

For some minutes in my room I grew angry at the situation I had allowed to happen. Then turned out the light and lay in darkness with my jaw set. If she must do this to me she must go. But now that she was here I couldn't think of it being any other way.

A noise. The door had opened. "Do you want to play?" she whispered, as the conspirator she had so many years before.

She switched on a small lamp and placed it on the floor. "Can time go back, Mr Perrin?"

It was the grass on the hill again, the sea cave, her bedroom in the quiet of the day, so many places. She looked the same. It felt the same. Exploring these depths went on for hours. Not able to leave each other alone for a moment. Wanting more and more and more.

"I wonder if our boy knows or will ever know? He may come looking one day. Was your mother beautiful? I only remember her as angry?"

She must have packed that night, before she came to my room. The note said, 'I don't know. If you do, then wait for me. Please don't hate me if I never come.' The paper was unsigned.

It is a year. This house on the clifftops, previously owned by a bitter old fishing couple suits my needs. The other three houses are all for sale. Susan's new owners only lasted six months. I could make an offer. They'd be cheap. It would be fun to own the lot.
With the paraphernalia of my profession at hand I can communicate and work quite successfully. At nights I walk down the cliffs and look at the sea caves. Stand for hours with my eyes closed into the wind. So far she has not come though I think at times I hear her nearby.

THAT WEEK

Oh how they dragged their feet. Those long and tedious
summer days in the early years of the seventies.
Of course the sixties and seventies have become an icon
for outpourings of creative fervour and self-indulgence.
In the suburbs of Sydney we had not completely
experienced the rush of rebirth that was supposedly
enveloping us all. Well, most of us. It was yet unrecognised.
Simply a rumble of indeterminate source or function.

TV was dreadful, even for those who knew no better. It had
to be better. My father kept his lawns flat. Trimmed into
submission, they lay level and ran soul-less to the paling
fence. My mother baked bad, dry cakes, my sister did
dreadful things to her hair with dye, curlers and spray and
my brother sat, up to his neck in grease, surrounded by the
innards of his car.
Other cars roared distantly as they accelerated from the
lights on the highway. Someone had the races going on the
radio.

I lay on my bed with a damp forehead, trying to read
philosophy without really understanding a word of it.

The weekend hung over our street like a smothering, maiden aunt's blanket, wrapping us up with no escape and little comfort.

Then Davey arrived.

He scraped the gate as he swung into the drive. He always did. My father advised him to be a bit more careful. They discussed whether or not he had actually made contact with the pale blue painted wrought iron. Dad discovered evidence in the form of a faint tinge of paint on the door of Davey's car. Dave countered with the point that it was an old mark done on some previous occasion when Davey HAD hit the gate.

Father was rendered speechless by the sheer balls of the guy just long enough for him to slip round the back, pat our dog, knock off a few grapes from Dad's prized vine, get his hands on a hot biscuit from my mother with a combination crack about her fabulous looks and cooking and make it down the hall and into my room.

Dad had come back to life outside with added acrimony. "It's not the bloody point ...." While his adversary had decamped he directed his reply to the empty space then returned, muttering, to the weeding.

I had not moved. It always took a while. Davey never got past Dad. Even on Dad's good days, Davey knew it was sound value to comment on and show interest in the lawn or a bush or anything he could locate in the barren landscape.

"What's this shit you're reading?"

"Kant."

"Can't what?"

"Are you doing that deliberately?"

"What?"

"Forget it."

"Hear it?"

Having known Davey since we messed nappies together (Actually he's a bit older than me.) I knew what I was supposed to hear.

"Reckon they're big do you?"

"Fucking huge, mate. C'mon, grab your gear, let's go."

"David, watch your language," Mum called from the kitchen. He pulled a face at me.

We actually lived quite close to the beach. It's always the way. When something is on your doorstep, you take it for granted.

Davey drove as if on a death wish. He was on first name terms with all the local police. Scared as I was I said nothing. Willing to die rather than show signs of weakness or cowardliness. My foot rammed down on the imaginary brake pedal on the floor.

Davey chatted amicably as he weaved a path through holes he would not fit.

"I went to confession yesterday. Slate's clean, so the local talent better watch their pants tonight mate. Might find ol' Davey's apparatus making it's way in the side door."

Sex obsessed Davey. We all had the usual teenage hormone driven urges. Davey was one endless urge.

"You bloody Catholics. Hypocritical bastards. You can't wipe the slate with a couple of quick Hail Marys and a dollar in the box. You're supposed to mean it."

"How do you make a hormone?" asks Davey. "Slip her six inches and punch her in the nose."

"That's not funny. Just crude."

"Then stop smirkin'."

There is a moment, heading along the Pacific Way, that you know you've arrived. As you breast the hill the ocean is suddenly there. It hits you in the eye. The hot white trail of road, the park, the shops and the big, blue beautiful ocean beyond. And today I can see the surge of swell way out, rolling in giant green pulses into shore.

"Fuck, look at 'em go. Look at those baby's go. It's shit-hot" Davey punches my arm. He is given to bursts of great passion when expressing himself.

"Yeh, you guessed right. Good waves."

"No guess man. Me and the ocean, we've got this thing." There is that feel, the smell, the noise. This strip of shoreline is alive.

Today the beach is packed. It is hot and there are bodies everywhere. Miles of beach but everybody drops on the sand at the first available spot. We hop across the sand with burning feet. Lots of kids in the shallows. There are board-riders out the back. One gets smashed as I'm watching.

On the surf club's loudspeakers the 'Atlantics' are pumping out 'Bombora'. What a great day.

"Which of you babes wants me tonight?" Davey asks in general, arms extended.

"Piss off, ya drop-kick." That will be the protective grunting of the primate males, replying to Davey's challenge. It's this intellectual banter that endears the beach scene to me. I've had the Davey deprogramming lecture.

"You're a bloody snob, Rory. I mean you're a good bloke but just a little up yourself. Lighten up, ditch all those books and shit and grab the nearest blonde by her left tit. You might get slapped, the boyfriend might appear and cream you but there's a bloody good chance you might get a root."

The distressing part of this mindless 'life force' philosophy is that he's partly right. And though I'd never stoop to admitting it, I'm jealous. If I had the necessary front to actually pinch a girl's breast and God I'd love to, there's the terrifying chance that she might smile and move closer. Then where would I be?

It's a mate thing. Davey gets into everything in sight. Some of them actually good looking. I have never had the pleasure. Of course I've lied my way through several erotic encounters. If nothing else in life I have a balanced talent for creation. Does Davey know? Hard to say. But he does have a missionary zeal for seeking out girls that have a girlfriend in tow. One for his good mate.

"Fuck, yours is ugly." And he's generally right again.

It is some strange female pack mentality thing that a desirable mating partner must be accompanied by a dwarf or mentally imbalanced or massively obese person. Combinations of these shortcomings are known to occur.

Does it make them look better, feel better or do they just have a penchant for finding incompatible friends?

Many times I have made difficult small talk in the loungeroom, faced by some creature from hell while cries of animal intensity emanate from the adjoining bedroom. We both pretend not to notice. Their faces always give it away and their eyes widen at particularly loud cries of ecstasy.

"Why didn't you give her a poke?" Davey asks afterwards.

"I wouldn't 'poke her' with yours, mate. Did you see her?"

"Fussy bastard."

So today we pick a patch. Make great ceremony of laying out towels and dumping gear so as to casually check out the area. Laying back, hands behind heads.

"What do ya think?" Davey moves his head to indicate the surroundings.

"They all seem to have blokes attached."

"Yeh, wouldn't it shit you. I clocked that little darling over to the left and next the boyfriend is glaring back at me."

There follows the traditional period of silence enjoyed by all surfers. It is time to adjust to heat, sand, salt, ozone, noise, smells and allow eyes to recalibrate for the glare factor.

With eyelids down the senses strain to focus on the nuances of beach culture. Waves hitting on to the sand, children crying out and skipping about in the froth, gulls calling, the relentless DJ on the loudspeakers, smells of pies, chips and other low-end food, conversations partly heard, squeaking sand as people walk past. It is a collective whole that is the beach.

We're brown. Everybody is brown. The occasional pale skinned person stands out. They will return home in the evening, blistered and in pain, having been trapped with their friends and afraid to admit their difference.

Now back to girls. Davey is well-built. I'm on the slim side. No, I'm not skinny. That bony guy with the teeth, down by the water, now he's skinny.

I was at this party two years back when I was fourteen. It was the first party I'd ever been to where the parents had left the house. A few girls set up a room and invited the boy's in one at a time. Nothing spectacular was happening, they were just giving each entrant a bit of a kiss. My turn came. I go in with my heart pounding so much I thought they could see it. The lights are out and there's a chair in the middle of the room.

"Sit down," they say.

Then this girl sneaks up from behind, swings her head round mine and starts kissing me. Then she stops.

"Hey, this one's nice." She's talking about me! Her hand slides inside my shirt. Is she going to grab my heart as it breaks through my rib cage? She moves around, still kissing me, all over my face like a vacuum cleaner. By now I'm brave enough to have put my hands round her waist and I'm getting a bit involved. She sits on my lap. A slight shudder goes through her. She leaps up, out of my arms.

"Err, what's that?"

I realise she's referring to the considerable lump in my jeans. What can I say. I have no power over the little bastard, who is now quite a big bastard.

Over the intervening years I have consummated that evening many times in my mind. Rearranged the circumstances, altered locations to add spice to the event, always with a similar result. No one can fail in their fantasies. Life and its aspects of reality is the leveller of dreams.

"You better turn over, mate. As the actress said to the bishop."
"Uh?"
Davey's head is inclined to my crotch. Damn this uncontrollable appendage. I roll over and reach down to dig a small hole for it to rest in.
"Having a bit of a think about something were you?"
Davey is particularly obnoxious when he adopts that man-of-the-world superior tone in relation to matters sexual.
"Yes, Dad."

About half an hour into the beach day there is the mutual grunt as participants become hot and decide by some silent telepathy to cause each other to head for the water. It is 'de regueur' to plunge straight in thus enhancing the shock factor of hot body in cold water. While the water is in fact quite balmy, the body entering it is practically cooked. It is the difference between the two that causes the heart-stopping moment.
"Jesus Christ."
The scream is always silent. It is considered particularly 'cool' to dive right next to a pair of young girls timidly making their way into the waves. They may think you're

a moron but at least they notice you. You should not run
over somebody's kid in the effort to get to the girls first.
After all we were all young once and having some great log
knock you spade over bucket can be distressing for a little
person.
Diving of course puts large numbers of healthy young
males into wheelchairs for the remainder of their lives
but ego is everything when you're young and foolish.
Accidents only happen to your mate's, mate's friend, twice
removed.

Back on the beach with your body desperately clawing its
way back to the ambient temperature for handling the sun,
there is the equally silent mind-wrestle to allocate 'shop
duties'. In this ritual I normally accede. I'm hungry and
Davey would rather starve than lose so 'what the hell'.
Davey gives a snort of victory as I wander off. Let him have
these tiny prizes. My life is on a grander scale.

"I got told to 'fucking watch out," I tell Davey on my return.
Dancing across the sand I sidestepped onto a girl's hand.
'Ouch' she said. For the briefest passage of time our eyes
met. Her's under a single brow. God she was ugly.

The boyfriend added the advice.
"Must be a good root," observes Davey glancing back,
"she's got a face like a smacked arse."
We're both into hot chips and a large can of pineapple
juice. It is part of the current Davey health plan. He has
deduced that the acidic drink will counteract the grease

of the chips and thus restore a balance to our internal
workings.

"Also coats your gut for handling beer," he enthuses.

We've both been 'drinking' for about a year. Though still a
little way off the official drinking age we're tall enough to
get away with visits to pubs. In a busy bar, a sale is a sale,
they don't ask questions.

One memorable session last summer involved bringing
beer to the beach. So excited were we by the ability to get
some of this mysterious nectar that we drank a number of
cans each in the blazing sun then decided to swim.

For one so young, this near death experience as I struggled
about drunkenly, trying to fight the waves, left a permanent
mental scar. Just as I had prepared myself for being
dragged under and away forever my feet clawed their way
onto swirling sand and I was able to stumble out of the
water.

Laying on my towel with my head spinning, trying to take
in enough air to survive, I heard Davey flop down next to
me. No words of terror or triumph were uttered. No words
at all. No alcohol came to the beach again.

After eating you must wait before going in the water, due
to the possibility of cramps. I have never heard any of our
group or any other group actually mouth those words but
everybody waits. It is a beach philosophy drummed into
all of us by our parents. Of course at our advanced years
we have ceased obeying any parental guidance but hell,
you never know, they might be right.

The day drags past midday and into a hot afternoon.
Lifesavers wander down the beach, watch the surf for
a while and then move the flags about two feet to the
left. They then blow a whistle at a couple of board-riders
encroaching on the flagged area, intent on decapitating
some surfers and having justified their existence, retreat to
their little lifesaver's bunker to idle away the afternoon.
They're probably a bit pissed that despite the large waves,
nobody has required rescuing, especially some young
thing with great tits.
Lifesavers at tourist beaches get to rescue lots of visitors
who haven't got a clue about surfing or even swimming
but here its pretty much locals who've all been swimming
since they could walk.
Almost asleep, I'm aware that the sun has vanished and
water is splashing on me. Malcolm Lutz, 'Big Mal' is
standing over us with his dripping board.
"You guys going to Kenny's Bash?"
Davey shades his eyes. "Yeh, we might give it a go."
"Are we invited?" I inquire.
Malcolm glares down at me, bending his great thick neck
as far as it will move.
"Fuck Rory, you just turn up. Ya fucking gold invite got lost
in the post."
After he's gone and the sun is restored I hear Davey
snigger. "Invite." Another social faux-pas. When will I get it
right dealing with the mentally impaired.

Back in the water it's time for some serious stuff. We're
only body surfing. There's a whole thing about board

riding and board riders and their groupie girlfriends who sit on the beach all day pretending to be excited about the waves they ride. We've checked it out and decided it's all too much effort.

Trouble with the waves today, they're such a great shape that they carry you right into the beach. No need to bail out to avoid death, they're big and friendly. Following each sensational ride there is the onerous task of swimming back out through the breaking surf to take up a suitable position for the next run. After a while Davey sums it up eloquently.

"Christ, I'm fucking knackered. You can stay here Tarzan, I'm going in."

Aha, I've outlasted the bastard.

"No, I'll come in."

We're heading up the beach back to our patch when we both look ahead and see that we have interlopers in our territory.

Approach with caution. They are standing on our towels. Each has a small bag. Dancing from one foot to the other. Females. Young, desirable. We're gaping at this scene.

"Fuck, yours is gorgeous," says Davey.

"So is yours," I reply.

Continue approach. We have a situation here of some considerable delicacy. They haven't seen us yet. What is going on? God is not this kind.

"It's the sand," I say.

"What?"

"They were burning their feet on the hot sand."
Davey sums it up. "We better move fast mate, they'll be
off." He circles quickly, like a predatory animal, moving in
from the side.
"Well hi, hullo, how are we today?"
They look slightly surprised. Where did he come from?
The old Davey boyish charm wins through.
"Great day. Heading in for a swim are you? Best time of
the day. The surf's amazing. Sand's a bit hot but you can
generally find somebody who'll let you stop."
There is a flicker of recognition. She is simply beautiful.
Deep brown eyes, delicate features, slim.
"Oh, are we on your towels?"
"That's fine, lovely to have you drop in. I'm Davey, this is
Rory. Here sit down for a minute. Make sure your feet have
recovered."
Her friend is slightly smaller and younger. She has similar
deep brown eyes.
There follows a period of manoeuvring. Great tactical
battles take place while Davey, desperately aware that
one slip could break the tenuous claims we have on our
visitors, tries to appear casual and jointly charm them into
submission. I am a bit player in these proceedings but feel I
contribute the soft, less confrontational angle.
A variation of the 'good guy-bad guy' routine, to give the
yet unassessed quarry room to breath.
By the unrecorded rules of engagement, the dominant
male has jurisdiction over the choice process and opts
for establishing rapport with the older female. As the
unspoken subordinate in negotiations I am left with the

'other' party. In this case it is a solution from heaven.
As Davey works on his chosen one, I struggle to find
sentences that string together, are witty without being
acerbic and elicit a favourable response, from this
adorable thing parked so close to my skin.
We are sharing my towel, side by side, with knees up to
keep our feet off the sand. This is particularly helpful. Our
arms, legs and shoulders brush ever so casually together
at times and this has produced a response in my groin.

Her name is Bree. She has just left school early and is
thinking about what she wants to do in life. She does some
work in a chemist to earn the rent and food share. Her
friend, Angel, is an illustrator. She might do something
similar. I tell her that I have cadetship with a newspaper.
That is at least vaguely creative. My planets are in the
ascendancy. For once, Davey the wordturner is the odd
one out.
Planned with the precision of a bombing raid, my glances
at Bree only add to my library of favourable impressions.
She is in the smallest of string-tied bikinis. In fact they both
are. Her hands, her feet, her knees, the flock of curled light
hair that surrounds her face. Oh God, I want to grab her
and roll about right here on the sand. She's talking and
I'm flashing pictures of her soft, dreamlike body curled on
white sheets. Skin I want to own.
In the crease of her thighs her tan has a series of tiny
lines. I'm exploring, cutting through this new, untamed,
wilderness, searching. Don't let it fade. It is real.
"Do you like them?"

A question has been directed at me. Three sets of eyes are
cutting a path in my direction. I'm still in the wilderness.
It is a long way back. Silence. Davey throws a life line.
"Rory has pretty odd tastes. This group .....", his eyes
indicate the surf club's loudspeakers, "aren't classical
you see." The content of Davey's life line is a somewhat
dubious revelation that will probably bury me.
There is hand on my arm. Those deep brown eyes are on
mine.
"Do you like classical music?"
"Well, yes." I may as well go out in style. This baby will live
on in my fantasies.
"Dvorak's 'New World Symphony'?"
"Yes, I particularly like that." Where the hell did she ever
hear of that? The hand is still there, on my arm. The grip
is firmer. She even pronounced the composer's name
correctly.
"I lay on my bed and it just takes me away. Images of
forests, pools, huge skies. I close my eyes and I'm there."
Her enthusiasm is startling.
"Finlandia?"
"Yes."
"Apalachian Spring? Four Seasons?"
"Yes. Yes"
Her eyes narrowed ever so slightly.
"Mahler's No.5, Puccini O mio babbino caro?" A little out of
left field but I knew them.
"Very moving stuff. I love them."
Her hand turns to a claw. Excitedly she gasps, "Oh God."
Not a time to look at Davey. His knowledge of the classics

extends to once having heard the opening bars of
Beethoven's 5th as he skimmed the radio dial.

"What the fuck was that?"

Here he is on the outer edge again. People like me do exist.
Angel sweeps her long hair back. "I'm a bit more Dylan
than Debussy but my tastes are quite catholic. "

"Oh mine too," says Davey, saving himself with a
misinterpretation of her religious bent.

Bree has my arm, still.

"Want to come in for a swim, now. What else do you like?
You ought to come back to our place for dinner. We can
listen to some of my stuff. Angel uses it for inspiration.
With her painting."

It is as if the leprechauns' have got together with my fairy
godmother and have taken over the arrangements for my
life.

There is a glance between Bree and Angel.

"Yes, Davey, do you like Greek?" Angel asks.

"What was good enough for Pythagoras."

They live quite close to the beach. A big rambling brick
place, heavy and squat. It has a dark foyer, large rooms
with high ceilings and a great deal of stained wood and
white walls.

I am still recovering from the brief drive from the beach.
Davey owns a ute. Angel slides in next to Davey and there
is room for one more.

"I'll sit on your lap." Bree is indicating that I should get in.
With timing that could gladden the heart of a Swiss I am
able to get a folded towel onto my lap before this virtually

naked, golden child, drops ever so gently into my arms.

Looking about, amazed. Bamboo screens, soft lounges,
books, drawing boards, huge paintings on the walls, grass
matting on the floors, chinese paper lampshades, tulip
glasses half full of red wine. Here in the depths of suburban
beach boredom sits this oasis of sophistication.
Angel's illustrations are taped on a drawing board. Mainly
pencil roughs for a book concerning an enchanted forest.
They are rich in detail, confident and accurate.
Their kitchen is all wood and garlic cloves in bunches,
spices in various jars, bunches of celery and cuts of
coriander laying about as if prepared for a magazine cover.
A big scrubbed wood table centres the room. Bree has
draped a fine cloth half-shirt about her shoulders. It is
gossamer thick. The effect is to gift wrap my desire.
Davey struts.
"Some bloody good stuff comes out of this kitchen I bet."
Instead of food Angel hands out cold glasses of white wine.
We sit and sip, about the table. Silly talk. Whether brown
eggs boil quicker, how to spell geranium, why leather
thongs are long strips and rubber thongs are footwear,
who invented the violin.
Angel is refilling the glasses yet again. She starts to hum.
A long even soft sound. Her beautiful, full lips pursed,
eyelids fluttering. Seating herself in the doorway, she
crosses her legs, continuing the chant. Davey has his lip
curled. Her eyes spring open.
"Come David." Her long slender finger curls.
Bree has my hand. We are slipping away. Davey is seated

behind Angel, his legs crossed and his hands considering the options of mantra or massage. Perhaps both.

In the hallway Bree whispers, "We'll listen to some music." Her room is at the front of the house. Giant windows pour in late sunlight through the curtains. The clothes-rack is simply a pole hung from the ceiling. Grass matting, cushions everywhere. A big double bed with brass fittings. She lights incense sticks. Sandalwood I think. What do I do? I don't want to appear untamed but I would like to be in command.
From speakers hung in the corners the first notes of Beethoven's Pastoral Symphony. It all seems so right. She has my hand again.
"Lie on the bed we can hear it better."
Here we are side by side on this Indian cover. I am frozen in position. Looking at the ceiling, eyes fixed on the plaster decoration. Not unlike a patient being wheeled to the operating theatre. I am aware that she is up on one elbow. Those eyes are close to my face. Don't look, concentrate on the music.
"You've got a roman nose. That's what I liked about you. Couldn't place the reason. Heroic statue."
Now she is closer. Her face is almost touching mine. Her perfect finger runs down my nose. It continues across my lips, chin, neck and travels down my chest. Her words are soft. Her breath, the music, almost drown in my ear.
"Want to undress me, Rory?"

On the way home Davey is unusually quiet. It is late.

The Greek Salad and strange oily bread sits in our stomachs. Both pissed. Wine, cheese. A lot of cross legged sitting. Each free of initial inhibitions, hands and bodies wandered. I have discovered sex, become an expert in one afternoon. Wanted to keep doing it and could. Drained of reproductive fluids for a month. Stunned, I decide, we're both stunned.

"We missed Kenny's party."

My observation is ignored.

"Are you in love, mate?" Davey asks, "Cause I sure fuckin' am."

He has a point. I think I am. Certainly all I want to do is be back there with Bree. It took the cool, controlled voice of Angel to show us out the door.

"I think Angel is older than you, mate."

"Wouldn't be much in it," says Davey, in a trance.

"She knows what she's doing, I'll tell you that for free."

Dad calls out when I stagger down the hall and hit the telephone table again.

"Is that you son?"

("No, it's a fucking burglar. I'm ripping off that flight of pottery ducks you have on the wall. They'll fetch a fortune on the black market.")

"Yeh Dad. Went to Kenny's party. Pretty boring. Just sat around and talked." Hold it. Too much information. He'll be suspicious. Shut up.

Davey is early.

"C'mon mate. Lost the urge?"

I'm trying to wake. Did I just go to sleep? Foggy figure

hanging over my bed.

"Jeans, shirt, hair combed. Davey, what's happened to you?"

"Just get your arse out of bed or I'm leaving without you."

Dad is standing in the doorway with a cup of tea and the Sunday paper.

"The surf must be exceptionally good."

Davey turns. It's a chance to slide out of bed and jump into some jeans. I've slept in the buff, too stuffed to care and enjoying the memories. Dad casts a disapproving eye over my bare butt.

"The surf is unreal, Mr Maddox. I'm worried that if me and Rory don't get down there soon we'll miss the early morning swell. Best time of the day."

Dad retreats.

"Have a good time fellas."

How much does he really know? Someday in the future I will have a real conversation with my father.

"Sure, I knew you'd had one. You change immediately, everybody does. Never look the same after you finally get it."

Bree and Angel are in the front lounge, sitting cross-legged on the floor eating slices of orange. Musk incense sticks are slipping lines of smoke away from the mantelpiece. Angel is wearing a long wraparound thing. It has this unwritten message, that the parcel can be unwrapped. Bree is wearing a man's white business shirt. Is it possible to have an orgasm while standing? Yes, I think so. Orange juice is running down her chin. It tastes fine. She is still warm from sleep.

"Today," announces Angel, "we're going on a picnic."

Now this is an area where Davey is a master. He locates
us in a glen of ferns and grass, buried deep in the national
park's thickest intestinal tract. There is a stream, heat and
dappled sunlight, black shade, seclusion.
"How did you know this place?" Bree asks, exploring the
perimeter. Poking with her bare feet.
"Oh I do a fair bit of bushwalking."
I am left wondering the number of deflowered virgins this
glen may have witnessed.
Angel has a large wicker picnic basket. From it she
produces an exotic array of items, some of which I have
never seen before. Davey to his credit utters no cries of
dismay, disgust or derision. He crunches away on his
carrot sticks, dipping happily into the goat cheese and
exploring Angel's rump with his spare hand.
Wine flows and we drop into a hot semi-conscious state of
well-being. Bree plays with my nose. Angel sketches. Davey
lays his head in her lap.
There is a painting. I can see it. A french impressionist?
A picnic, all terribly bohemian. In these trees. What was
it called? I throw the question open to the group. Davey
pretends to be considering the answer. He has learnt a
great deal in 24 hours.
Angel points her Conte pencil at me. "You must mean
Manet. Le Dejeuner something. Lunch in the field, on the
grass or something."
"That's it." She does not realise how impressed I am having

seen this image less than a week earlier.

"The women were undressed, the men retained their clothes," she adds. "A fair indication of the times."

Then Davey rises to the bait. "Sounds reasonable. Women have a higher body heat than men. They no doubt needed to cool off."

Bree is enthused. "It's a sort of tableau. Representative of the new, unabashed lifestyle that was taking hold in European society. Quite understandable, given the circumstances"

She's quoting. We all look. "Well it's true. I know, let's recreate the painting," she adds, eyes bright. Oh my little baby, what a clever idea.

So we are here in this forest. Bathed in golden afternoon sun with two naked girls, who are much more at ease than me. Can't help looking over my shoulder. What do Rangers do with naked picnickers. Is there a fine?

Davey can't sit with an unclad Angel and remain aloof. He begins to fiddle. It takes a time for her concentration to move from her sketchpad but given that time and Davey's intent, things begin to happen.

"We're going for a walk. Saw some interesting wildflowers." They depart, hand in hand. Angel looks back. "You take care, Bree." Odd thing to say. We hear them cross the stream.

The old Rory would now be left stumbling for words. Without a mate, the interlocutor, to bounce things off, stuck with some terrible person of low intellect. The new Rory has everything at his disposal. A gorgeous young thing at his side. Sans covering. Stylish conversation with a girl who understands, enthusiasm and unbridled lust to retain a full measure of the first two.

"What did she mean, 'take care'?"

"Oh she just looks out for me. It's okay, it's that time of the month. You didn't bring any covers did you?"

I'm only just keeping up with this. Still bloody naive.

Am I blushing?

"No." I've never had enough guts or the need to go into a shop and ask for 'covers'.

"It's okay. Really," she says, moving in closer. Her nipples brush against me. Did I mention her beautiful, soft little breasts?

Yes, now we're making love, on the sponge-like grass, under the sky. Gently, easily, no hurry. Let the Rangers come, I'll pay the fines. Yes, I'm in love. This must never end.

Laying back exhausted with hands still exploring each others bodies. We're actually panting. Bree looks across to me. A small giggle escapes her lips.

"What?"

"Nothing, my lover."

'Lover'. Wow!

Briefly I become conventional and consider the possibility that I am not the first of Bree's 'lovers'. (Though she assured me that I am.)

In those thoughts there is a reminder of past deeds.

One of Davey's more ignominious claims to notoriety was that he was the only person we knew who had actually been a customer of the 'special clinic'. Known to all by its familiar blue light and city location it hung in the back of teenage psyche as a beacon of last resort. Salvation for those who made a bad choice in partners.

After an initial coy period in which he refused to supply 'insider' details of his encounter Davey cracked and then ran on like a broken pipe. He scored beers and babes (yes babes) on the story for months. The 'babes' part of the whole episode was somewhat of a puzzle. We finally put it down to a combination of reflected glory, living dangerously and the perception that lightning never strikes in the same place.

Back at the girls' house, there is a dilemma. Tomorrow is Monday. It is evening. Time is interfering with my joyous, new lifestyle. In the front lounge. We hold Angel down until she shows us her etchings. They are very good. Various pieces of our afternoon scratched on cartridge paper. I am there. My ego is appeased.

A lot of this slothful laying about. It is in fact very practiced. If you appear relaxed you have achieved the high degree of precision required to carry it off.

Angel sits playing with a small cloth bag. A slight tingling runs up my temples as I realise what she is doing. Quickly there are four fat, rough cigarettes on the matting. Oh how incredibly wicked. This girl is an archetypal non-conformist. We are being dragged into a sea of wanton, lawless behaviour.

After lighting up and being shown how to draw the stuff in and nearly choking and getting the hang of it and having a second, it all seems so trivial.

I can also see clearly how the dilemma can be resolved.

"Bye Mum." I slip past and give her a kiss. Mistake. She is
touching her face.

"After all these years my youngest suddenly says goodbye.
And a kiss?"

Heading for the bus to the station, to work. Cross the park,
away from the bus stop. There is Davey's ute waiting under
trees at the end.

"You ever gonna get that thing of yours going again?"
There is no malice in the question. The 'thing' has not
worked at all since I had a little trouble with the tuning
and my brother plunged in to fix it. Now it is a jagged
nerve that does not like being prodded. He has buggered
it completely and wants it to go away. Eventually Dad will
consider that sufficient time has passed and will resolve
the issue by taking it to Seth at the local garage.

I picture the scene.

"I was gonna fix it, just needed to find the time."

"Well, it's done now son. Rory's back on the road and
you've got a bit more spare time, eh."

"Yeh, I think Dad might drop it off to Seth, soon."

(I'm not old enough to drive but according to Davey that
doesn't matter.)

On the beach as we swing past, two runners are the
only occupants. Empty and lonely. The rumble of life as
workers go off to work. At the house, the girls are still in

bed. Completely out of character and for the first time in our lives we prepare and serve breakfast. Considering the novice event it comes out reasonably well.

"You have to time scrambled eggs just right," Angel says, prodding the yellow, watery lump on her toast.

At 8:45am first Davey, then I ring in with tales of illness to our respective places of employment. Mine has a higher degree of inventiveness with suggestions of the simple headaches and accompanying dizziness being portents of some greater medical evil. This I feel leaves room for relapses and further complications at the end of the week should my penis, which is now running my life, requires still more gratification.

Angel disappears at 9:00am for a city appointment with a publisher. She is back by midday with the news that he loves the style she has chosen and a large cheque for advances on the illustrations. The week is ours. It is opening up and blossoming like a time-lapse flower. There are plans made, magnificent ornate beasts that quickly fade as the true nature of our getting together manifests itself. Is it possible to grow tired of sex? I am going to do my absolute best to investigate this theory in the coming days.

Small excursions are allowed as long as we are not too far from the house and its beds. I am to take Davey's ute for the first such outing. Armed with a list I will bring back supplies for the troops to maintain strength. At the last minute Davey joins me to 'help carry things'.

In the supermarket he borrows some deodorant and after

shave then places the used containers at the back of the
shelf.

"Didn't have time for a shower this morning," he whispers.
"Don't want Angel thinking her David is uncouth."

"Heavens no," I reply.

By the Tuesday of the week I have informed my parents
that I am staying with Davey because he has a job in the
city and can drive me in each day. Davey is, of course,
staying with me. No reason is required with Davey's folks.
Their mode of existence does not require that they pry
into their son's lifestyle. Our parents are not known to each
other. It is all so neat that I worry briefly then Bree takes
my mind right away from such minutiae.

On the Wednesday night of the week we are settled in
and life is elegant. What boy's dreams could conjure such
immense pleasure? A day of idleness at our virtually
private beach. It appears others may be absent from work,
due to the exceptional weather and wave forms but we
have eyes that do not travel far. They are fixed and slightly
out of focus, as our respective babies attract envious
glances and flaunt themselves. Akin to a doctor looking
for traces of disease I spend a great deal of time examining
Bree from every angle. She appears to enjoy the attention.
Big boy playing with doll. This one is warm and breathes.
Seems like a new car. Shiny, with no blemishes. All parts
working. That new car smell. While she lays back on a rug
I'm working my way over knees, thighs, navel, neck, lips,
ears. When I double check her teeth she gives that funny

giggle again, as if there is unshared knowledge.

At the house we're smoking our way through a large amount of Angel's stash. Overcome eventually with the cost consideration Davey broaches the delicate money subject. Can we help out with paying the supplier? There is that laugh again. Complicity. Angel shows us to a back room. It is a solarium full of long green plants. Good God, she has a jungle in here. It occurs to me that despite her obvious enjoyment of the mature product she has a great deal here for one person. My finger is raised along with a quizzical eyebrow, the question hangs on my lips but I leave it there. Is ignorance a defence? Or stupidity? Little Peter Penis says, don't rock the boat Rory.

After a strange pseudo Italian pasta and something dish and a lot of red wine and several sessions of sitting in a circle passing around Angel's fat cigarette's, we're lit up enough to resolve the world's darkest dreads and move onto more pressing problems.

Angel says, "Let's do a little painting. A joint effort. Sort of memorial."

In more enlightened moments when in full control of my neural functions I may have mentioned that memorials are generally constructed for dead people but I wasn't, so I smiled stupidly and everybody smiled stupidly back as Angel rolled out a huge piece of canvas on the floor. Appropriate music involving Ravi Shankar and a lot of frenetic drumming was placed in the background. Angel and Bree brought forth tubes and jars of paint.

It started rather conservatively with bold brush strokes

attempting a degree of style. Interpretations of the great struggle of some vague notion against the power of the universe and other themes.

An hour or so later (Time had lost its hard edge much earlier), we were imprinting various parts of our anatomy in bright acrylics on the work. Innocent hands and feet at first, then the inevitable progression.

Yes, here I am, Rory the inhibited one, slipping across the artwork, buck-naked tracing a line in Cerulean Blue with my dick. Apart from Bree, the only other people who had seen me naked to date were my parents when they gave me a bath at five years old.

Four paint covered people creating one of the great visual expressions of life in this century. It will be called 'Love' and Angel has this fabulous idea for the finishing touch.

I sit stoned, pissed and aghast as Davey and Angel go at it like rabbits. Her thighs squishing in Viridian Green, Davey's Vermillion Red arse rising and falling.

Old Rory is back. I'm next. I can't do it. More red wine. Feigned unconsciousness. So terrified, determined, numb that I'm able to stay limp when they tickle me to test the genuineness of my condition.

Morning is not good. The others had managed to wash their paint away. Bree lays next me soft, glowing. Being unconscious this was not an option for me. I am put to bed to 'sleep it off.' It hurts to move. Dry acrylic is amazingly elastic and quite waterproof. A triumph of technology for the modern artist. While not overly hirsute I remove most of my manly follicles during the next hour, smothering cries of pain through gritted teeth. Bree finally decides that drastic action is required and shaves my small patch of paint globbed pubic hair. I look like a hairless ten-year old. Four glasses of water and some coffee restores a modicum of balance to my physiology. Our masterpiece is still there on the floor. A rich range of colours and patterns somewhat muddied in parts by action on the surface. Refusing to be sick I crawl back to bed alongside Bree. An extra chance to sleep. So wasteful of life but necessary to live it. Bree opens her eyes, half-smiles then closes them again. Is the first heady rush of this relationship becoming mundane?

If there is a belief that some good must come from all adversity then it is when I wake again many hours later. Bree is examining me and the many red blotches on my skin. Concerned at the torn and battered body beside her she begins rubbing hand lotion into all the affected parts. What a great pleasure it is to allow her to do this. A reaction follows and this must also be treated. We surface and check the rest of the house in early afternoon, smiling broadly, to find Davey and Angel have gone to the beach. Hunger becomes a new need to be satisfied. Lots of eggs, bacon and bread. Bree supplies a salad for the sake of contrast and health. If brunch is a halfway point between breakfast and lunch then this meal of ours must be 'lundin' or 'lutea'. We discuss this and other aimless topics while eating, facing each other over the kitchen's wood table. Tired of talk we fall into silence.

It is a telling moment, without the necessary signs,
pointing the way and only clearer in hindsight. Bree looks
at me and a small shudder passes through her. Overcome
with a sudden clarity of mind I am forced, for the first
time in my life, to note that our world is one of change
and what is now can never be again. Bree must feel it too.
Our expressions must be truly dopey as we stare into
each other's eyes. She appears so incredibly young. So
unblemished and perfect. If I could preserve her now, as
she is, forever. Impossible scenarios race about. Setting up
life together on my apprentice wages. Holding on against
all that life may throw up by clinging to each other.
We both give a little laugh as if embarrassed by the depth
and sincerity of this unspoken moment.
It progresses no further as the rumble of Davey's ute
bumps through the walls into the silent kitchen.

Angel spends the rest of the afternoon working on her
illustrations. Davey hovers, drinking beer, occasionally
kissing her shoulder. Nothing is said of the painting on the
floor. It is simply stepped over like some embarrassment
from the past. In the acute afternoon light it takes on new
dimensions of ordinariness.
"How was the beach?"
"Oh okay, mate. Nothing to write home about." Angel
scowls and hushes us as she concentrates. Davey nods
towards the door.
Sitting on the front steps looking out to the sea. Another
day of summer. Shuffled out, still and clear. A giant dish
of blue over our heads. Distant sound, life's clock ticking

sluggishly and the boundless optimism of youth.

"We've got it made." I say to Davey, without perhaps the conviction the statement deserves.

"Yep."

He can feel it too.

"I'm going to devote my life to inventing a way to freeze time."

"Yeh."

Not the Davey I know. Reduced to a thoughtful, introspective, basically glum person. Watched carefully he does not leap up and once again take charge. He remains there on the steps, looking at the sea.

I wander off to seek out Bree. She is sitting in a deep lounge chair facing a tall window. Outside a mass of green ferns dotted with small palms. Sliding in beside her we have no words to say. She is in the bikini that she wore when I first saw her. A lot of skin is touching once again. Her cute curls brushing my shoulder. We just want to sit, to stare at the ferns.

Around the dinner table Davey has found and lit several candles. The food is whatever we can find. Various bowls placed about and each of us with a fork. Cold orange juice, rice, salad, pasta, bread. We forage in no great order, casting about for items that will be palatable.

Apart from politeness and mastication, little other sound ensues. Well into the meal Davey rises from his chair. He is holding a glass of orange juice and I prepare for a short toast to the last day or perhaps some ideas for our last day. Along the lines of ' the little holiday is nearly over but

this is the beginning of a great affair.' What he actually says
is ......
"I've been waiting for the right moment to say this. Now is
as good a time as any."
So far so good. A degree of the humility we both feel. Angel
makes to speak but Davey will not be put off.
"This last week has been the greatest time in my life. I've
never been so happy. Each day seems like a hundred
birthday parties rolled into one."
'Nice,' I think as he rolls on.
"I cant believe that we only met last weekend. Wow, it has
been just so good. Too good to let go. I know we've got
tomorrow and we can call back on the weekend but..."
Angel says, "Davey, look ...." But Davey is running now.
"Angel, I'm aware how young we are and that our parents
probably won't approve but hell I can't imagine being apart
from you ever again. In front of witnesses Angel I want to
declare my undying love for you and ask you to marry me.
As soon as possible."
Well that certainly brings things to a halt. Davey poised,
posed, looking toward the ceiling. The three other figures
at the table stock still. A small non descript sound does
come from Bree. Eyes move slowly to Angel. She has the
right of reply.
"I'd love to marry you, baby but I'm already married."

I have often tried to picture my face at this moment. I do
remember several pieces of pasta sliding from my open
mouth and returning to the plate, possibly with some
saliva.

What were you doing when Kennedy was shot? Ever been asked that one? It palls alongside the Angel revelation. Every moment following that husky voice issuing forth those words, is imprinted on my memory. The details of the explanation. Dumbstruck horror as I realise that it is all ending and for a very good reason. Crash, as each pillar holding up this world of ours is removed and the roof tumbles inwards. We must go tonight. There will be no tomorrow. Angel has been seeking ways to tell us. All trace of our stay is to be removed. We, for our own well-being, are obliterated.

An experiment in free living. Not meant to go this far. Some day the world will find a place for spirits such as ours but for now Tony the missing husband, the truckdriver, (he has five interstate trucks), is due home tomorrow and sometimes he comes back a little early, to surprise his family.

Family?! Further questions. Oh Jesus, Bree is Angel's daughter. Mum is thirty. Bree is what?! Fourteen!!

I turn to face my erstwhile lover. She has already fled the table. Locked herself in her room. And I'm left talking to her 'mother'.

To reinforce the gravity of the situation we are shown Tony's clothing, chattels and appurtenances hidden away in cupboards. He takes quite large clothes. We even help bring some larger pieces down from the roof to restore them to their normal position about the house. It is raped before our eyes as this unknown usurper moves in without so much as an angry word or challenge.

These actions are carried out in dumb silence. Davey is a

robot. Only Angel gives an air of apology and acceptance.
After all she has the maturity.
We could have stayed a little longer. Akin to hovering in the
dentist's chambers after an appointment.

Summer is not over. Davey vanishes from my life
for a month. I spend more time with Kant, tackling
Schopenhauer as well. Beating my brain against these
hard headed Germans has a soothing effect. There are
some glimpses of understanding. One of the sub-editors
comments that a small piece I am allowed to do has merit
and gives me a by-line.
I forget to tell anybody then decide to wait until I do
something major.
There are days when I feel suicidal. Then there is the day
on the railway station when I look down to an area where
buses are loading with school children. Bumping, noisy
lines of kids. There she is, my Bree, starched and neat in
uniform, carrying a violin case, chattering to other girls.
She sits at a window. Still involved in conversation. She
looks as young as she is. Light years plus two separate us.
So I pick up my briefcase and board the train.

That night I ring Davey. "I'm coming by to get you in the
morning, man. Seth got the car going. Word is the surf's
reasonable."

On the way to the beach Davey looks coy.
"I drove past their place every day for a week, ya know.
No sign of anybody. Fucking great truck up the side of the

house. I guess some truck drivers can have it all and then some more. Shame."

At the beach the surf club speakers are chugging away. The place is packed. Davey walks down the steps onto the sand.
"I'm here darlin's. Which one of youse wants a piece of this eh?"
There are several suggestions from the neckless brigade however I note a few favourable looks over to our right.

FRANKLIN'S DAY

Here with the sea rolling in at the end of the headland
road, two people are leaning against the bonnet of a quite
expensive car. Their casual dress has quality, european
overtones. It is winter and the area is deserted. except
for a pair of board riders, in dark wetsuits, waiting on the
morning swell. These people and their car look out of
place.

"It could be yesterday." The man has his shoulders
hunched. Fat cream sweater. A striped scarf flipping its end
in the breeze.

The woman finds his hand. Their attention is fixed on a
white weatherboard house, that sits by itself.

She glances up at her companion then back to the house.

"We all have our past. But let's not knock on the door.
You know you'll be disappointed. We'll leave it as
yesterday, it will be intact and we'll drive away."

Looking sideways briefly the man is unsure.

"You know how often I've caught myself thinking about this
place. Some things just won't go away. Hell, I've cancelled
engagements. It's a long way to come just for a look."

He takes a deep breath, exhaling slowly.

"This road, it's still unsealed. No large block of flats, villas, shops. The only difference is the new shower block. When we came round that last bend and I looked ahead, I felt faint. Childhood in a bottle."

Holding the man tighter, as if he may be in danger of slipping away, the woman waits.

"This is your little catharsis. I'm relaxed about being here. I'd like to have more involvement but I can't. I just don't want to see you hurt. You didn't write. There's little chance that she's still there. If you leave it alone then it will all be as it was .... and .....". Her voice trails away.

Salty, slightly burnt by the sun. It is a good, tired feeling. Sitting, laying, in wooden deck chairs of orange, brown, white striped canvas. Long angular legs of youth. Bony awkward shoulders. Chests without form. A boy, a girl, both staring at the sea.

The grass is lightly laid about the yard in the sandy soil. At the end of the sparse garden a tangled hedge affords protection from the sea breezes. There is a break in the hedge allowing access to the beach. It is through this breach in the defences that the two prone figures fix their gaze.

"I'm buggered."

The girl squints, shading her eyes, looking at the boy.

"Your face is white."

"Uh." He rubs, It is sea-salt, caught in the fuzz on his cheeks.

The girl is digging her toe into the soil, aimlessly poking a hole. She has pretty feet, slim legs. Brown and smooth.

Like the boy her tiredness is drug-like and is enjoyable.
Their youth knows no other state of being but fit, with all
the active accoutrements of youth.
"Want to go again?"
"I'm too tired. Beat you to the water." She is up and
running, the first wave in sight.
He is chasing, male ego and cheating to be avenged.

The day is wasting away, slipping past Miss Carter's white
bay-windows like a handful of sand from that white beach
beyond the hedge. A jacaranda tree near the verandah has
begun to move gently in the mid-morning breeze.
Franklin looks at his hand. (The fine, hot beach sand
escapes no matter how tightly it is held.) He intakes a
deep breath to let it escape slowly through almost closed
lips. Lips that perspire. From his hand he extends an index
finger. He slides it inside his collar and tugs at the white
shirt and tie he has been forced to wear.
"I can't hear the Brahms, Franklin." Miss Carter's sing-song
voice floats down the wooden hall. Everything in Miss
Carter's house is wood, white and sparkling.
On the verandah the piano teacher's dog is perched on a
chair. One ear is stupidly cocked as if it is half listening to
something in the distance. This does not amuse Franklin.
The dog's panting has its tongue fully extended. So far
out that the tongue slips to the side of its mouth as if it is
about to fall out. Franklin manages a furtive smile.
It is a Silky Terrier named 'Himmel'. Miss Carter's form of
protest at the war her father endured in Europe. That was
many years ago. Now the dog and the joke are old.

Franklin jumps. A glass of lemonade has appeared beside
him. It is tightly grasped and in control of the stern lady
that stares down at her pupil. Ice tinkles, the glass is frosty.
He reaches for this mirage of comfort. It moves from his
range.

"When I hear the Brahms, Franklin, the Brahms. It won't
happen while you're imagining yourself out of my
windows."

"It's so hot Miss Carter." Franklin's narrow eyes view his
tormentor, silhouetted by her windows.

"Your parents pay for piano lessons Franklin and I have
just chipped a quantity of valuable ice from my ice chest to
aid your comfort. Now, let me hear the Brahms.

"Why don't you buy a fridge Miss Carter?"

"Because dear old Len Parrish has very few people left to
whom he can deliver ice. The Brahms, Franklin."

There is a period of silence while wills collide and
strategies are briefly contemplated, then the small fingers
begin to work their way across the keys, climbing over the
ivory desert, squeezing out the Lullaby, closing many gaps
the composer had placed in his music.

"You rushed it. Once more. I want to hear some feeling. It is
supposed to rock a babe to sleep, you know."

The boy, perched on the high piano stool sets his mouth
hard. Miss Carter waves the glass before his eyes and
points at the keys.

He closes his eyes. Tilts his head back. This time the notes
flow and blend in semblance of their original intent. They
are gentle, clean, without hesitation, filling the room with
melody then easing their way to a soft conclusion.

For a moment the music teacher is still. She notes her student stretching for the glass and places it in his hands. She places a hand on his tousled black hair as he drinks thirstily.

"You can be remarkably good at times, dear Franklin. What a pity your heart, soul and motivation come together so rarely." Quickly out of her reverie she takes the empty glass from the boy's hand.

"Now, having given me another glimpse of your true hidden depths, we shall press on with chords, scales and then your next piece." A finger is pressed against his pouting lips, about to issue forth another tirade at the injustice of the situation. She takes the finger away and opens the fat book of exercises on the pianos music stand. He protests anyway.

"My two best friends were sitting out there just five minutes ago."

"I saw them. They treat my yard like a private lounge."

"They went in for their second swim. Their SECOND. They're blessed with good fortune. I'm imprisoned. Where is the justice of it all."

Miss Carter is impressed by the eloquence but dares not indicate any weakening of her position. It is perhaps time to consolidate.

"You have your SECOND lesson this afternoon."

They swoop together into a green wall letting all its energy roll over them. It is easy. The surf roars about them but it is a known power, one that is used and contained. The boy is away picking up the next wave. He lets it lift him then tucking in below the crest, he shudders down its face with a yell of ecstasy.

Swimming back, grinning, he is about to brag when the girl in turn is lifted away and cuts past with a finned curve revelling in the propulsion she suddenly enjoys.

They have exulted and out-achieved each other for an hour. The girl swims back and takes up a position beside the boy. Treading water in that vital part of the wave system just where the swell starts its run into the beach. It is not something anybody told them or ever showed them. If you live in this world, on this coast, it comes along with eating, breathing, running and riding a bike. From this point each lift of a wave as it rolled under them gives a view of a near empty white beach. Occasional dots on the shoreline indicate another human presence but they are few.

"You want to go back?"

"Yeh."

Ashore, with nothing to pick up, they make their way across the cool wet sand, run the hot white dry stretch and then work up the face of the land over dune-grass to the house on the very edge of the low rise. The white weatherboard house with the ragged hedge. When they reach the deck chairs they are dry, perhaps a shade browner and the salt of the sea has left its streaks of white on their limbs.

They feed each other a dribble drink of warm odd-tasting water from the garden hose, then flop down and close their eyes.

The piano, this instrument of child labour, has been rung
with all its combinations of scales and taken every chord
to which the yet undeveloped pianist's small hands can
reach. Now he is finishing, with some delicacy, the ever
increasing repertoire that his years of tutoring have
installed.
This last torturous, traditional task must be carried with all
the precision he can muster. The teacher's ears await the
slightest hesitation so that they can force him to repeat the
piece to iron out any aberration that may have crept in.
The recital is proceeding with quality when a tug at his
concentration drags the player's mind from the keys. They
are back. His friends legs hang from each side of the chairs.
"Franklin."
His eyes are back and the mind is focussed but it is too
late.
"No, no, no. That passage is beautiful. You just committed
a horrible crime in its name. You were going so well. Now
let's work on that. It is rather difficult."
Miss Carter enters the room. Her charge has his face
buried in his hands.
"Franklin? Are you alright my dear?"
For the first time since he came to her at the age of six,
years before, she sees something new in this child in whom
she places so much hope.
"Ah you unwell?" Then she hears the noise. "Are you
crying? You are, you're crying. But why?"
Miss Carter knows the answer but it is not her role to
encourage dissent. She does however give into an urge she
has carried for a great time. She crouches beside the piano

stool. Tugging at the boy's shoulder, he is pulled round. She unfolds his arms and places them round her neck then pulls him to her. Rubbing his back, feeling his wet cheek, there is loss of control. The teacher has given ground, she has shown a degree of compassion. It will be hard to drive the child and his talent after this. Still she does not let him go but hugs him tighter.

When she does at length pull his head back, his eyes are pools. This boy with his pile of dark curly hair.
"All I want is for you to play, all you want is to play. It's all to do with interpretation. Go on, your friends are outside. Come back for this afternoon's lesson if you wish. I'll be here."
To her surprise he does not rush out the door. His exit is quiet. He packs his sheet music and workbooks, then places them on top of the piano. With dignity he loosens his tie, unbuttons the shirt collar and then pulls his shirt over his head. She realises that his swimming costume is under his shorts.

Salty, slightly burnt by the sun. It is a good, tired feeling. Sitting, laying, in wooden deckchairs of orange, brown, white striped canvas. Long, angular legs of youth. Bony awkward arms. Chests without form. A boy, a girl, both staring at the sea.
The grass is lightly laid about the yard in the sandy soil. At the end of the sparse garden a tangled hedge affords protection from the sea breezes. There is a break in the hedge allowing access to the beach. It is through this

breach in the defenses that the two prone figures fix their gaze.

Crouching down between them a third person, a boy, slightly smaller than the other two. He looks from one to the other.

"You still want to swim?"

The girl asks, "Have you finished?"

"Yes," he grins back.

"Your eyes are red."

"Can we swim now? Thanks for waiting. Miss Carter doesn't approve of her chairs being used."

"We just want to listen."

Franklin looks at the faces of his two friends, from one to the other. "Listen?"

"You're so clever." The girl's face is sincere. "It's so beautiful. When we're swimming we can hear it in the wind but it couldn't carry that far."

"Can you ask if we can still listen? We'll sit very still."

"Yeh," says the other boy.

"I have to do lessons. Practice all day, every day. You can just swim, lay on the beach."

"You're so lucky to be able to do something so perfectly."

"C'mon please. I really want a swim."

The three figures move through the hedge and down the slope to the water. In the glare of white sand the smaller boy is hopping pulling off his shorts. He drops them and sits to take off his shoes and socks while the others survey the water.

"Don't worry Franklin, the waves are better than this

morning."

They stride down to the water together. It rushes to meet them curling round their feet. A shock of cold on their warm skin.

"Are you going to be playing again this afternoon?" Franklin is running, splashing to dive into the first big wave.

"Yes," he calls back.

At the car the man has reached a decision.

"You're right. I'm too scared. It could all be ruined if I knock on that door. I've seen it, that's enough."

"You know, Frankie," says the woman, "when I rang Albert to tell him you wanted to cancel Zurich and Berlin, he said he'd sit on them until the last minute. After all, two giant symphony orchestras awaiting your presence."

"Let me guess. We haven't reached the last minute yet." The woman smiles as they climb in.

At the house the owner is watching quietly through her curtains. As the car in the distance drives away she frowns briefly then turns her head to look through the glass panelled doors at the two rotting old orange, brown and white striped deckchairs.

ME AND ANGELINE

The night had been, in fact still was, cold and black.
What right does the father of a twelve year old, have
to announce, that he has earn't, at weekends, the right
to sleep till daybreak? While his son, still callow and
vulnerable, goes out, alone, into the darkness, to take care
of farm chores. What right?

Once free of the house, Curtis warms as it were, to the
allotted tasks.
Boss the fifteen cattle in the second paddock to the front
holding paddock. Can't see them too well but a count
shows fifteen have gone through the gate. No doubt using
their 'grass is greener over the fence' mentality to urge
themselves on.
Back to the sheds. Muck out the stables. Put 'Thresher' in
the round yard. Check the hens. Three lousy eggs.
And in passing untangle 'Gilbert' from his tether. Some
lawn mower. Big mistake, Dad.
Fill the wood box. DO 'NOT' LIGHT THE FIRE!
The boy squints under the single globe at the back door.
His father's neat script on the note makes a clarification.
'The day will be warm.'

'My father is never wrong.' Curtis considers this later as sunlight across the valley has already turned the moist air to cotton-wool mist. Lumps hang in trees and glow as the day heats rapidly.

He angles down a steep path overhung by grandfatherly white gums. Huge complicated trees, firmly set in their ways. Through the fence and along beside the river.

He drops his flannelette shirt and pulls off his boots and socks. He has already left his jacket back up the path hanging on the fence. And here in just his jeans in the deep glassy, black-green pool of the water he lowers himself in with half breaths and small exclamations letting the cold water creep up his chest. Emersed at last with head wet and hair pushed back it is a time of peace. To float and envy the sky reflected in his world, hearing nothing through water filled ears.

A few bright coloured birds flit about overhead in their anxious way. Unsure whether to squawk, preen, feed or flee.

Little arcs move out each time Curtis moves. For a time he lays back and thinks of nothing in particular. It is an odd world without sound. The water is a giant mirror. So still and all encompassing. It is a copy of the world around. Then there is a flicker of movement in the image.

She is there, on the bank.

He had hoped it would be so and it has happened.

Lifting his head the water drains from one ear in time to hear, "........... my little Adonis, floating in your kingdom." Angeline! Oh, she is beautiful. The long lacy white dress.

Delicate clever hands. A mass of straw coloured hair that
frames her dark eyes.
The artistic daughter of a gifted family. Spontaneous,
rapturous, given to bursts of enthusiasm about virtually
anything.
A visit to their house is to experience wonder. As if a portal
existed to another world, where perfection was the norm
and intellect the bread and butter of daily life.

For months now the boy has, like some miraculous
sponge with unquenchable powers, soaked up the
atmosphere of their new neighbours. And the diamond
in this box of jewels, laying over the paddocks in the
white weatherboard house, is Angeline. She has told him
he is her hero, her knight, the core of her being and soul
partner. She has spoken often of destiny. He has listened
to poetry delivered with passion while the mother played
Chopin in the next room. He has been sketched many
times, had scones with jam and cream on the patio.
Had his mouth wiped with fresh linen napkins. Had his hair
tousled and his forehead kissed.

Today she has him in the pose of a figure of Greek
Mythology, his jeans dripping about his knees. How quickly
her delicate fingers work the charcoal on the pad.
She moves her eyes, those deep green eyes. Her long hair
glints. Her eyelids flick.
"Chin up, Adonis," she says and he returns to the pose.

When it is finished he is allowed closer. He leans over

her shoulder from behind in admiration at himself on the cartridge paper. He knows the moment is right. This is the time and the place. He knows because he has run this very scene so many times in his mind. It has flitted in and out of his imaginings as he has done his chores, idled on the back steps, even staring vacantly out the window of the school bus.

His hand hovers over the sketch. She takes his wet hand and briefly kisses it.

"Cold like a magic fish," she says, in that accent.

Now. It is time. Moving closer he brings his face down to hers and in an embrace, he leans round and places his wet mouth on hers. He kisses her passionately on the lips, to seal their unspoken love.

On the way back along the track, under those old gum trees, crumpled like the charcoal drawing in his hand, he feels the bitter scar of rejection form on his retreating back and unseen by all, a steady watering of the soil with tears takes place.

On and away from Angeline. Through the wire fence caught with tufts of roo and into the bottom paddock. Then the long haul up the hill towards the house in the distance. The day is still and the track feels even steeper. Curtis finds it hard to swallow.

Silhouetted on the horizon is a tractor. It makes its way down to the boy.

"Want a lift?" his father enquires.

The boy climbs silently onto the back behind the seat.

Increasing the power slightly to climb the slope the man says, "Y'know you really shouldn't go bothering the neighbours too much, son. They're nice people I agree. How old is that Angeline girl, she must be twenty two or three?" He pauses. "Yeh, better get some of your school mates round a bit more, eh. Do what boys do."

Curtis views the back of his father's brown neck. He is bouncing slightly as they bump over the ruts in the field. Standing perched high, holding the metal rim of driver's seat he stares up into the empty blue sky, swallows at last and considers the continuing phenomenon of his father always being right.
But then there is the matter of Gilbert the lawnmowing goat.

BARGANS

Those from elsewhere call it Dals-hart but local people
know it is pronounced Dal-shart.

Created as a suburb in the 1920s, Dalshart had always been
a bastion of the white man's ideals. Good professional folk.
Upper middle-class. Erudite, polite and well-mannered.
Lawns, tree-lined streets, tennis courts, patios and pools.
The main street had a lot of shops selling most of the
goods and services that such people desired and needed.
A quite extensive layout in quality and quantity.
For 'special' items the people of Dalshart traveled
elsewhere.Days, seasons and years passed. Children were
born and grew in their comfortable cocoon of suburban
bliss. They left and moved into the world. Many returned,
refreshed by their experiences but still more than happy to
continue their existence in the clutches of Dalshart.
Let us not assume that Dalshart was unique or in any
way isolated in its quiet progress through life. The people
were as well informed as most. They were very much in
touch with world events and the various winds of time and
change. The storms that came and went in international
affairs were interesting and worthy of discussion and
comment but they all seemed quite remote.

Over a dinner at home or at a barbecue or one of the local restaurants, over a good beer in the local pub garden or a refreshment at some sports event the world regularly formed part of the range of topics that found their way into the mouths of the people of Dalshart.

At times, the local high school had exchange students from foreign countries. There had, in the past years, been some delightful children from Sweden, a group of young French children who spoke excellent English and a lot of teenage boys from California who had tried to enthuse the local Rugby team about American football.

It seemed Dalshart was destined to just keep reinventing itself each year with different colour schemes, new whitegoods, a little sprinkling of the latest technology and a whole lot of goodwill to all.

In the early Spring about a decade ago, Archie Nettles mentioned at the Chamber of Commerce monthly meeting that a decision had been taken and it was time for he and good wife Laura to 'hang up their aprons'. The phrase was a metaphor of course for retirement. Archie and his wife ran the 'Columbine Tavern' near the post office. This was not an earth shaking event. People in Dalshart had retired before. Though the news was rather unwelcome for all those people who had over the last thirty years enjoyed Archie's excellent steaks, casseroles, chicken dishes and fine soups. And also Laura's tempting pastries and rich cakes. Many a waistline in Dalshart was in need of a trim because of the Columbine Tavern.

So, the first question after the initial joking and

congratulations and commiserations was the not too subtle one of self-interest.

"Are you selling the business, Archie?"

"Yes, I've found a buyer."

"Oh good, then it will stay a restaurant."

"Yes, that is the intent. The man's name is William. He says he can use most of the equipment and kitchen setup."

"Well of course he can Archie. One thing's for sure, you kept a very modern and well equipped kitchen. Anybody would be delighted to work in your establishment."

"William," the people said. "A good sturdy name. Sounds European trained. Might be even better than before."

About one month later the Columbine Tavern had a grand farewell dinner. The place was packed. At the end of the night Archie gave a brief speech in which he thanked all the people of Dalshart, told them they were lovely people and that there would be no charge for the whole dinner and beverages for the night. Both he and Laura would be away early the next morning in their new motor home.

How quickly it all seemed to happen. The next morning the Columbine Tavern was closed and its windows covered with newspaper. Thirty years of memories and wholesome food were in the past. A day later a group of workmen were busy inside the building. Little of their effort was available to the casual or even persistent observer. Everybody would just have to wait and watch. For two weeks they carried on their activities. Then a truck arrived with boxes and crates which all moved swiftly inside. Anticipation grew that soon the new shinier Columbine Tavern would be open for business under the guidance of masterful European chef 'William.'

The next day another truck arrived. It had a small crane mechanism on the tray at the back. Electrical wiring was poked out through the upper part of the building's facade. Holes were drilled in the masonry. A large box sign covered in protective wrapping was hoisted from the back of the truck and fixed in position.

"Wow", said some, "the Columbine Tavern name in neon. Archie would be impressed at that."

A workman peeled back a layer of wrapping from the right hand side of the sign. A long red curled object appeared. Those watching screwed up their eyes and tilted their heads.

The workman moved along the temporary scaffold to the other end of the sign and cut away the remaining cords so that the covering now fell to the ground.

At the same time a workman below tested the switch inside and the whole bright, magnificently gaudy object leapt into life.

The red section at the end, it turned out, was a mythical beast, rearing up and breathing fire. 'The Lucky Dragon', the sign said.

In smaller letters underneath, 'William Tong - Proprietor.'

It took some weeks before a customer arrived on the doorstep of the Lucky Dragon. William Tong opened his doors only two days after his new establishment was revealed. He opened for lunch from 12 till 2pm and then again for evening meals from 5.30pm right through until 10pm. He had fresh produce delivered every two days.

He lit his lights and even some scented candles at the tables near the windows.

His wife Janet Tong watched her husband as he paced and smiled confidently and the nights slipped by.

It was not that the people of Dalshart were not interested in the new cafe or that they were not interested in the taste of Chinese cuisine, it was more a jointly felt need for a period of mourning. The Columbine Tavern had a place in their collective psyche as a safe haven for both food and gossip. A protected corner where business could be discussed, plans made and problems resolved. Now it had gone. The leather nooks were now an open plan and the quiet, conservative timberwork was painted in bright reds. It was as if a small part of Kowloon had transplanted itself in their midst.

On the Thursday night of the third week with misty rain falling, Max Casey arrived home from the city to find his wife was away suddenly. Her mother was unwell. She and the children would be gone for a week.

He read his wife's note one more time then put on his hat and coat and headed out his front door.

Max walked into the Lucky Dragon and William Tong's first reaction was to ask, "Are you lost, sir?"

"No," he said, "I'm hungry."

There was a pause. A silence while the proprietor considered the answer.

"Well," said William at last, flapping a napkin and guiding the man to a seat. "You've come to the right place, sir." He placed a giant red covered four page laminated menu into the man's hands and started by pointing out the specialty of the house.

The next night was clear and pleasant. A good night to be out.
With Max Casey an immediate committed regular and placed conspicuously in a front window seat the ice was broken. Thirty two people dined that night. Like a broken dam wall the Lucky Dragon sprang to life. Janet Tong took over all duties in the front while William handled multiple woks in the kitchen.
And thus the Lucky Dragon became a part of Dalshart.

Of course being accepted by a community has its complications. William became a minor celebrity. His food was very good and faintly exotic for the people of Dalshart. His name was quickly given that all too familiar workover by well-meaning fans. He was now called Bill rather than his preferred William. As there were other Williams and Bills in Dalshart, it had to be differentiated. This was accomplished by calling William Tong, Billtong. Then the laziness of the human tongue set in and the Billtong morphed into Billong, Bilong and finally Blong. William smiled graciously as people called him Blong, slapped him on the shoulder and shook his hand at various times but he secretly wished it was not so. One night as he sat with his last customers for the night before closing he confessed that the name Blong disappointed him.

"It doesn't even mean anything," he commented. Fortunately that night his last customer was Rennie Simpson, a member of the media and PR industry.

"Doesn't mean anything." he exclaimed. "Mate, I thought you knew. That name is a tribute to you mate. As a newcomer the people of Dalshart decided to call you Blong for a reason. It means …… it means 'belong'. You know, you belong, you belong here. You're one of us mate. That's why you're called Blong."

Rennie was quite proud of his effort in diplomacy and inventiveness. He told everybody how he had avoided a 'difficult situation.'

William bought the idea. He was very happy and felt proud of his acceptance in his new country. So Blong became a part of the locality. As fixed as the war memorial or railway station.

Time, in it's annoying continuity, gave normality to the whole Lucky Dragon scene. Such was the enjoyment of the rich Asian dishes at the establishment that when Blong moved two sets of his relatives to the area, to take on the burden of the kitchen work, there was not a flicker of concern or the raising of an eyebrow.

One Friday night in early Spring while the Lucky Dragon was packed with the good folk of Dalshart in what had become a lazy tradition for the end of the week, Blong suddenly appeared above the mass of diners. Slowly the rumble of happy conversation and the click of chopsticks and forks for the less adventurous, all came to a halt. Blong stood on a chair, his arms raised. His face wore a huge smile.

Blong smiled a lot. The locals did not understand the Asian habit of perpetually smiling so they assumed that Blong was just an extremely happy fellow. In the most part they were right, however tonight the smile was a beam that could guide a ship at sea.

"I have an announcement," he began, moving his head and arms so as to encompass all the customers.

Some thought, "Oh no, he's closing down." But they were wrong.

" I'm going to be a Daddy." And as a seemingly necessary addition to the news he added, "My lovely wife Janet is going to have a baby."

Slowly and then with increased momentum a round of applause made it's way through the room.

Blong held up his hands once more.

"To celebrate this momentous event, all meals tonight are free."

The Lucky Dragon erupted in cheering and whistling. Blong was carried round the room. His back was slapped, his hand was shaken and eventually somebody found Janet Tong and dragged her out to the centre of the celebrations, to point out that her efforts were in no small part the reason for all the noise.

And so, some eight months after the announcement, a boy, who would be called Warren arrived and became the third member of the immediate Tong household.

Even the rivals at Johnny's Pizza and Cafe Parisienne sent their warm congratulations.

The boy was named Warren to fit in with the notion that a western forename helped with assimilation and acceptance. It took the local aficionados of wit a mere couple of weeks to decide that Warren Tong could be mangled and shortened to 'Wonton'.

Smiling and secretly horrified Blong accepted the inevitable and carried on with his business and the upbringing of his first child. It was a boy after all. And he was a proud father.

Wonton was constantly in the Lucky Dragon. There was little choice. When he cried the diners would lend a hand and take turns at cooing the child back to happiness or sleep.

Janet Tong decided that this arrangement was not ideal. One Saturday night at the Lucky Dragon the diners noticed that two elderly Chinese folk were seated in the corner, holding and doting on baby Warren.

"My parents," Janet explained. "They have come to live with us. They speak no English but they love children. They will stay at home and mind Warren."

All plans are only plans after all. Janet was right about her parents. They did indeed adore children. However she was quite wrong regarding their acceptance of being stay at home babysitters. Fascinated by the old couple, the children of several diners approached the couple for a closer look. They were beckoned forward. They were then captured, by arms and smiles and knees to sit on.

At the evenings end, the children knew a number of words in Mandarin or Cantonese or something and could sing with confidence at least two old favorite Chinese nursery rhymes.

Janet and Blong looked on with weak smiles of resignation. Somebody thought they heard Blong say, "Why you bring them in here at all. You know the danger of letting them near children."

Thus the Lucky Dragon child minding service began it's unofficial life. It added another layer of enjoyment for diners who could now unload their children and enjoy a peaceful meal, free from guilt. Listening to a few Chinese ditties on the way home was more than acceptable, in fact most parents found it quite fun.

It did briefly occur to Max Casey that the songs could be about bordellos and bad behavior rather than bunnies and butterflies but he dismissed such thoughts as preposterous.

At the age of three Wonton was pressed into service. Dressed in a tiny pair of patent black shoes, black trousers white shirt and an apron he began carrying dishes to tables on a purpose built tray.

Blong investigated the noise and was about to call a halt to the whole charade, (The obvious work of his parents-in-law) when he took into account the delighted reaction of his customers and was forced to accede to this addition to his staff.

A compromise was reached and Wonton only appeared as

a tiny waiter on weekends.

The next major event in the boy's life occurred at five years of age when Wonton began his schooling. By now he had twin three-year-old sisters and another brother on the way.

The kids at Dalshart Primary all knew Wonton. They liked him. He was that kid at the Lucky Dragon. The one with those lovely grandparents. Most of his classmates had been handled and led astray by the old couple. His entry into the education system was painless.

The kids did not however like his name. No, not Warren. That was of no consequence. Wonton, it did not please them. They pondered the problem long and hard while Wonton became a bystander to his fate.

They asked the teacher if a Warren had a meaning.

"Well, of course," replied the lady, delighted with the children's curiosity, "It's a place where rabbits live. A series of burrows."

There was more information in the teacher's reply but the seed had been sown. Wheels were in motion. Older, wiser children added their input.

By the end of the day, Wonton was no more. The boy Warren was now to be known as 'Burra.'

Warren proudly told his parents of the events that led to his name change. They looked at him. His father gave a strange strangled sound. His mother briefly closed her eyes and lowered her head.

Then they both said, "That's nice dear." And so it was official.

Burra was a bright lad. By the time he was seven he was top of his class in all subjects. A gifted and talented pupil. Despite his academic achievements he was still liked by the other kids, perhaps because his knowledge was not flamboyant or nerdie. He just knew things.

The great hole in the life of Burra was in the area of sport. On weekends the children of Dalshart all hurried off or were driven off to a veritable cocktail of sporting events. Some managed to play football in the morning, tennis in the afternoon and perhaps baseball or cricket on Sundays. Both male and female. Dalshart people did love their sport. But for Burra, the boy from the Lucky Dragon, the cornucopia of sporing choices was unavailable. He was in the family business and that meant being available for duty at all times.

At best he was allowed to run and play in the park in unofficial made-up games or quickly organised off-shoots of the real thing but there was not the time for full commitment to a sport.

Of course this denial of a sporting outlet meant that Burra craved the very thing he was denied. And Blong and Janet were aware of their eldest son's longings and felt suitably guilty. But Asian people have a great work ethic and a great sense of family so the dream of sporting excellence by their boy would have to remain unfulfilled.

Besides there were two sisters and a little brother in the busy household now. Oldest boy's were expected to be unselfish and lead by example.

At eight years of age a great calamity took place in the

life of Burra. Gathered in the loungeroom of their now
quite substantial house the father, the head of their
clan, announced to the whole family that he was about
to embark on a new enterprise. The restaurant business
had been very good to them but with their good cousins
running everything so well he felt it was an ideal time to
branch out.

While the others sat in awe of the words of Blong, their
son Burra had mixed feelings, wondering how this new
direction might further complicate his life.

The announcement it seemed concerned the new
phenomenon of the cheap shop. An emporium that sold
low-priced goodies and gadgets and a thousand and one
other things that people needed or thought they needed or
discovered they needed for their everyday existence.

The site had been chosen. Conveniently only two doors
from the Lucky Dragon. The new wonder shop would be
known as 'Blong's Bargains'.

Who would man the counters in this new shop? Why we
would of course. The family. A roster would be produced
with each person's alloted time behind the counter, inked
in for reference. It seemed that Burra was about to be
sentenced to a lifetime of family business servitude.
Gloomily he watched as the rest of the family greeted the
news with excitement and enthusiasm. Surely they could
see they were being manipulated? Led into a cunning trap?
Well, apparently they couldn't.

It took an amazingly short amount of time for the new
store to become a reality. A fact duly noted by Burra, who

realised that his father had been planning and organising the whole operation for some time. Boxes began arriving, then more boxes. Soon the Blong household was awash with boxes. They seemed to have all originated in China. Marked in varying levels of legible English. Tableware, tumblers, tennis balls, makeup mirrors, maps, message boards, spoons, scent, saucepans, plates, pliers, paints, brushes, bon bons and bamboo back-scratchers. The quantity and variety seemed endless.

It was revealed that cousin Jiong who knew somebody who worked in a similar store in the city had 'acquired' a copy of their stock list. Father had simply contacted the warehouse in Shanghai and ordered the lot.

The shop was painted and vast racks of shelving arrived to be laid out in long aisles, each running from the front to the back of the store. A single counter and cash register was positioned near the door. All you had to do, according to Blong, was sit at the counter and collect the money. Restocking and tidying would be done by the night-shift. Yes. He said 'night-shift.'

Cousin Jiong knew a signwriter who would do the front of the premises at night for a special price.

So while all the family toiled at night sorting boxes, unpacking, loading shelves and adding prices to everything, a little old man teetered outside on a very high ladder, humming to himself as he painted a giant name across the shop's facade.

After two weeks and very little sleep for everybody the shelves were all dripping with irresistible merchandise. Blong had another relative print up some bright pamphlets

to be distributed to every letterbox in Dalshart and
surrounding areas.
Burra was greatly relieved to find that this task was to be
undertaken by a professional distributor. He had been
found a few times in the last week asleep at his school
desk.
"Blongs Bargains' the pamphlet read. It gave an exciting
story about the volume, quality, variety and low pricing
of goods on offer. The first one hundred shoppers would
receive a bonus bag of amazing items to take with them as
a joyful gift to celebrate the store's opening.
(The contents of the bonus bags had come about as a way
of clearing out the large array of left over items following
the shelf stacking. Nobody in Blong's extended family
could work out what most of the items were or what they
did. It was assumed the happy customers would have
better luck.)

All too soon it was the Saturday of the grand opening.
The pamphlet drop had certainly worked. A large crowd
had gathered, eager to grab a bargain and a free bonus bag.
Blong stood on a step ladder and welcomed everybody.
He hoped they would enjoy shopping in Blong's Bargains.
With more than a little showmanship he pulled a cord to
drop the large shiny cloth covering the front of the store.
As it fell to the ground he announced the store open for
business.
The crowd looked up. There was a strange pause, a silence,
a little muttering but then the lust for bargains and free
bonuses overtook them all and they poured forth and into

the store. Trade was brisk. Although most people bought
one item then came to the counter to pay thus ensuring
their bonus bag.

After the bonus bags ran out the store remained
comfortably well attended with people searching along
the aisles, discovering trinkets and treasures they simply
could not do without.

Round about 1pm an elderly lady waiting for her change,
held out the letter box pamphlet and said to Blong, "So,
which is it?" She pointed at the front of the pamphlet.
"Haven't you decided?" she added.

Blong looked puzzled. "Decided on what?" he asked as he
handed her the change.

"The name," she replied. "I guess the other one will grow
on me," she added as she left the store.

Blong looked at Burra. The boy shrugged his shoulders.
Blong began to carry on with business as usual but the
old lady's words could have actually meant something.
She had pointed to the pamphlet. He looked at the piece
of paper then peered about, like a detective on the scent
of a breakthrough. His manner became almost serpentine.
He walked through his front door onto the pavement and
hands on hips, lifted his head to stare up at the second
storey heights of the front of the building.

He stood looking for some time then lowered his head and
walked back inside.

As he passed his son at the counter he muttered, "Bloody
cheap signwriter." He continued out the back and stayed
there in a black mood. Burra had never heard his father
swear.

The boy took a lull in between sales to run outside.

"Oh", he said to himself when he looked up.

There for all to see. 'BLONG'S BARGANS' it said in crimson and black letters. Huge letters that could not be missed.

Back at the counter Burra considered the consequences. He knew this would involve more drama in the household. It would not be good. More stress.

As luck would have it, the next man through the door was the well known local marketing identity Rennie Simpson. Although not yet nine years old Burra could spot an angel of mercy when he saw one.

It took twenty minutes but when Rennie emerged from the rear of the store he gave a surreptitious thumbs up to Burra.

A little while later Blong returned to the counter and busied himself once more with the activities. After a few minutes he casually announced that he had considered the spelling of the name on the storefront and decided he liked it. It had style. It was unique. It had chutzpah. It had that x-factor so often lacking in modern marketing. A fortuitous event that would give them the edge in the cut and thrust of bargain store supremacy. They would henceforth be known as 'Blong's Bargans.'

So began the Blong's Bargans phase of the life of Burra. In the day he would work hard at school, at night he would eat, study and then either pack shelves or serve tables. His ninth year was approaching. Winter was approaching. In the cool sunshine of autumn Burra sat with two of his closest associates during the school lunch break. Tums, a blonde-haired kid whose real name was Armond and whose parents were Belgian and Lop whose real name was Arnold and whose parents dated the family back to convict times.

Both these friends played for the Dalshart Tigers. A well established and quite successful local Soccer Club.

Both had been working on Burra since he was five, to join them in their team. It would soon be time for the Under-Nines Comp to begin signings for the year.

"Look at you," said Tums. "Your father owns a restaurant, yet you are slim and super fit. That shows willpower and discipline. You are made for sport."

(Tums had a future in PR.)

"Actually, that's because I never stop working and I forget to eat," explained Burra.

But this rather tragic information would not deter the two Dalshart Tigers.

"We gotta come up with a scheme," interjected Lop, the more grounded and practical of the trio.

"Something that will get you off the hook for good. It has to be terribly clever and your Dad can't know he's been tricked."

"Well, there's a problem," said Burra, "My Dad got where he is by being foxy smart. He can spot a scam over the horizon. Chinese people spend most their time trying to con each other."

Lop clumped his hand on Burra's shoulder. "Like I said mate. Terribly clever."

Two days later they had a plan. After looking at it from all

angles they decided it had more holes than a fly screen.
Similar conclusions were made for Plans B, C, D, E and F.
It was becoming depressingly obvious that any attempt
to outwit leading citizen Blong was probably beyond their
undeveloped nine-year-old brains.They parted that day in
an advanced state of incommodious glum.
There seemed no way out of the situation.
In the night Burra slept uneasily, dreaming intermittently of
sporting glory, beef with black bean sauce and Great Uncle
Bo. It took some minutes for his body and unconscious
state to snap out of it's slumber and for Burra to sit up,
take a number of deep breaths and then sit on the side of
his bed as he pondered the amazing content of his dream.

At the lunch break Burra said nothing to his mates.
He purposely led them away every time their talk turned
toward any form of physical effort. Things were already
in motion and Burra, being a smart lad, was in shutdown
mode. 'Trust no one,' he thought.

It went something like this -
As a small child, back in the old country, Blong had been
a favored child. While his parents toiled he was cared for
by a truly wonderful man called Uncle Bo. As a relative
twice removed Uncle Bo was the only one to step up when
needed to spend weeks and months looking out for the
tiny child and allowing his parents to navigate their way
through the troubles that beset the country.
Uncle Bo told stories that would delight the gods. He
made meals that never failed to please and leave young

Blong wanting more. He showered the boy with love, ideals, passions and wisdom. Not a moment of the day was wasted. Not a moment was spared.

"Time" said Uncle Bo, "is so very precious. We never know how much we have until it is gone."

There came a night when Blong was woken from his sleep and while still trying to comprehend the matter, he was bundled into a van wrapped in a blanket. He fell asleep on the long journey. When he awoke he asked his parents where they were. They said it did not matter. He asked them when Uncle Bo would be arriving and they averted their eyes.

Then there was the boat, the late night moves, another boat. Somewhere along this journey Blong's parents disappeared. Others on the journey took Blong.

Many years later he was here in Dalshart.

As a teenager he had learnt of the death of his parents on the journey. He had to admit he hardly knew them. It was not the same with Uncle Bo. Blong had a hole in his heart. He pined, he ached he wanted to see Uncle Bo once more. His efforts were fruitless. A wall of bureaucracy stood between any inquiry and any result. It was impenetrable.

Burra's plan went something like this -

Have grandparents who are sympathetic to the boy's issues, (they wre from his mother's side of the family), find an aged Chinese actor. Coach him and give him lines to learn. Fill him with every fact and nuance known about Uncle Bo. Advise him on mannerisms, verbal tricks and family history. Give him a story about his potential arrival and then have him wait.

In the meantime Burra will casually drop the name of Uncle Bo into conversations with his father. After several bouts of reminiscence Burra suggests that he may know a way to find Uncle Bo. There is a new secret program for finding relatives that can be accessed but only after working out their secret coding. This will require a great deal of mathematical calculating and trial and error. If he can crack the code he will be able to apply.

"I tell you what Father," says Burra as they stand at the counter of Blong's Bargans, "If I can do this for you, will you let me take up and play the game of soccer."

Now normally Blong would be highly suspicious of any such vague and rather dubious proposal but his longing to make contact with Uncle Bo once more overcomes his mind and blinds him to the oddness of the whole operation.

He agrees. Perhaps he doubts his son or doubts the whole strange mechanism but what has he to lose?

Now as he sits at the front counter of Blong's Bargans the boy watches his mates go past heading to their first trial games with the Dalshart Tigers, he fills a school exercise book with strange pages of calculations, codes and symbols. When his father appears he continues to calculate and consult reference books.

Occasionally Blong will enquire as to the progress of the work.

Burra replies always that he is making some progress.

After several weeks Burra is ready to fit the final part of his plan into operation.

At the family dinner on a Saturday night, just before Blong is heading off to check on the Lucky Dragon, Burra announces that he has a surprise.

As the grandparents look on with benign smiles of approval Burra says, "Father, I cracked the code for the Sino-Reunion Society. I entered a search through their organisation last week. If you will dial this number, I believe they have Uncle Bo on the line."

Blong stood quite ashen faced, his eyes wide. He silently took the piece of proffered paper. He stared at the number while in silence, his family looked on.

"This is a local number," he said at last.

"Of course," said Burra. "You ring the society and they connect you. Just say that password when they answer. That's vitally important."

With a trembling hand Blong dialed the number. His son watched and considered the possibility that he had gone too far.

Blong said the password. He waited. Then he said hullo to someone.

Fifteen minutes later, he carefully and deliberately placed the phone down. He stood for a short while with his head bowed.

When he looked up he had tears in his eyes.

"It is so sad. He has forgotten things and has other events confused. He must be very old now. It is forgivable. But he remembered me and the time we had together. It was a great joy to him as well."

Blong turned to his son. "I'm not sure how you did this

thing but you have made me so very, very happy."
Blong hugged his son who felt so very, very guilty.

The next day in the store with Sunday trading fairly
light, Blong approached his son at the counter. He had a
package.
"I am a man of my word," he said.
The package contained boots, socks, shorts, shinpads and
the shirt of the Dalshart Tigers.
"How did you do this so quickly, Father?"
"It was your grandparents. They knew all about the club
and the manager and where to sign up and your boot size.
They amaze me with their knowledge sometimes. Now go,
your friends are waiting for you outside."
And sure enough they were.

Blong had several more conversations with Uncle Bo. None
of them all that satisfactory due to his memory problems.
He agreed to send some money via the secret Sino-Reunion
Society post-office box. After that Uncle Bo became hard to
contact.
Despite his athletic build Burra was to prove a fairly
ordinary soccer player. His skills lay elsewhere. The team
did okay, everybody liked Burra and life was pretty good.
He was a welded-on member of the Dalshart Tigers.

Three years later, Burra was at the front counter of Blong's
Bargans giving some of his time before his afternoon game
when a fairly bright, well-dressed, very senior Chinese man
entered the shop.

"Hullo young man," he said to Burra, with a real twinkle in his eye and a smile to match. "I'm looking for a person called William Tong. Do you know him?"

"I certainly do, sir," said Burra smiling back, "He's my father."

"Oh, how lovely," replied the man. He took Burra's hand and shook it vigorously. "I am most very pleased to make your acquaintance." He smiled infectiously with one gold tooth showing. "Is your father here?"

"Yes, he's out the back. I'll get him for you. Who can I say is calling?"

The man stepped back and spread his arms, smiling even more broadly than before.

"Why you tell him, it's a man who's just arrived from China and has been searching for him all these years. Tell him it's his Uncle Bo."

BLIND DATE

Even in daylight ..... at No.75, the children quickened
their pace. Looking, not sideways, they ran past the next
house. Stupid Francis Millett always screamed, in that
piercing, penetrating way that children have.
The run was considered okay but the scream was bad
form.
It could be heard. It exposed their behaviour.
Finally Mrs Kempt, a large woman with very broad
shoulders and a way of cutting across niceties of life to
grab the throat of the problem, went up and knocked on
the door of No.77.

"It's that the children are scared", she explained. "Bearing
in mind their immaturity and inventive minds ...... could
he be so kind as to leave one light at least burning at night
and switch one on when he rose in the early morning.
A house in total darkness all the time, well it wasn't
normal."

The man agreed readily. She thought he tried to smile.
Could she be so kind as to tell him if the lights in fact
worked? He, after all, had no way of knowing. He indicated

vaguely to his face.

Reluctantly she followed him from room to room.

Two were out. He located the globes, dusty in the back of a laundry cupboard and changed them easily, standing on a chair.

She thanked the man with a handshake which required taking his hand. He seemed startled then pleased.

The porch light, she noted, was now on even though it was mid-afternoon.

She caught Francis in mid-stream at the gate.

"Look you stupid child, he's a nice man and he's left the light on for you."

"I'll tell my mother you called me stupid."

"It's okay dear, she already knows. Now continue home quietly please."

For a time the new arrangements appeared to allay the fears of local children and a degree of peace reigned over their undeveloped, over-inventive minds and the street upon which they passed.

Spring came upon the town somewhat early and caught the flowers, the bushes, the trees and the people who dwelt amongst them out of step.

At mid term a series of subtle events, (Francis visiting an Aunt in the city, Spikey sick in bed, Brian Goodge held back on detention,) brought Geoffrey Marks to the edge of that house, alone on a perfect, still day.

It was the first time he had ever walked home without companions. Although ten, Geoffrey was slightly small for his years. A quiet boy who happily listened rather than project himself into the front part of proceedings, he now found himself locked in terror as he noted a man right at the edge of the front fenceline of that house.

The figure was kneeling. At first Geoffrey assumed he lay in wait, no doubt in preparation for a pounce on some poor passerby. Then he noted that the figure was in fact digging in the garden with a trowel and further more he had pots of flowers next to him ready for planting.

At this moment as Geoffrey hovered in a mix of plans, thoughts, worries and nerves the man looked up.

"Hullo," he said. "Are you lost or just walking home at a nice slow pace?"

Relief flooded through Geoffrey's frame, from his rubber-soled shoes to his hefty backpack. This was not the crazed blind person, it was a gardener. He was staring straight at him.

"Just who I need," the man continued, "I'm in a bit of a hurry. Can you shake these blokes out of their pots while I stick 'em in the ground?"

Now Geoffrey moved forward. He liked working with men. Perhaps it was to soak up some of their maleness and take in a little of their companionship, in place of a long vanished father. He squatted beside the man, full of interest completely forgetting that he was inside the yard of the ogre he had only moments before been trying to avoid.

"These are nice. Mum has these at our place. Which one first?"

"Oh heck, I don't know," the man replied, poking out

another hole with the trowel. "You choose, I'm no gardener." He turned to Geoffrey and held out his hand. "I'm Tex. Silly name isn't it. My parents were big country music fans."

Politely, Geoffrey held out his hand while his thought processes applied themselves to the information concerning the 'no gardener' aspect of his companion. With the man firmly gripping his hand he met the stranger's eyes for the first time. They seemed normal but they went through him to a focal point somewhere behind his head. Frozen in terror he thought, 'I'm frozen in terror.' 'That's why I can't run.'

Tex held Geoffrey's hand and with his left hand he reached out.

"Do you mind?" he said, "If I check you out? I can tell by your hand you're a little fella but I'd like to know some more."

He ran his fingers softly across the boy's forearm and to his face. Like an annoying moth, his fingers fluttered about then he let go. Mere moments but Geoffrey flopped back on the grass.

"Well," said Tex, "I know all about you except your name." A key turned. This man had unlocked the one abiding passion that ran Geoffrey's life. He was a ten-year-old knot of curiosity.

Instead of fleeing he asked, quietly, "What do you know? We just met."

"You have blond hair, spend a lot of time outdoors, normally don't wear shoes and can run very fast." There followed a tiny silent period.

"How?" said Geoffrey, squinting up at the man's eyes,
trying not to be obvious.
"Kids with blonde hair, especially those who are outdoors
a lot, all seem to have this fuzz on their cheeks, you're light
and your muscle structure indicates speed and agility. Sort
of guessed my way through it really."
"Wow." Geoffrey was hooked.
"Hey, was I right?" asked Tex.
The boy sat forward and held out his hand. "I'm Geoffrey
Marks." Then looking down he took Tex's hand and placed
it in his for a second handshake.

Mrs Kempt had watched this little play run through her
kitchen window and now eased back noting all appeared
well.
"The other kids are going to give you hell Geoffrey. Poor
bugger's an ogre. You don't make friends with ogre's."
A further thought added to her burden. "And for Christ's
sake don't tell your mother."

Heather Marks spent two days and two nights of
indecision, mixed with guilt, fear and bouts of terror before
she woke at 3am from a dream involving the mutilation of
her little boy by the man from that house.
Prepared by her dream for the worst possible reality she
marched in the gate and up the path of that house to
confront her only child's potential slayer. Only a mother's
love could have driven her on.
Mrs Kempt noted the arrival. "Oh God," she said, in
resignation, "Here we go."

When Tex opened the door he knew there was a woman standing on the threshold but his polite enquiry brought no response.

He had been playing the piano when the doorbell sounded. Heather Marks, mother of Geoffrey, noted the man's strong arms, his defined face, the clean shirt, his hips, his age. He wasn't old at all. Perhaps forty-five. Handsome almost.

"Oh." Further silence.

"Are you, Tex? By any chance. I mean ....."

"I am."

There was a hand extended. A large fine hand. The woman caller took it awkwardly.

"Oh right." Tex nodded. "You're Geoffrey's Mum."

He added, "You have the same hands as your son."

"What a lovely man." Mrs Marks was in an expansive frame of mind. Geoffrey sat at the kitchen table with some after-school toast and a drink.

"He said that he was so pleased to meet me and what a nice son I have. He understood that I must be concerned with my boy talking to a stranger, especially a single guy who is blind and lives alone. He assured me that he is quite harmless and you are welcome any time to drop in for a chat. He said you were a real help in the garden the other day and he hoped he put the flowers in the holes the right way up. We laughed.

I had a cup of coffee. He knew exactly where everything was in the kitchen. He even makes his own biscuits. They were very nice.

Do you know, he had perfect vision until his mid twenties.

He woke one morning and nothing. Total black. The eye
doctors told him it was some nerves that no longer worked
and there was nothing they could do to help. Isn't that
terrible Geoffrey."
Geoffrey nodded. It was pretty bad.
Mrs Marks continued.
"I asked how he occupies his time through the day. He
said, 'I practice.'
That's why he's always around through the day Geoffrey.
He's a musician. He works at night. One of the members of
the band calls by and picks him up when they're playing.
It all makes sense now. I asked what instrument he plays
and he rattled off about ten things.
There's a lovely piano in the front room but he said his
real passion is the guitar. When he plays blues in his band
that's when he's happiest. He showed me his studio. It's
quite impressive. All soundproofed and tricked up with a
lot of gadgets and dials and things. Lots of lovely looking
guitars. There's even one that's chrome plated."
It was round about now that Geoffrey was transformed
from a boy who might occasionally say hullo to their near
neighbour, to a boy who was absolutely focused on every
word his mother uttered.

Geoffrey had a secret. At times, in his bedroom with the
door closed and the blinds down Geoffrey would cease to
be Geoffrey. With his collar turned up, the top button of his
shirt undone and his long blond hair slicked back, Geoffrey
became Trent Maddox, rock star.
The music had to be loud enough to rock the stadium for

his adoring fans but not so loud as to bring his mother knocking on the door.

He played his imaginary guitar with such passion. His talent was immense. He had all the movements, all the twists and shrugs just right. They sent the girls in front of the stage into a swoon and made his mates incredibly jealous.

But, for all the work that Trent Maddox put in perfecting his act there was one glaring omission. Geoffrey had never actually handled a real guitar.

Oh he had dropped enough hints. And when they hadn't worked he came right out and pleaded for a guitar. His mother checked things out and finally had to tell her son that she just couldn't afford such a thing. Her job barely paid the bills and put food on the table. So the whole guitar idea faded away.

But now. There was this guy in the same street who had, not only lots of guitars but a whole damned studio. If only he'd known sooner. Plans needed to be made immediately.

The next day Geoffrey was relieved to find that his only companion for the walk home from school, along their quiet, tree-lined street, was Brian Goodge. Brian was a bit of a hell-raiser. The kid your parents told you to stay away from. The whole scary house thing had never really troubled Brian.

As they walked past Tex's house, Geoffrey actually slowed down.

"Isn't this the bit where we run?" asked Brian.

"Nah, I'm over that. Apparently the guy's okay. Look, he planted some nice flowers in his front garden." Geoffrey pointed to the sad jumble of mismatched plants near the gate.

"Must have been in a hurry," suggested Brian.

Geoffrey's walking companion lived about ten houses past his own, so Geoffrey gave a casual "Seeya," as he turned into his gate.

"Seeya," said Brian ambling onwards.

Too easy, thought Geoffrey as he crouched behind the hedge just inside his yard. He gave Brian enough time to get well and truly into his house then, checking that all was clear, he headed back up the street to the house of Tex.

"Hi," he said, as Tex opened his door.

"Geoffrey, if I'm not mistaken," said Tex, staring way over the boy's head.

Putting aside the uncanny puzzle of how Tex knew it was him at the door, Geoffrey launched right in, trying to sound positive and upbeat.

"I've been thinking. You know you planted your garden out the front with those nice flowers."

"I'll have to take your word for it, that they're nice," Tex smiled.

Not to be distracted Geoffrey continued. "I was thinking, I could look after them for you and tidy your yard. As a sort of neighbourly thing to do."

Silence followed.

"Did your Mum tell you to do this?"

"No."

"Did you decide to do it because you feel sorry for the blind guy?"

"Hell no."

"Perhaps a little obtuse Geoffrey but I get the point. Do you want to be paid? Are you short of pocket money?"

"No, it's free. Just being neighbourly."

"And you expect nothing in return? Gratis, obligation and conscience free?"

Geoffrey hesitated. This was not going as well as expected. He hadn't anticipated suspicion on the part of the recipient of his fake largess. If he agreed he'd be stuck doing gardening and pretending he was nice.

"Well, perhaps there is this one thing."

"Aha," said Tex. "We have arrived at the crux."

"What's a crux?"

"There's always a crux old sport."

Geoffrey blabbed. As the words tumbled from his mouth, he could hear rock star Trent Maddox becoming a has-been before he'd ever been. In his mind he heard the inevitable reply.

"Yeh look I'm kinda busy kid. Don't have the time for teaching guitar. And do you even own a guitar? I mean hell, how's that gonna work?"

He'd be shown the door before he was even through it.

However, Tex just stood there. Looking, not looking. Though this time it was one of those distant looks that people take on when they're wrestling with a problem.

Finally he said, "Okay, trying to con me is probably not a good start. On the other hand it shows a certain keenness." He paused again.

"I'll be up front with you Geoffrey. Twice before I've been asked the question you're asking me now. And twice I've, against my better judgment, said yes. I don't like teaching. I find it boring because I want the person I'm teaching to be good. In both these cases they were not. Which made it real difficult to explain that they were musically dumb. You see you've either got it in you or you haven't. If it's not there it can't be implanted."

Geoffrey stood staring at Tex trying to get a hint of which way his fortunes were leaning.

"So, this time it's no Mr Nice Guy. I'll give you a go. A few weeks only. If you're no good I'll tell you and that will be the end of it."

Geoffrey was assessing the offer before him.

"I'll be damned good. Honest I will."

"Yeah well, I'll be the judge of that. Now seeing as you want to fix up my front yard and make it pretty, that will be your payment for services rendered. And you try to do a half-arsed job, I will know."

"How?"

"I'll ask the lady across the street. She keeps an eye on things. I'll ask her if my yard is lookin' good."

Tex paused once more.

"Well you better come in. I guess your mother trusts me or you wouldn't be here. Right?

Geoffrey let the query go by.

As they walked down Tex's hallway he asked. "How long

have you been playin' anyway? What sort of guitar have you got?"

This is not getting any easier, Geoffrey thought.

An hour later Geoffrey Marks came walking down his street. In one hand was a sheet of paper showing chord diagrams. In his other hand was a slightly battered guitar case.

His mother was at their gate looking to see if her son was about.

Tex had said don't come back for a week or when you've mastered C, F and G7.

A couple of days later it was Saturday. As the evening light settled over the neighbourhood Geoffrey hovered behind the hedge in his front yard. Curiosity had him there.

He was right. At 7pm Tex emerged from his house.

He was carrying two guitar cases. Geoffrey recognised them immediately. One contained a Gibson ES335 and the other held a Fender Jazzmaster. Both were finished in a beautiful sunburst colour. Geoffrey had been allowed to touch them briefly before Tex put them away and told Geoffrey that they were decades away from his abilities and bank balance.

A black sedan rolled up to the kerb and after a few muttered words Tex loaded his guitars onto the back seat and then climbed in next to the driver. Then they were gone, to some magical place where music is played.

Sitting on his bed holding a severely road worn acoustic

guitar with no famous brand Geoffrey slogged his way
through the three open chords he had been assigned to
learn. He had been practicing so hard the skin on the end
of his fingers had become frayed. His hand ached.
Geoffrey's mother had heard his elaborate story of
gardening in exchange for guitar lessons. Despite having
met the man she was slightly concerned about her only
son spending time alone in his house. To balance this she
was impressed by her boy's entrepreneurial spirit and the
thought of him perhaps having some musical talent.

The next morning, Sunday, at 9am, as the warm early sun
was filtering its way through the trees and birds were
attempting some early morning calls, the doorbell rang at
the house of Tex.
After a considerable time a shuffling noise came from
within and the door opened.
"Hullo. Is there anybody there?"
Tex was barefoot. He wore a pair of jeans, a very crumpled
t-shirt and a grubby dressing gown. He looked equally
crumpled, tired and unshaven.
Geoffrey winced but he was here now.
"It's me, Geoffrey," he said brightly.
"Jesus kid, what time is it?" Tex had one eye closed as he
yawned, his face screwed up.
"It's after 9. I have those chords ready. You said to call back
when I was ready.
Tex took a deep breath.
"Now you see, this, is what I was talking about. Geoffrey,
until the other day you had never even held a guitar.

There's no way you have suddenly picked up a guitar and in a few days got any sort of mastery of even some basic open chords. It takes a lot of time and practice. When I first started on a guitar it took weeks to get even my fingers in the right place. Can I suggest ...."

"Can I show you? I think I've got them."

Tex took another slow, deep breath.

"Okay," he said, "Yeah, why not. This will prove my point and then you can go home and come back in a month."

They walked through the house to the studio.

"What time did you get home?"

"None of your business Geoffrey but 3am. Musicians work late."

"Oop sorry, you're probably a little fragile."

Tex smiled to himself. "A bit," he said. "Did you bring the guitar?"

Tex slumped back in a chair while Geoffrey positioned himself on a round stool. He put the strap round his neck, stretched his back up straight then leaned over the instrument. His fingers dropped into the open C position. He began strumming. Four beats of C, four beats of F and then four of G7 before ending on C.

"Wow," Tex exclaimed, "I'm impressed ...."

Geoffrey had put down his pick and started finger picking the three chords. He then improvised by adding in little single notes and runs. He took parts of the chords and blended them in neat little harmonies to make the whole three-chord progression quite melodic. It lasted a couple of minutes.

When he stopped with a nice ringing C major, Tex sat for some seconds in the silence then said, "Son of a bitch."

At what moment potential rock star Trent Maddox was consigned to history it is hard to say. Perhaps quite early when Geoffrey had mastered some great blues riffs and intros in E or when he discovered the simple joy of 12 bar blues. It could have been when Tex played and sang some stuff by Muddy Waters or Robert Johnson or BB King or when he and Tex played a couple of Stratocasters together to some backing tracks. Whatever it was, it continued to be a source of amazement for Tex. Every so often he would question Geoffrey.

"Are you sure you're ten?"

"You definitely never picked up a guitar before?"

"And you're white like me? I mean no coloured folk in your background?"

Then there was the time when Tex repeated, after a particularly good session, "Are you sure you're ten?"

Geoffrey answered. "Tex, I'll be twelve next week."

"Has it been that long? A year and a half?"

Geoffrey then asked another question he'd wanted answered for over a year.

"Tex, when can I see you play? You know, on a stage."

Tex sat up. He turned down the sliders on the mixer.

The backing faded out.

"Geoffrey, the places I play in ain't real kid-friendly. I doubt your Mum would be comfortable in some noisy club.

I don't think you'd be safe by yourself. Plus you're under

age."

Geoffrey, as was his nature, had an ace up his sleeve.

"I know a way round all those problems."

"Oh yeah, and what would that be?"

"Onstage with you and the band." Geoffrey held up his hand and said, "I'm holding up my hand. Before you say no, not ever, the band wouldn't be in it. Let me show you something. I've been working on this for a while."

Tex leaned back. "Oh God, what now Geoffrey."

The boy picked up an acoustic guitar. Played a nice intro then launched into the angry riff that is Catfish Blues. He played it through a few times. And then .... he began singing.

Now anybody familiar with this song will tell you that it needs a rough, dirty voice made of gravel and bourbon and hard livin' before it can ever have a hope of sounding authentic.

Geoffrey Marks had such a voice. It was hidden under his normal adolescent squeak. He played and sang the whole song with a nice bit soloing in the middle. When he finished on a slowly picked out major 7th, Tex sat silent. Then he said, "Son of a bitch."

It took some planning. Geoffrey was now twelve.

Tex organised a backing track. He let Geoffrey use one of his prized Strats. Found a nice squealy overdrive sound for the riff. Then he fiddled with his deck and mike and managed to bass out Geoffrey's voice and make it mildly dirty then added a little reverb.

He taught him a few other standout pieces like Hoochie

Coochie Man. The kid was a natural. His voice was powerful.

They got Harris Bones, the band's bass player over to listen. When the boy had finished Harris raised his eyebrows.

"Shit" he said. After a long pause he said, "Okay here's my slant. Great gimmick. Would definitely get more backsides on seats. Rest of the band would be okay. Problem one. Tex mate, you ain't lookin' at Geoffrey. I am. No offence kid but you're real cute with your long curly blonde hair. You'd knock 'em dead in a tweeny surf band. I'm not sure we could make you ugly enough to play blues."

Geoffrey looked at Harris. All black jeans, leather and tattoos, not to mention his gut.

"I could get a tattoo," he suggested.

"Yeah right," said Tex, "your mother is already a little weirded out by this whole thing."

"Problem two," added Harris. "He's twelve and guess what, he looks eleven. With a fake beard and dark glasses he could look twelve and a half."

The trio sat for a while glumly assessing the situation. Tex finally spoke.

"I know you're thinkin' it Harris, so I'll say it. Marco Dragovic."

Since the day that Mrs Kempt had knocked on the door and asked the blind owner of No.76 if he could be a little less reclusive the whole street had evolved. The children no longer screamed or hurried past the house.

Occasionally they actually saw the owner out and about. They all knew that Geoffrey Marks did some gardening for the man and in fact the lawns, paths, trees and bushes all looked quite tidy now.

Initially they had tried to make a big deal out of Geoffrey associating with the man but when some found out he was a musician they admitted a grudging respect for such a person and the whole thing became old news. Children do not have great attention spans.

One thing that had alluded the best of the school's rumormongers was Geoffrey's music lessons and aspirations.

Except for Mrs Kempt who was very good at putting two and two together. Geoffrey made sure his mates never saw him coming and going or carrying a guitar case but his movements did not get past the lady in No.77. Still she was basically a kind soul and was happy to see how well everything had worked out for the blind man and the boy and his mother.

Mrs Marks had grown to like and trust Tex and was secretly pleased that the boy had a man in his life, even if he was blind and was a musician. She often listened at her son's door as he practiced and while the strange, often miserable songs he played were not to her liking she had to admit he did them well. When Geoffrey began singing she shed tears listening to his beautiful voice. If only he'd sing some 'nice' songs.

With his musical improvements came a new confidence, a sunny, happy manner and an improvement in his grades. Mother and son rarely mentioned his music. It just happened. He was over with his friend Tex a lot.

Then one day her doorbell rang. When she answered she found her near neighbour Tex standing at the entrance.
"Is that you Mrs Marks?" he asked.
She felt awkward. Despite her son seeing so much of the man she saw very little.
"I have a question to ask. Could I come in?"

Seated on the lounge sipping a cup of coffee Tex now looked a little awkward. But it was good coffee.
Being bold Mrs Marks started by saying. "You know if I have to call you Tex, umm Tex then it seems only fitting that you call me Heather."
Tex smiled. "I haven't heard that lovely name for a while. Okay, it's a deal Heather."
"So what is it you wanted to ask? Geoffrey's not bothering you is he? He loves his guitar playing." For a moment Heather Marks thought that maybe Tex was there to tell her he didn't want the boy around anymore.
"It's like this Heather. Geoffrey is a very talented boy. I mean musically. In fact I've never heard anybody like him. He's also a very fine blues singer. Professional level in under a couple of years is remarkable. Now as you know I play in a band. A very good friend of ours has heard Geoffrey playing and singing and he'd like him to appear with us on stage in his club. Now Marco runs a fine quality, high-end establishment called 'Marcos'. It's famous for showing off new talent. Only the best people go there. I'd deem it a great honour and privilege if you'd allow our

band to give Geoffrey some guest spots in our upcoming gigs at Marcos. He'd have the very best of care and be with us at all times. I think he'd love the experience."

There, he'd done it. Tex had fired his best shot. He had to rely on Geoffrey's mother having no knowledge of the city club scene or the age restrictions on minors. Or having ever heard of Marco Dragovic.

The next day when Geoffrey arrived Tex was waiting.
"What?"
"Long talk. I have to stick by you and do as I'm told by the band. I can eat but mustn't drink anything but water and come straight home after the gig. I said I'd be nervous if she was out front and I'd rather leave it for a while till I was really confident before she came to see me."
Tex held up his hand for a high five.
"Good goin' kid. We'll get round the comin' to see you thing later. Now I'm bein' straight with you, as I explained, we're doin' this for the money. You'll be a great gimmick. Marcos is a big club. But it's a nasty place. Marco don't give a shit about age restrictions or anything else. The cops won't go near the joint. He knows them all personally. We have a sort of love/hate relationship with the guy but we always do well there. With you on board we'll pack the place."

Two weeks later in the dusk of a Saturday night, Mrs Kempt observed the boy Geoffrey standing at the edge of the road outside No. 76 together with the blind musician Tex. Both were dressed in black jeans and black shirts with black

shoes. The boy had on a white tie. The man had three
guitar cases next to him. The boy one.

As she watched a large black sedan pulled up in front of
the pair and they climbed in with the boy in the back.
Just as he opened the door the boy turned and smiled
and waved. Mrs Kempt leaned forward and noted that
Geoffrey's mother was standing at her gate returning his
wave.

As the car pulled away Mrs Kempt smiled. Perhaps that
boy's mother was not quite the worrier she had assumed
her to be.

The club was empty. It didn't open its doors till 8.30. The
sort of people who went to Marcos expected to do their
thing until late into the night.

The band set up on stage. Tex fiddled with the guitars and
took care of the tuning. He had brought along his National
steel guitar. It was tuned to open G. There was talk with the
sound engineer. An extra amp was added to the backline
and Geoffrey's borrowed Stratocaster set up in front of it.
Then they did a sound check. Geoffrey stood off stage
with his mouth open. He had never heard the band in
action. When he asked once where they rehearsed he
was told that they'd been together so long they'd given
up rehearsing. The rumble and roar of the full throated,
precise punchy sound got right into the boy's gut. The sax
had a go, the keyboards, the drummer, Tex tried his three
guitars out with National having to be miked up for his
slide work. Even Harris on the bass sounded great. They
were so good.

Then they stopped and Harris turned to the boy and waved a finger beckoning him out. Geoffrey walked out to his amp. He picked up his guitar and walked to the front of the stage next to Tex. He slipped the guitar strap over his neck, turned the volume up to about 6 and looked at the shiny mike in front of him. His head buzzed. He swallowed. "Now would be a good time to start, buddy." It was Tex sitting on a chair next to him.

He looked down at the guitar neck. His vision was swimmy. It seemed out of focus.

Another voice behind him said, "Sing your arse off kid, an' don't forget to give me a solo."

It was old Louie, the sax player.

Geoffrey smiled. It was going to be alright. He launched into the riff for Catfish Blues, shocked at how loud it sounded. Then the band joined in and it just felt so good. Oh God it felt good. And when he sang he expected to be drowned out but his voice powered out of the foldbacks and he could hear it all. He found that even a faint nod of the head in somebody's direction meant they launched into a solo. For his neighbour he whispered Tex and that was enough.

When they finished. Before they had time to speak. A man in a cream coloured suit appeared in front of the stage.

"Hullo Marco," said Louie.

"Jesus," said the man in the suit, "this is not gonna work."

Tex said, "What?"

"Nah, nah, the kid's fuckin' brilliant. But Christ he looks like some bumpkin angel for God's sake. It'll be even worse

with the spotlight on him. It won't sell to my crowd. I
gotta dirty him up a lot or he don't go on. You guys grab
somethin' to eat, I'm turning the kid over to Dolores."
Tex leaned over to Geoffrey. "Don't worry mate. Dolores
will sort you out. I'll have some food sent into you. How
does a burger sound?"

Dolores walked around Geoffrey several times as he sat
on a high stool and ate his burger. It came with a glass of
beer but Dolores had tipped it out and replaced the beer
with tap water. Several young ladies were getting changed
into their uniforms and putting on their makeup. Geoffrey's
presence didn't seem to bother them.
"If you'd been born with greasy black hair we'd be okay,"
Dolores exclaimed. "I can fix the cuteness but these long
flowing golden locks, Jeez." She flicked Geoffrey's hair.
"Okay, I'll start with the face. Hurry up and finish eating,
There's work to be done."

It was eight fifteen. The band sat around a large table,
talking, drinking and relaxing. Their first set was at 9pm.
Harris snorted. "Holy shit. Oh Tex, if only you could see.
You'd love this."
Walking towards them was Marco. His hand was on the
shoulder of a small figure with a dark visage. It's eyes
were surrounded by grey black makeup. The skin was
sallow. The collar was turned up and the rest of the hair,
now oiled up and swept back, was mostly hidden under a
wide brimmed black fedora. One of the waitresses black
waistcoats had been added to the ensemble.

"He'll do," said Marco, who wandered off to yell at the bar staff.

The keyboard player Jimbo, stroked his chin.

"Well Geoffrey. Ya look like an ol' blues player with a habit. It's destiny."

Then he added, "Oh shit no, don't grin. It kills the effect."

At the kitchen table at 10am Geoffrey was finally eating breakfast.

"2.30 in the morning mister. That's awfully late for a growing boy."

Geoffrey just smiled an incredibly wide smile and spooned the cereal into his mouth. Luckily Harris had the forethought to have the boy's face and hair cleaned up before the trip home. He looked sparkling when they dropped him off to his waiting mother.

"So, how was it? I want to know all about it. Are you famous?"

Geoffrey told his mother all that he felt she should hear. When he'd finished, the club sounded not unlike the local town hall glee club.

One part where he did not hold back was his admiration for Tex. For the first time he had seen his mentor in the element that was his life. As he played and sang and blasted out solos and added soulful blues harp melodies he had the audience right there with him.

When his voice cried out in some of the slow blues numbers, he watched the faces of the audience and saw their enjoyment as they felt the sadness of the song. Tex

had a voice that made people weep.
And when he sat there on stage with Tex he was not afraid.
He could give it his all and feel the connection. When
they applauded and asked for more he mopped up their
enthusiasm and it gave him strength and confidence.

Marco loved them. The club was packed each time.
He wanted them more than once a week but they declined.
"Don't want to have the masses getting tired of us. Leave
'em wanting more," they said.

One night as Geoffrey belted out Dust My Broom he
squinted past the spotlight checking the audience faces
and nearly forgot the words. His hands lost their place and
he butchered the riff.

The next morning his mother explained as he ate his
cereal.
"I'm not a complete dummy, my love. That imaginary club
you described sounded like something run by the church
fete. Marco gave me a table right up front and refused any
payments. He thinks you're wonderful. Probably because
he's making lots of money. Dolores told me she keeps a
close eye on you and you have lovely chats when she does
your makeup. We both agreed it could all go belly-up if the
vice squad or somebody find out there's a minor at the
club. Marco got all flustered when I mentioned that. I said,
"As long as my boy's having fun and doing something he
loves, what's the harm?"
By now Geoffrey had ceased eating his cereal and just sat

with his mouth hanging open.

He couldn't wait to tell Tex. After waiting a while for Tex to
rise he ran to his house.
But Tex was different. He received the news with no
reaction.
"That's good isn't it Tex?"
"Yeah, it's good." Then he fell silent again.
After a little while he spoke.
"I had a phone call a little while back. Some mail might
have come through the week. Listen, can you go down the
path and check if I have any mail?"
When Geoffrey returned he had one white envelope.
"That must be it. Can you read it to me mate?"
Geoffrey slid his finger under the flap. He watched Tex who
seemed agitated as he sat on the lounge his thumbs under
his chin.
The letter had a crest and a name. The Kensington
Institute. Geoffrey cleared his throat.
"Dear Sir. I am writing to confirm our offer as discussed in
our recent phone conversations. While I appreciate that
you will not be able to read this correspondence it is our
way of formalising our proposal to you. As explained, we
have read your medical notes and made ourselves totally
cognisant with your case. As with others who have your
particular problem it is not the eyes that are failing to
provide you with sight but nerve damage behind the eyes.
In the past this damage has been impossible to repair but
with several major advances in techniques and treatment
over the past decade we can confidently predict that,

should you take up our offer, we will be able to restore full
functioning eyesight to you.
Because this is a breakthrough in eye surgery developed
by the Kensington Institute we are offering ten people
the chance to have the procedure at no cost, as a way of
proving our credentials. We have already performed the
operation on six patients with complete success.
Of course you already know all this from our long phone
discussions. Please be assured we have your best interests
at heart.
I would appreciate your final answer to proceed asap next
week.
Best Regards
Professor Keith Mellot."

Marco was devastated.
"Three freakin' weeks. You guys are killin' me. What am
I gonna do for three freakin' weeks? Yeh, I know it's real
great news about the eye thing but hell. Do you know
how many nosy reporters I've had to pay off to stop them
running a story about the band with the kid wonder?
Normally I'd sleep with the editor to get publicity and
instead I'm having to keep it under wraps. Thank God for
rumours and word of mouth. Okay already, I'll see you in
three weeks. Don't be late. Hey, an' good luck with the op
Tex. You'll finally be able to see how goddam' handsome I
am."

The operation took place near the start of the first week.
Heather Marks was waiting outside the school when

Geoffrey came out the gate.

"Well?"

"C'mon let's walk a bit. Your little friends can be too curious."

Once they were away from the crowds of children, Geoffrey said, "Mum, c'mon."

"He can see. Tex can see. The operation seems to have been fine. They have him in a dark room. Over the next few days he'll gradually have the light increased. For the next week he has to keep his head as still as possible to allow some of the healing then he'll be home. In the meantime he's not allowed visitors. Imagine seeing nothing of the world for twenty years and then suddenly it's all back there in front of you. So simple, it just needed reconnecting. I'm sure it's much more complicated than that but its wonderful. Anyway, Harris will pick him up when the time comes."

Geoffrey walked past a week later. Harris's car was out the front along with Louie's. The whole band must be there. It could only mean that Tex was home. He stood at the gate for over thirty seconds with his head down. He was scared. What if Tex didn't like him anymore? It was too much. He couldn't go in.

He'd taken a dozen steps onwards when he heard a whistle. It was Harris, standing on the front steps of the house. He was waving his arm.

"Where are you slinkin' off to ya little rat. Get in here."

When Geoffrey walked in Harris said, "I think you're the dude he most wants to see."

As Geoffrey entered the front room the band all fell silent.
There was Tex sitting in his big 'relaxing' chair. He was
looking at him. There eyes met for the first time.
Tex the big rangy guy in jeans, boots and a t-shirt with his
rough looks and dark features. The boy with his bright
face, golden locks and delicate frame. They stood and
stared. It was quiet. Everybody was watching.
Geoffrey felt his eyes start to sting. Oh no, not now. Not in
front of the guys. Too late a tear ran down his cheek.
He angrily wiped it away.
Tex stood. He said, "Guy's I know this is probably
inappropriate but ……"
He walked over, knelt in front of the boy and wrapped his
arms around him.
"Hullo Geoffrey." he whispered.

"Well hell Marco, you really are a handsome bastard."
Marco looked at Tex.
"Listen Tex, I'm glad you got yer eyesight back an' all.
I mean it's a wonderful thing but I can do without the
bullshit. When I first looked in the mirror many years ago I
said listen Marco fate hasn't been kind to you in the head
department so you gonna hafta get by on yer wits an'
charm. I took my advice an' I'm doin' okay."
Marco looked down at Geoffrey standing beside Tex.
"An you can quit grinnin' ya wholesome little creep. Go see
Dolores and get uglied up."
He clipped Geoffrey across the ear.
"I tell ya Tex, the only act could get for three weeks on
short notice was the 'Templetons.'

I've lost half my customers. You gotta get 'em back for me tonight okay."

Tex patted Marco's shoulder. "We'll do our best."

After the show everybody was quiet. The place had been packed. Word had got around. Geoffrey was still a big hit. In fact the band extended his stage time.

In the green room afterwards Tex said, "I'm sorry fellas. I don't know what's happening. I can't concentrate. Bloody people, lights, it's so confusing. Couldn't handle it. Every time I fluffed a line or missed a cue it just got worse."

The man was shaking.

Louie clapped his hands together and broke the silence. "Hey, everybody has a bad night. Hell you just got your sight back after twenty years. You'll be fine next week. Just a bit of adjustment. That's all it is."

After the show the following week, Marco followed the band into the green room.

"Fellas, what the hell's happening out there? My patrons are complaining. They're sayin' the band has lost it. An' don't think I haven't noticed Tex is doin' a lot less. Listen Tex you're the man they come to see. You an' little Mr Pintsize over there. The other guys in the band sound okay but you're the man, the star and you are really crappin' it up. Some very awkward moments. I'm sorry, another night like tonight an' I'll hafta pull the pin."

The band talked but nobody could think of what to do the get Tex back in the zone. They couldn't hide him up the back. He was their frontman. They agreed to leave the man in peace and said it would all be okay next week. Of course none of them thought it would be alright at all.

When Tex and Geoffrey were dropped off, Harris said, "Take it easy, man," and waved goodnight.

The man and the boy stood in silence on the pavement in the dark for a some time. Finally Tex put his hand on Geoffrey's shoulder.

"Better get inside, buddy," he said in a husky voice.

At his door Geoffrey looked back. It had always been an unsaid understanding that Tex would make sure Geoffrey was in his front door before he went home.

Tonight, when Geoffrey looked back he saw Tex walking up his path, his head down, his shoulder's hunched. Miserable and alone.

Geoffrey did not sleep well that night. After he'd looked in on his mother he went to bed and lay staring at the gloom of his ceiling. He worried and tossed and punched his pillow till daybreak. Then he lay staring some more at his ceiling.

At breakfast he asked his mother if he could go shopping. He had a nice little bank account from his music work.

His mother was worried that he was going to do some foolish child-like thing and spend the lot.

No he said, he only wanted one item. He would not say what. But she would have to drive him to the giant super-centre some distance away.

Just after midday, Geoffrey knocked on the door of No. 76. Tex looked terrible. His eyes were bloodshot. The boy hoped it was lack of sleep and not any post-operative problem.

"So what can I do for you bud?"

"I want to come in. I've bought you a present."

With some misgiving Tex stood aside to let the boy past. In the front room Geoffrey took a small package from behind his back.

"I think I know what's wrong," he said. So I've bought you the answer."

Tex rubbed his face and sighed then ripped off the brown paper of the present. Inside was a brown box. Bennett & Brown it said on the box. He'd heard the name but couldn't remember where. He opened the box. A pair of sunglasses?

"Not sunglasses," Geoffrey explained. "Glasses for blind people. To hide their eyes. Totally black. There's a shop in the super-centre that has this stuff. Try them on."

Tex looked at the glasses. "A blues man wearing sunglasses. It's so pretentious. I spent all my blind years with no glasses. I don't know if I could do this."

"Please Tex, just try them."

Tex held the glasses in front of his face then slipped them on.

"Well okay, seriously dark."

"You're back where you were, Tex" said Geoffrey, "you're blind again. No more lights, people's faces. Back in your old world. No distractions."

Tex stood looking about. Then he lowered his head brought his hands up as if he was holding a guitar. His fingers moved unseen on the fretboard. He turned his head in the boy's direction.

"You're a good friend Geoffrey. And I thank you."

As they sat in the green room that Saturday night, not saying much, Marco put his head round the corner of the door.

"Hi guys, the sound check was great." He paused, looking slightly embarrassed. Then he turned to Tex. "Are we okay? No more bogies?"

Tex looked back. "Yeah man, it's all good. Gonna knock 'em dead tonight." He sounded flat.

"Well perhaps not dead," said Marco, shrugging his shoulders, "the deceased don't pay their bills."

He looked around for some appreciation of his humorous effort. None came.

"You know …… when they're dead …..   Aw forget it. Just play well."

Geoffrey noted that Tex had the glasses in his shirt pocket.

At nine they started their first set. The crowd was good though not packed in. Perhaps with a note of caution Harris took the first two songs. Good crowd pleasing blues that suited his rumbling low voice. Then they launched into an extended version of the instrumental Blues in E. It went over well. Finally Tex walked to the front of the stage and pulled up a chair. The crowd moved forward and gathered to listen to the man. He had a slide on his finger, his National resonator guitar in hand and a double mike setup. After some leadup slide work he began the vocals of the Leadbelly classic Black Girl. Tex was leaning back trying to stare down the audience.

From the edge of the stage Geoffrey could see he was not wearing the glasses. It was then that Geoffrey noted Tex pause fractionally. He sang the first verse again. His fingers did not move confidently on the slide. Meanwhile the crowd in front of the stage were pressing closer, trying to see if something was wrong.

Geoffrey took a step onto the stage. He peered. The glasses were not in Tex's pocket.

He ran down the corridor to the green room. The glasses were sitting on a bench behind where Tex had been just minutes before. He'd left them behind on purpose.

On stage the band were getting worried. Tex was struggling. They couldn't stop in the middle of the song. They'd have to see it through.

Somebody in the crowd said, "That doesn't sound right." Tex looked at him and realised the guy was correct. He'd fluffed the simple phrasing. He was sweating and breathing fast. Tex never panicked. He was totally professional. He blinked in the spotlight and shook his head.

Then he was aware of movement to his left. He looked round as Geoffrey pulled a chair up and sat beside him. In his hands he held the Stratocaster guitar and the dark glasses. He began playing a nice slow solo that filled the hole Tex had been digging. Out of the side of his mouth the boy growled, "Put on the frickin' glasses Tex."

Tex stared at his companion as the kid played along confidently.

"Geoffrey. Did you just swear at me?"

"Just do it!"

Tex slipped on the glasses. There was a murmur through
the crowd. The guy that had spoken before said, "Hey cool
man. You look good."
Encouraged, Tex replied, "Yeh look it's nuthin' personal.
I just can't stand your ugly faces."
That brought a great cheer from the crowd.
By now the sound man had organised a mike in front of
Geoffrey. He looked at Tex as he finished his triple solo.
"If you don't take the song back, I'm gonna start singing.
You said my voice don't suit this song. I may murder it."
Tex leaned forward and hunched up over the mike. He was
back in his own world.
No distractions. Alone in the dark. Just him and his music.
Everybody said it was the best version of 'Black Girl'
they'd ever heard.

In the happy and relieved green room after the show. Tex
walked over to Geoffrey and put him in a headlock.
"I have two questions for you fella and I want the truth.
Where's that glasses shop? I want to buy some spares. And,
are you sure you're thirteen? You're not some incredibly
wise and talented little midget who just looks like a boy?"
He let go. They both grinned.
Louie said, "Welcome back Tex. It's good to see ya again."
Tex hadn't finished. He walked Geoffrey by the shoulders
over to the band instruments, stacked ready to leave.
He pulled out a Fender Stratocaster case. He turned and
held the case out to Geoffrey.
"Here," he said in a low voice, "I figure this is payment for
saving my life. I'll throw in a decent tube amp as well."

Geoffrey stood with his eyes wide.

Louie said, "Wow, you done well kid. That baby's vintage."

Then Marco's head appeared round the door.

"What are you boys doin' for the next six months?"

They did two more packed shows at Marcos with Geoffrey, then some woman from the audience decided to check on the legitimacy of allowing a minor to be playing in the club at all hours of the night..

Once that happened Marco lost control of the press and they all did articles on the whole scene. Wonder-kid Geoffrey, the band, the club, the miraculous eyesight of Tex. One even wrote a nice little piece about the night the kid made Tex wear the glasses.

Child welfare got all excited about the 'neglect of a minor' and interviewed Heather Marks with a view to intervening in Geoffrey's life and upbringing. The whole street and even the local school turned out in protest, threatening to lynch them if they ever came near the boy again. So child welfare settled for a stern warning and dropped the whole thing.

The publicity made the band famous and they toured extensively. Tex wasn't allowed to appear without the glasses. They were his trademark.

A year later he married Dolores. Marco cried during the ceremony because he was that sort of guy and because he was losing his top girl. But he paid for her wedding dress.

At the wedding Heather Marks met the younger brother of Tex. The less flamboyant one who was a physiotherapist.

Six months later they were married. Geoffrey was very happy. He had a Tex lookalike as a Dad and the real Tex plus Dolores three doors up the street.

At the age of fifteen Geoffrey wrote a song called Bluesy News. He showed it to Tex. They tidied it up a bit and the band recorded it. As we all know it became a smash hit worldwide as was the followup album with four more of Geoffrey's songs.

In a television interview when the album was selling millions, Geoffrey was asked what the future held for him. He stared straight ahead for a moment then said,
"I honestly don't know but I think it's going to be a lot of fun."

Bluesy News

Key E major
Slow steady blues beat

Riff
B E E Db G A B Bb G E

E
Heard news today from far away
A   E
I was there, I heard him say
B7
I can't be sure
A7
I may be wrong
E
Did not delay - did not stay long.

Riff x 2

E
But he described the terrible scene
A   E
The wreck, the smoke, the devil's scheme
B7
It may be true
A7
I cannot know
E
If none survived - perhaps a few.

Riff x 2

E
That was the train, the very one
A   E
Bringing my wife, my life, my son
B7
Could it be
A7
Can it be so
E
That all I loved - now has to go.

Riff x 2   then Wailing blues harp

E
I can but wait - a tortured soul
A   E
For a word and hope, that is my goal
B7
Can they walk in
A7
My life again
E
Or will I see the hatless men.

Riff repeats